Saved by Noel

TRACY BAACK

Christmas in Noel **BOOK ONE**

Saved by Noel
Copyright © 2024 by Tracy Baack
All rights reserved.
ISBN ebook: 979-8-9905554-2-6
ISBN paperback: 979-8-9905554-3-3

Cover Design by Parker Spencer at Author's Best Friend

Saved by Noel is a work of fiction. Names, characters, and incidents are products of the author's imagination and intended to be used fictitiously. Any resemblance to actual events or persons, living or dead, is entirely coincidental.

For Layla Noel

Know that your dream of being a writer someday is possible
Or a professional ballerina
Or any other dream you decide to chase

CHAPTER ONE

Clark

I should have slept. Instead, I spent the midnight hours convincing myself that this bewitching attraction I experienced last night is merely that: attraction. I mentally cataloged a list of explanations to dismiss my reaction to her.

A list I recite as I walk up to the front porch and ring the doorbell.

But the second she opens the door with wide eyes and a warm smile, every self-preservation alarm in my body begins blaring out code-red warnings.

I am in so much trouble.

Chapter Two

Clark

Four weeks earlier...

"Tell me you're kidding."

I'm met with silence, despite fixing my deepest scowl on Beau's face. I set down my wrench on the new bathroom sink I installed in Beau's half-bath.

"Beau, tell me you're kidding. You can't seriously be thinking of moving," I press again when he still hasn't answered.

"We're not just thinking about it, Clark," he finally responds. He swallows hard before continuing. "Abby and I have been talking about it for a while now, thinking through our options. And we decided that moving on is the best choice for our family. The house is going on the market next week."

I narrow my eyes at him. "Hold up—so you made me party to your abandoning our town? You finally called me out here to install a working sink in the bathroom, not for *your* use, but so you can sell the house?"

Beau drops his eyes to his shoes, unable to hold my gaze. "Look, man, I wanted to do the right thing and tell you in person. Make sure you heard it from me and not just see the sign go up in the yard."

"You mean, you think it's the *right thing* to leave behind the town that raised you? Leave behind your best friends since childhood, not to mention your parents?" I take a step closer, arms crossed over my chest, daring Beau to look me in the eye again. He's about three inches shorter than my 6' 3" frame, but he stands to his full height and stares me back down. I'll give him credit for that.

"Actually, our folks are moving with us. I got a reliable job in Joplin, and our parents will stick with us to help Abby with the kids. It also gets us all closer to Abby's sister in Springfield," Beau says, the hesitance gone from his voice. "I'm sorry, Clark, but I have to think about my family. I have to provide for them. With the plant closing down, there aren't enough opportunities left. We don't have a choice."

Beau's words are a gut punch, knocking the wind out of me. I grab my wrench off the sink, leaving behind the water pooled in the new cabinet from the installation process. Beau can clean up the mess himself after roping me into beautifying his house so he can sell it. Traitor.

I pick up my tool-box and stomp through the house to the front door. Beau's announcement sinks in more with each step. Not only are he and Abby leaving, but both sets of their parents. Three more families skipping town. I don't even want to add up what that brings the tally to this month.

Tucked in the woods along the Deer River in the northwest corner of Arkansas, our little town has plenty of beautiful scenery to enjoy. Tourists do just that, giving us an economic boost during the summer float season. Visitors make their way to the cabins and campgrounds around the area, renting canoes and kayaks to float the Deer River.

The rest of the year, the permanent population hovers around 2,000 people, making for a tight-knit community. A community that has been largely fortified by employment at the Byers meat-packing plant in town.

That is, until Byers shut it down four months ago, sending shock waves of panic through every corner of the city. Almost every household had at least one family member working at Byers before they announced the company was consolidating and closing our plant. They may as well have detonated a bomb on Main Street.

Peak tourist season over the summer kept a lot of families around even after the plant shut down in May. People picked up extra work where they could while they tried to find new permanent opportunities. Unfortunately, no one thought to plant any extra opportunity trees, and families' options have dried up. This month, we've seen the beginning of a mass exodus, particularly among the families newer to the community.

But Beau and Abby *aren't* new to the community. They were both born and raised here, same as me. Our parents and grandparents grew up here together too. Beau and Abby choosing to leave cuts deep. Too deep.

"Clark, come on, don't leave here all ticked off," Beau's voice booms as he catches up to me in the foyer. "I never wanted to leave town, never wanted to leave you and the other guys. But sometimes in life we don't get what we want—we have to accept what we're given and make do with the change."

As angry as I feel, as tempted as I am to paint Beau the traitor for leaving us behind, I do understand his predicament. He and Abby have three kids to provide for, whereas I'm a single man with stable finances and no one else to worry about. I sigh as I turn to face him. "Have you told Davis yet?"

"Yeah, I let him know yesterday," Beau answers. Davis Baker is my closest friend, even closer than Beau. The three of us grew from boyhood to manhood together, playing along the river as kids, then playing every sport throughout school. Although there are other guys I've known most of my life, Beau and Davis are the only ones I've let get close. The two men who really know me.

And now one is leaving.

"I'm sorry, Clark," Beau says as he grips my shoulder. "I'm sorry to catch you off guard, sorry to leave you and Davis, to leave everyone here. I wish there was another way."

I relent and clap Beau's shoulder back. "It's not your fault, man. Stupid Byers execs making these sweeping decisions from their cushioned office chairs. They don't think about the families and communities they're imploding in the process. I can't blame you for being collateral damage."

Beau squeezes my shoulder in acknowledgment before dropping his hand.

"When do you leave? Once the house sells?" I ask.

His face turns sheepish as he answers. "Actually, we'll likely be gone before the house sells. Who knows how long that will take? We've already found a house in Joplin to rent along with Abby's parents while we wait for the houses here to sell. I start my new job in three weeks, so we'll be moving the week after next."

I swallow hard and rub my hand along my bearded jaw, trying to keep the emotion out of my voice. "I'm sorry for being a jerk about you tricking me into installing the new sink. If there's anything else I can do to help out these next couple weeks, let me know."

I give Beau a quick clap on the back to avoid him trying to hug me. I need to get out of this house before my ability to mask my emotions falters. Beau may be one of the two closest people in my life, but I still don't want him seeing how much it's tearing me apart that he's leaving.

Stowing my tool box and gear in the back of my truck, I climb inside and drive away as quickly as possible. Panic bludgeons me on the short drive home.

Beau is leaving.
So many people are leaving.
Who will be next?
This town is all I know.
This can't be happening.

CHAPTER THREE

Clara

"Tell me you said no."

I expertly avoid making eye contact with Madison, my coworker and best friend. After all, my salad isn't going to mix itself. Focused attention required.

"Clara. Tell me you said no," she repeats more firmly while sliding my plate away from me.

I clear my throat and reach for the plate. "I will tell you I said no. . . problem."

Madison huffs in frustration. When she pauses to pull her long brown hair into a ponytail, I know I'm in for it. She begins, "I cannot believe you. You have to draw some boundary lines at some point, Clara."

I return to my zealous salad mixing.

"You're the head of our department. You're supposed to be editing everyone's work and keeping deadlines on track. You can't keep bailing Michael out every time he fails to manage his work-load."

My left thumb twirls the tanzanite birthstone ring on my index finger as I chew an overly-large bite of salad. I take a long drink of water after swallowing to further delay responding to Madison. To her credit, the unblinking glare of her brown eyes never falters throughout my stall tactics.

"But I *am* keeping the deadline on track, Mads," I finally reply.

"By writing Michael's article for him. Again."

"But I enjoy writing, so what's the harm, really?" I respond with a shrug.

"You mean other than you spending your free time doing an employee's work for him rather than writing what you *actually* want to write?" Madison counters. She takes a bite of her chicken salad sandwich but continues staring me down as she chews.

"I couldn't just say no—Michael's had a rough couple of weeks with his girlfriend, and his landlord is being difficult, plus that carpal tunnel keeps flaring up. It's not like it will take me long to whip out an article about winterizing your home and lawn. Chances are, it will take me less time to write it myself than to edit his version," I list out quickly, justifying myself. Madison simply rolls her eyes.

It's exactly the type of article I used to pump out in bulk on a weekly basis when I started working for WritInc straight out of college. With a bachelor's in English but no clear career direction after graduating, I fell into copywriting newsletter content for WritInc's clients. Customers include businesses ranging from retirement communities to real estate offices to insurance companies. And everything in between.

All in all, I can't complain about my job. I've managed to work my way up to overseeing the writing department. Now my primary duties involve assigning content to writers and copyediting their work before it moves to the graphic design team. Fewer creative tasks with a side of management headaches, but slightly more pay. Still a win, I think? WritInc is also where I met Madison, and that's definitely a win.

She's not only my work bestie, but my best-bestie, even if I'm technically her boss. Unfortunately, that means she has no problem telling me when I'm doing my job wrong, because she knows I'd never seriously reprimand her—or anyone, for that matter. Her attention to detail as the final proofreader also means she misses nothing regarding my team management . . . challenges.

"You do realize that he's probably searching 'excuses for missing work' and feeding you the responses every month, right?" Madison says. I play with my salad rather than answering. "You cannot let him do this again next month, okay, Clara? Hold him to the expectations and set boundaries."

I sit up straighter in my seat. "Yes. You're right. I'll do it . . . next month."

Madison sighs, probably not believing me, but loving me anyway. She mutters, "It'd be even better if you would talk to your boss about firing Michael and hiring someone better."

Deep down, I know she's right. Half of the articles Michael submits I wind up practically rewriting. The other half are often passed off to me entirely when he doesn't have enough time to get them all done. But I'd much rather jump in to do the work myself than have to have the uncomfortable conversation to *fire* someone.

Even if it means I never have any free time to work on my passion project.

I redirect Madison's attention by asking about her latest roommate drama. She launches into a detailed story involving waking up to a strange guy in the living room, a broken toilet, and unauthorized cats. One of Madison's two roommates, Ivy, is constantly causing issues. Madison frequently tries to convince me to move in with her and her good roommate so they'd have an excuse to kick Ivy out. But they live in the trendy area of Brookside, while I prefer to stay closer to my parents in the suburbs on the Kansas side of the Kansas City metro.

I share an apartment in Overland Park with a roommate who is almost never home between traveling for work and staying over with her boyfriend. Which pretty much gives me the place to myself. Plus, I'm only a ten-minute drive away from my parents in case they need anything.

I've finished my salad by the time Madison is banging her forehead against the table, groaning about Ivy's new preoccupation with ASMR videos in the early morning. I suggest we head back to the office, anxious to catch up on my recently expanded work-load.

Walking past the open cubicle workstations, I note that Michael is mysteriously missing. I'm stopped by three of the other writers to answer questions before finally making it back to my small office an hour later. I rotate my Pilea plant on the windowsill before sitting down at my desk.

Everyone else has long since left the office by the time I finish writing Michael's article and editing submissions for the homeowners newsletter sent out by real estate agents. Slipping my thumb and forefinger under the rim of my glasses, I rub my tired eyes. I use the last of my brainpower to send the compiled articles to the graphic design team before powering down my desk monitors.

The silence is startled by a text notification. I open my phone to see a message from Dawn, a friend from college who recently got her real estate license.

DAWN

> I've found it, Clara! I'm sending you listing info. Let me know what you think. Bc I think this is THE ONE.

My heart pounds in my chest. *Could this really be it?* For the past two months, Dawn has been searching for a small property to serve as a writing retreat for me. My list of qualifications was short, but I wasn't willing to budge on any of them.

One: Must be within a four-hour drive from KC

Two: Must feel secluded, but not actually be secluded—close access to a grocery store and coffee shop required

Three: Must have reliable Internet for remote work

Four: Must give cabin in the woods retreat vibes

When my late Aunt Gloria, my father's sister, passed away from pancreatic cancer a few months ago, she left a large inheritance to me. She had never married and always doted on me like her own daughter. Aunt Gloria also built a name for herself, pursuing her passion as a member of the Kansas City Ballet and later an instructor at the school. Apparently, that legacy also included wise investments that resulted in a large chunk of money.

What she didn't donate to the ballet, she left to me. But I was burdened by guilt that she passed it to me and not to my parents. I tried to insist on sharing it with them or donating it to help fund the Living Nativity my parents run at their church every Christmas.

However, shrewd Aunt Gloria had left one stipulation attached: I *had* to spend the money on something for myself, something in line with my passions. The executor of her estate would have to approve my plan for the money before it would be released to me. My parents also wouldn't hear of me bypassing Aunt Gloria's plan to force me to pursue my dreams.

It didn't take long to know exactly what to do with the money. I would purchase a writing cabin. A place I could run to and hide away in while I wrote what I *wanted* to write—Christmas movie scripts for the Heartmark Channel.

I've watched *every* single Heartmark Christmas movie *every* year for as long as I can remember. When I was a girl, my mom would make cookies and hot cocoa, and we'd watch love stories play out to the backdrop of snowy scenes and Christmas wonderlands. Sometimes Aunt Gloria would join us if she wasn't busy teaching ballet classes. We never cared that the same handful of story lines got remade over and over. It was the magic of the season, the magic of falling in love that drew us in each time.

Ever since high school, it's been my dream to create a little bit of that magic for other moms and daughters watching together each holiday season.

My fingers tremble as I click the listing link Dawn sent. *Could my dream come true?*

The first photo that pops up is the exterior of an adorably quaint log cabin nestled among mature trees. I swipe through the images to find one bedroom and bathroom, a small but adequate kitchen, and a living room with vaulted ceilings and an inviting stone fireplace. The photo that stops me in my tracks, however, is a sunroom on the back of the cabin with ski lodge-style windows. Upon zooming in, I see a sliding door leading to a small deck and fire pit. I can already envision myself curled up in that room with a cup of hot cocoa, my laptop, and a view of the trees inspiring my writing.

DAWN

Look at the name of the town, Clara. It's FATE!!!

I click out of the photos to the listing information to see where the cabin is located.

Noel, Arkansas.

My heart pounds even harder.

Noel?! A town named for Christmas?! This has to be it.

I immediately call Dawn on speaker as I continue swiping through photos.

She answers mid-ring with a cheerful, "Is it perfect or is it perfect?!"

Chuckling at her enthusiasm, I can't help but agree. "It does seem perfect. Is that a bad thing? Is it too good to be true?"

"I haven't seen it in person," Dawn says, "but all the listing info checks out. The finishes are outdated, but the bones are good. It's not quite four hours away from KC, and although it's a small town, there's a grocery store and coffee shop. All straight from your must-have list. It's the perfect size for you! Plus, it's under your budget, so you'd have plenty of money left to make updates."

My heart rate picks up with every point she places in the "pro" column. *This might really be it.*

"Not to mention, the town is called Noel. *Noel,* Clara! You're the biggest Christmas fanatic I know," Dawn continues. "If that's not a sign, I don't know what is. What do you think?"

"I think . . . I love it," I say with a happy sigh, and I hear Dawn clapping. "But wait, we were looking in Kansas and Missouri—are you even licensed in Arkansas?"

"Yep," Dawn replies. "My broker made us all get licensed in Arkansas for precisely this reason. Lots of spillover from southwest Missouri to Northwest Arkansas properties. I can broker the deal for you, no problem. I think if we go in with an all-cash offer, we'd have no issues getting it. You could be moved in before the Christmas festivities! Want me to write it up?"

I mull it over for a moment. I'm usually a frustratingly slow decision maker—just ask anyone behind me in line at a coffee shop, ever. Exactly zero people who know me would place bets on me purchasing a house sight unseen. But this *feels* right. I pull up the photo of the sunroom again, the golden glow of the sunset casting brilliant warm light through the room.

"Go ahead and draw it up," I surprise myself by saying. "I'm going to talk about it with my parents at Thursday dinner tomorrow, but have it ready for me to sign. I want that cabin."

Chapter Four

Clara

"**G**o for it, Care-Bear," my dad says with enthusiasm.

I've just finished showing my parents the photos of the cabin in the woods. I came to Thursday dinner fully expecting a barrage of questions and precautionary sentiments from Mom and Dad. At the very least, I expected them to pump the brakes on such a big decision.

"I agree with your father," my mom adds as she clears away our dinner plates. I jump up to help, but she waves me back to my seat.

"You don't think it's a bad idea, purchasing a property sight unseen?" I ask.

"There will still be an inspection, of course," my dad replies. "You can always back out if there are major issues uncovered. But the photos look like exactly what you're hoping to find, and it's under your budget. Plus, can't beat that town name!" he finishes with a wide grin. I come from a long line of Christmas lovers—generations of Yuletide fanatics on both sides of the family.

"Not to mention, I've never seen you so willing to take action on something that *you* truly want, Clara," my mom adds. She pauses to briefly cup my cheek before sitting back down at the table. "It's not a lifelong decision that can't be undone. I say seize the moment!"

I take a monster cookie from the platter Mom set on the table. She cooks dinner on Thursdays, but I *always* bring dessert. I stayed late at work today and didn't have time to bake something from scratch. It felt like cheating, but I picked up a cookie box from McLain's Bakery, one of the many amazing bakeries in the Kansas City metro area. I chew a bite of peanut butter-oatmeal-M&M goodness while I consider my parents' words.

"It still seems a little . . . I don't know . . . selfish to spend so much money on something for only me," I admit.

"Which is precisely why Gloria left the money to you," my dad says, patting my hand. "She knew as well as we do that you're always looking out for other people. She wanted you to invest in your dreams. Your mother and I want you to invest in your dreams. It's not selfish if it's what we all want for you."

I take in the familiar dining room of my childhood home. The beige walls and the 90s golden oak trim, the sideboard filled with fancy dishes and covered by framed family photos. There are pictures of the three of us throughout various stages of my childhood. My physical appearance is a perfect blend of my parents' genetics—my strawberry-blond hair is the same shade as my dad's, but with my mom's curls. Dad's blue eyes stare back through mine, but my smile mirrors Mom's.

My gaze sweeps to the several photos of me posing with Aunt Gloria, her smile always wide. Hot tears pool in my eyes. *I miss her.* I think of her letter to me included with the will, the letter I've reread so many times I have it memorized.

Dearest Clara, my little Nutcracker,
I know you're going to huff and puff and try to find your way out of spending this money on yourself. But this is what I *want. I lived my dream, chased my passion into a fulfilling career. Now I want you to chase* your *dream. Become the writer you've always wanted to be. This is my way of being there with you, cheering you on to the stars, even if I won't get to see you make it in this life. But I'll still see. Do it for me—but not just for me. Do it for* you.
I love you with everything,
Aunt Gloria

I nod to my parents and send a text to Dawn.

"I'm going to submit the offer tomorrow," I declare to my parents, who respond with enthusiastic cheers.

I'm doing it, Aunt Gloria. We're *doing it.*

CHAPTER FIVE

Clark

"**B**e careful with that, would ya?! I don't need you two ruining my masterpiece!" Pops yells from the bottom of the stairs.

"Calm down, old man! It's your fault for making this thing so dang heavy," I yell back. "Hold on," I add to Davis, who's holding the other side of the massive headboard several steps up from me. Grunting, I shift my grip before nodding to Davis to continue down the stairs.

Bill Allen, a.k.a. "Pops," is a master carpenter who specializes in custom-made, high-quality pieces of furniture. Translation: furniture that's heavy as all get out.

At least, he *was* a master carpenter. Right up until arthritis took away the thing he loved most—aside from Bev, the wife he'd already lost. With no kids of his own to check in on him, Davis, Beau, and I have taken turns stopping by. We generally sit and shoot the breeze with him, keeping him apprised of town goings-on. It's no skin off our backs, considering that Pops functioned as a surrogate grandfather to every kid of our generation who grew up here.

Now the arthritis is taking away his ability to climb stairs, but Pops would never hear of moving out of the home he shared with Bev. Instead, I helped him convert the formal dining room into a first-floor bedroom to eliminate the need to use the staircase. Today, Davis and I are moving everything from the upstairs bedroom to Pops' new quarters.

The solid walnut headboard truly is a masterpiece, but I know it holds even more sentimental value to Pops. It was his wedding present to Bev. I'm not about to ruin it on purpose, but darn-it-all if this thing isn't impossible to maneuver down the narrow staircase.

We reach the bottom of the stairs and carry it straight to the new bedroom. Pops mutters under his breath the whole way. I know this extra-cantankerous show is a mixture of his regular personality, plus his grief over losing his capabilities coming out sideways. Normally, I'd smart-mouth him right back. But for today, I bite my tongue.

An hour later, Davis and I have replicated the layout of Pops' original bedroom, complete with a framed photo of Bev on his nightstand. I set the pair of whittled blue birds next to the frame. Pops carved and Bev painted them decades ago, before Pops got too busy with all the furniture demands.

Pops invites us out to the front porch for a cold drink. Chase, my one-part Golden Retriever, one-part mutt mix, is already lying at Pops' feet. It may be the first week of October, but the weather still clings to summer in Arkansas.

We sit down in custom-made Pops rocking chairs and accept tall glasses of sweet tea. Bev always had a pitcher of tea so sweet, I think she must have been paid under the table by the town dentist. Pops has kept up the tradition. Although, he somehow manages to add even *more* sugar than Bev's original recipe, making it closer to pure syrup than tea. Still, I'll never turn him down—Pops is pretty much the only "family" I have left.

"So, Beau's gone," Pops announces, like it's breaking news.

I take a swig of tea rather than responding.

"He came to see you before leaving town, right?" Davis asks Pops.

"'Course he did," Pops answers. "Such a shame. Gonna miss him and Abby and their folks."

Only my loyalty to all Pops has done for me keeps me sitting in this chair instead of heading to my truck. Discussing Beau leaving isn't on my wish list today. Or any of the other families who have left. My comfort zone is slowly shrinking day by day, and I don't want to think about it.

Davis must sense my mood and changes the subject. He entertains Pops with a story about his four-year-old son, Davis Jr., trying to sneak a toad into the house past Sydney, his wife. "Junior practically squeezed the thing to death trying to hide it behind his back," Davis laughs.

Pops chuckles. "Reminds me of you boys when you were young. Your poor mamas never could keep the outdoors from coming indoors with you. You two and Beau practically lived in the river."

Davis still practically lives in the river, running Deer Floats, the largest float trip company in town. Some customers rent kayaks, rafts, or canoes for day trips, while others pay for guided overnight experiences. Thankfully, Deer Floats is well-established and successful every summer, meaning Davis won't be abandoning us. At least, I don't think he would.

"Yeah, my mom probably gets déjà vu every time she's over helping with Junior. We'll see if Addie grows up to cause as much mischief as Junior. She took her first steps right after her first birthday, so she's becoming more of a handful," Davis says.

A tiny pang stings my chest, the same one I get every time Davis or Beau talk about their close-knit families. But I quickly bury it away. Like I always do. I might not have any blood family around, but I still have this town and the people in it.

At least, the ones who are still left.

Davis announces that he should get back home to Syd and the kids. As much as I want to retreat home to some solitude, I know this is a tough day for Pops. I shake Davis' hand goodbye, but sit back down and pour a second round of tea syrup for Pops and me. I give Chase a scratch behind the ears, but he stays where he is, head in Pops' lap. Chase can always tell who needs him most.

I sidestep around the day's reality for Pops. "Gonna be real nice, having everything on one level. Next thing you know, you'll be having breakfast in bed every morning," I say with a smirk.

Pops scoffs. "Not till I'm bedridden on my dying day would I stoop to eating breakfast in bed. A man's gotta get up and go in the morning, start the day's work with the sun."

His statement, although delivered with bluster, sobers me. I can't imagine what it must be like to have your body betray you, to slowly stop obeying your commands to do what you've always done. I should swing by daily for the next couple of weeks, come up with something to have Pops do that will let him know he's still competent and needed.

This town is losing too much right now—we can't afford to lose Pops.

CHAPTER SIX

Clara

"White chocolate raspberry mocha and matcha latte for Clara!"

I make my way to the counter to claim my drinks. "Thank you!" I chirp to the barista as I hand Madison her latte. It's 1:00 p.m., well past my typical 10:00 a.m. coffee cutoff time. Even decaf after that point in the day somehow keeps me awake at night. But desperate times call for desperate measures.

And these are desperate times.

Madison and I have spent all of this beautiful October Saturday shopping to outfit my new writing cabin. Or, *almost* mine.

Dawn submitted my offer on the cabin in Noel. Although it was under asking price, the all-cash offer with no contingencies must have been appealing enough to the sellers to accept. The inspection didn't turn up anything alarming, and we officially close in two weeks.

It's exhilarating and terrifying and every other extreme emotion all at once. More than anything, I can't wait to sit in the sunroom, enjoying the peaceful scenery. And hopefully, start writing. I'm taking the Friday of closing day off work so I can spend a long weekend there. Maybe I'll even work remotely on Monday to extend the time.

But first, I need to buy a chair to sit in. And a bed. And couch, and table, and dishes, and linens, and all the other things you need for a functional living space.

Luckily for me, Madison is a thrifting queen. Unluckily for me, thrifting royalty apparently comes by way of patience and digging through multiple stores. I'm more of a one-stop-superstore type of shopper. But if I want to have leftover funds to slowly add my personal style to the cabin, I need to lean thrifty.

After the first four secondhand stores, we've purchased most of the furniture and kitchen supplies I need. We grabbed gourmet grilled cheeses from a food truck outside of the last location, then dropped off our first load of purchases at my parents' house. Dad is being generous enough to lend us his truck for the day, in addition to temporarily storing my new belongings in their garage.

Now, we're caffeine refueling before hitting up the next place on Madison's list. "The holy grail of thrifting," she called it, which makes me wonder why we didn't head there first.

I'm encouraged by our progress, but I still haven't found the two pieces of furniture I'm most excited about: an overstuffed chair and a writing desk. Possibly because I'm being rather picky about finding the *right* chair and desk. But they're the two central features of the cabin in my mind, so I think my choosiness is merited.

Taking a long drink of mocha before starting the truck, I already know I'm going to regret this decision when I'm lying wide awake in bed tonight. Madison gives me directions, and fifteen minutes later, we pull into the parking lot of a giant flea market. As we walk up to the front doors, my attention is sidetracked to the store next door—a plant shop.

"Oooo, let's stop here first," I say, irresistibly drawn to the chloro-phyll like a spider mite to an alocasia.

"Nu-uh, I knew this would happen," Madison chides as she steers me toward the thrift store. "This is precisely why we didn't come here first. I knew you'd detour to plant world and never come out."

I pout, sticking out my lower lip. "You're so bossy."

"Cabin shopping first."

"But plants can also count as cabin shopping. I have a whole sunroom waiting to be filled with plants, Mads."

She's undeterred, quite literally dragging me through the front doors of the sprawling secondhand store. I take another fortifying drink of my mocha and follow Madison into the kitchen aisles, searching for a set of dishes.

"Look at these, Clara! They're perfect!" she says, holding up plates painted with herbs. Mads places them in my hands as she digs around the shelf, pulling out matching bowls and coffee mugs. "Someone must have dropped off an entire set! This is incredible!"

My excitement matches hers this time, because the dishes really are adorable. We add every piece to my cart, double checking the surrounding shelves to make sure we've found them all. "I'm going to get you a good discount on those for taking the whole set, just you watch," Madison preens.

We make our way to the furniture section, and I stop dead in my tracks. The door to heaven opens and a ray of light shines down on the perfect chair and writing desk placed right next to each other. The chair is sage green with a high back and curved arms—the perfect seat to curl up in. The desk is beautifully distressed wood, wide but not deep, with a thin drawer. Ideal for functionality without taking up too much space in the room.

"I told you this was the holy grail," Madison says with a beaming smile. She tosses her hair and brushes off her shoulder in a gloating sort of way. There will be no living with her after this. Good thing I don't live with her.

"You're right, you're right, Queen Madison," I acquiesce, checking the price tags. A furrow forms between my eyebrows at the higher-than-thrifty numbers on the tags, but Madison simply makes a loud *pffft* sound.

"Please, like I'm going to let you pay full price. I didn't earn the 'Queen of Thrifting' title without elite bargaining skills," she says.

Thirty minutes later, we're supervising employees loading my new chair and writing desk into the truck bed. Madison convinced the owner to knock a third off the total price. I reward her by spending a mere thirty minutes wandering the plant store before purchasing a beautiful Ficus Tineke.

"You're going to love your new sunroom home, my little baby," I coo to the variegated rubber tree. I carefully place the ten-inch pot in Madison's lap in the passenger seat. She rolls her eyes, but she's used to this by now.

When we pull into my parents' driveway, my dad and I make quick work of unloading while Madison takes my new plant baby inside. After neatly arranging everything in the garage, I give my dad a hug.

"Thanks again for letting me use your garage. And encouraging me to do this. I'm truly grateful for everything you do for me."

"You're welcome, Care-Bear," Dad says, squeezing me back. "We're beyond excited for you. I can't wait to see it in a couple of weeks."

My mom stuffs us full of chicken pot pie and homemade rolls, her payment to Madison for helping me out today. We sit around the table laughing at Madison's latest Ivy story involving a Cockatiel loose in the mudroom.

Now that I've made all my crucial cabin purchases, I can water the seed of anticipation sprouting in my heart into full-blown excitement. *This is happening. I'm really going to have a writing retreat.* My thumb absentmindedly twirls my birthstone ring, a gift from Aunt Gloria for my sixteenth birthday. I wish she could be here to see this gift she's giving me.

I'm just going to have to make the most of this opportunity in her honor.

CHAPTER SEVEN

Clara

C losing day finally arrives, but it's already off on the wrong foot.

Although I hired a moving company to transport and unload my furniture, my parents were planning to drive down to Noel for the day to see the cabin and help me unpack. Unfortunately, my mom came down with the flu yesterday. Of course, I insisted my dad stay home to take care of her. Madison is out of town visiting her sister, so that means I'm flying solo for the first major purchase of my adult life. Well, minus that college degree I'm still paying off.

My nerves are buzzing as I make the drive down to Noel. Dawn will meet me there to sign closing papers, but then she has to head straight back to KC for an open house this afternoon. The moving truck is supposed to arrive at the cabin around 11:00 a.m., giving me enough time to sign the papers and hopefully walk through my new "home" for the first time before the chaos of unloading begins.

As I get closer to Noel, I'm slowly immersed in woodsy scenery. I leave the interstate for a smaller highway, which occasionally winds along the Deer River. The fall leaves are still hanging on to the trees even in late October, so lovely they bring tears to my eyes. Or maybe it's the overflowing wellspring of emotions causing that moisture.

I slow down as I enter the city limits of Noel. Although, "city" might be a generous term. The town appears to be tiny, but I do notice the grocery market and small coffee shop right next door as I drive down Main Street. Paint is peeling on many of the buildings, some showing even further signs of neglect. But it also looks to have all the trappings of a tight-knit community. On the bank of the river are several picnic benches and a playground, while a bar and grill advertising "drive-up boat service" connects the edge of Main Street to the river bay.

Dawn's car is already parked outside the small real estate office, so I park behind her and head inside. Twenty minutes doesn't seem like nearly enough time to sign away part of your life. Yet that's all it takes to finish the closing papers and receive the keys to my new cabin. This surreal moment deserves more fanfare than a simple exchange of signatures for keys. But Dawn's enthusiastic hug will have to suffice.

"I'm so, so sorry I can't come with you to see the cabin," she says when we walk out to our cars. "I'll already need to speed a little to make it back in time for the open house."

"Please, Dawn, since when do you speed a little? You always speed a *lot*!" I tease. She laughs with me. "Seriously though, thanks for making the trip down here for closing. *And* for finding this place! Words can't express my gratitude."

She gives me another quick hug before hopping into her car. I take a moment in mine to stare at the new keys in my hand, smiling to myself. Maybe I was crazy to do this, to buy a house I've never seen before. But right now, all I'm experiencing is excitement.

I punch in *my* new address and follow the GPS on a winding road to the outskirts of town. The layered cliffside juts out over the road in one section, creating a shaded canopy and dripping spring water on my windshield. I take a left that turns into more of a U-turn onto a steep road leading up to the top of that cliff. The driveway is poorly marked, causing me to drive right past it. *To-do item one: new numbers for the mailbox,* I mentally note.

Reversing the car, I pull into the drive and follow the beaten path around a wide circle to park in front of the cabin. I scooch as far to the side as possible to leave a wide berth for the moving truck. Hopefully it can make it up that steep incline—I'm extra glad I hired professional movers now.

Body trembling with adrenaline, I walk along the rustic stone pathway to the front porch. The cabin looks just as cozy as it did in the photos, at least from the outside. The full, mature trees give the illusion of total seclusion, although I know I drove past a few neighbors' houses along the road.

The front door has both a traditional lock and a keypad, so I make another mental note to update the code today. I turn the key in the lock, take a deep breath, and swing the front door open.

Daylight streams through the windows, and I survey the open concept living room to the left and kitchen to the right. The fixtures and hardware in the kitchen are outdated, but with time I can replace them with my style. The hardwood floors give that true log cabin ambiance, while the large stone fireplace adds a homey touch to the living room. I walk behind the central fireplace to the hallway behind, where the sunroom is the first space you see.

Tears fill my eyes again as I step into the room, fully able to appreciate the warmth of the sun flooding through the windows. The fall leaves create a backdrop so picturesque it could be misconstrued as computer-generated.

This is even better than the listing photos.

I continue down the hallway to see the bathroom door on the left, most of the space taken up by a gigantic soaking tub. The previous owners must have been fans of hot baths, a circumstance I'm happy to capitalize on. Beyond the bathroom is the single bedroom, with the perfect amount of space for a queen bed, night stands, and a small dresser.

A massive sigh of relief escapes my lungs. Although the inspection didn't turn up any structural concerns, it was still a gamble to purchase this place without seeing it in person. But I feel as though I'm holding a royal flush—I can't even imagine a more perfect writing retreat.

Returning to the sunroom, I open the sliding door and step onto the deck. *To-do item three: find some cozy porch furniture.* Closing my eyes, I listen to the silence, punctuated only by a pair of cardinals calling to each other. My mouth widens into a grin as I tilt my face to the sun and twirl in a circle, arms held wide.

Thank you, Aunt Gloria. This is better than any dream.

I'm ready to collapse from exhaustion after a long day of directing the movers. Okay, let's be honest—I carried half the boxes in myself. I couldn't idly stand by while they were working. I heat a cup of noodles in the microwave and quickly devour it, eager to take a long soak in that giant bathtub.

I kept shower cleaner in an easily accessible box so I could give the tub a good scrub first. After using the attached shower head to rinse away the cleaner residue, I turn up the water temperature and add a healthy dose of pumpkin spice bubble bath to the running water. I don't prefer drinking pumpkin spice lattes, but I don't mind smelling like one. Humming to myself as the tub fills, I arrange my hair products and soap along the ledge. I hang a fluffy towel and my favorite cozy robe on the nearby hooks.

I queue up my Dave Barnes Christmas playlist on my phone, turn on the overhead heat lamp, and ease myself into the sudsy water. I close my eyes and lean against the back of the tub, grateful for the large size accommodating my 5' 8" frame. The standard shower/tub combo in my apartment doesn't lend itself to relaxing baths for tall-ish people.

I did it. I'm doing *it. I'm making my dreams real.*

After thirty minutes of bliss, my pruned fingers tell me it's time to get out of the repeatedly reheated water. I use the shower head to wash and condition my hair, carefully brushing through the curls while wet.

While the water drains, I wrap myself in my velvet robe and use an old t-shirt to scrunch water out of my hair before working in curl cream. I wipe my hand over the fogged mirror so I can apply serums and night creams to my face.

After such a long day, I should be ready for bed, but I'm wide awake now. I smile at my reflection in the mirror, picturing myself in my overstuffed chair in the sunroom with a cup of hot cocoa and a good book. *Or maybe my laptop? Are the creative juices flowing to write tonight, or should I wait until I'm mentally fresh tomorrow?*

I turn off the heat lamp and twist the door-knob.

The door doesn't budge.

Brow furrowed, I pull harder. Nothing.

I wipe my hands on a towel, ready to put my full strength into my next effort. I turn the doorknob, then pull as hard as I can. This turns out very unfortunately for me when the doorknob comes clean out of the door. I topple backward with the full force of my pulling strength.

Oh no.

I try to put the knob back into the hole in the door, jiggling it around, as if that would magically make it click back into place. I then abandon the knob altogether and try to grab through the circular hole to pull on the door.

No. No. Nonononononono. This can't be happening.

It's my first night in my perfect writing retreat cabin, and I'm stuck in the bathroom. Literally *stuck* in the bathroom. The small window opens, but it's clearly made for ventilation, not escape purposes.

I quickly dial Dawn, praying she'll answer. Just when I'm certain I'm about to hear her voice mail recording, she picks up. "DAWN! I'm trapped in the bathroom and the doorknob came off and I can't get out and I don't know anyone in town to call to help me and what do I do?" I frantically ramble.

Dawn slows me down for an explanation, so I give her the specifics of my predicament.

"Well, that's . . . unfortunate," Dawn replies.

"Yes, fully aware how unfortunate this is, Dawn," I retort. "Now tell me what to do."

"Let me call the seller's agent and see if she has a suggestion of someone who can come over to get you out," Dawn says. "I'll call you right back."

I pace the approximate distance of a 5K back and forth in the bathroom waiting for my phone to ring. *I can't believe this is happening. Of course, this day was too good to be true.*

I'm staring at my phone, so the ring tone doesn't even sound before I've answered Dawn's incoming call. "Well?"

"Don't worry, Clara. The agent gave me the number of the town handyman. I called him to see if he could help. He's going to come over and get the door open for you. I just need you to text me the code you set on the front door so he can get in," Dawn tells me.

"How do you know this person is trustworthy? I'm supposed to hand over the proverbial keys to my house to a complete stranger? What if he's a serial killer?!" The octave of my voice rises as a new wave of panic sets in.

"The seller's agent was perfectly nice—you met her, remember? I hardly think she's going to risk her reputation, or the town's, by sending a serial killer after you. Text me the code, and then text me later to let me know you're alive and not in a ditch somewhere," she replies, an eye roll in her voice.

"How will you know it's me texting you and not the serial killer throwing you off his track?" I counter.

"Use the code phrase, 'My nonsensical imagination had nothing to fear' when you send me proof of life," she says.

I huff, but don't argue.

"Code, please?"

"Fine, two-five-one-two."

"Okay, just hang tight. Help is on the way—and his name is Clark."

CHAPTER EIGHT

Clark

I pull into the dirt circle driveway and park behind a blue Honda Accord. Although I knew this high ridge on the edge of town contained a handful of small houses tucked off the beaten path, I've never been inside one. This particular cabin was owned by a couple who had downsized to the small property after their children moved away as adults. I guess they decided the town wasn't worth sticking around for anymore. Not when so many people were leaving. Not when they could be closer to grandkids.

No outdoor lights pierce the pitch-black night. I use my phone flashlight to guide me along the stepping stones walkway to the front porch, then to illuminate the lock on the door. Punching in the code I was sent, I hear the electronic slide of the deadbolt and open the door.

This isn't the weirdest call I've received as a handyman in this town—that prize is reserved for the Edleman family. They tried to install a toilet in a tree house, and I was the lucky one to get to uninstall the mess.

Still, a person who's supposedly brand new to town unable to open an interior door? Seemed a little odd, so I'm slightly on the alert as I step into the cabin.

I slowly enter the living room, stepping over a pair of women's tennis shoes. Boxes cover the kitchen counters and are stacked against the walls, confirming the story that she recently moved in. "Ma'am?" I call loudly to announce my presence. I was told that the occupant is a single woman, so I don't want to alarm her. "I'm Clark, the town handyman. A woman named Dawn called me about getting a door unstuck."

"I'm back here, in the bathroom," I hear a muffled voice respond. Following the sound, I walk behind the fireplace and past a dark room with a wall of windows. There's a closed door before the open bedroom. I set my toolbox down and give a soft knock.

"Just letting you know I'm here," I call through the door. "What seems to be the trouble?"

A burst of exasperated laughter. "Well, I'm being held hostage by the bathroom door. The doorknob came off in my hand, and the door seems to be wedged shut. I can't get it open."

I quickly scan the door frame, noticing an uneven lean. "It appears the top hinge has gotten loose, causing the door to lean against the frame and get stuck. Do you have a screwdriver in there that you could use to tighten the hinge?"

"Uh, nope. No screwdrivers in sight. Which is silly, considering I always kept one in my shower caddy in college. Not sure why I stopped being such a good Girl Scout now."

I pause. "You kept a screwdriver in your shower caddy?"

"No, I did not. I think the sarcasm lost its effect since you can't see my facial expression. Courtesy of the devil door in the way." Even muffled, her voice sounds sweeter than a glass of Pops' tea.

The corner of my mouth twitches. "Sorry to ruin your punchline there, ma'am."

"You can drop the ma'am title," she calls back. "I'm sure it's just a Southern politeness thing, but considering I'm not even thirty years old yet, it's making me feel prematurely aged."

"As you wish," I respond.

"Was that a *Princess Bride* reference?" she asks.

"It wasn't *not* a *Princess Bride* reference," I muse, impressed that she caught it. I can't even count the number of times Davis, Beau, and I watched it with Pops and Bev. But that's not necessarily the norm for our generation. "You've seen *The Princess Bride*?"

"Oh gosh, more times than I could count. My parents loved it. I went through a phase where I refused to answer to anything but the name Buttercup. Unfortunately, my third-grade teacher, Ms. Smith, was a stickler for reality and wouldn't play along. It was a devastating time in my life," she concludes, a wistful tone in her voice. I can't stop the smile from widening across my face.

Who is this woman?

"I can relate. My best friends and I overused the 'I am not left-handed' line for a solid two years," I respond, half-laughing. Suddenly, I realize I've gotten so sidetracked conversing with her that I'd nearly forgotten my purpose here. I turn the door-knob and gently try to push the door open, but it's not budging.

"I could bust open the door Fezzik-style, but it might cause some damage. Are you okay with that?" I ask.

"Fezzik away. The villain door forfeited its right to long life the minute it decided to take me captive," she quips, doing nothing to temper my smile. "Please, just get me out. I can't spend my first night here stuck in the bathroom."

"All right, stand back as far from the door as you can," I say loudly, making sure she avoids injury. I shift my weight to my back foot, readying to give it a firm shove with my shoulder. "Uh, hold on. I, um, want to make sure—are you, uh, decent in there?"

"Oh." Her voice sounds startled, but in a positive way. "Thanks for asking. Yes, I had my bathrobe in here with me, so I'm . . . decent."

"Okay then, stand back." I wait a second to make sure she's clear, then put my full weight into a forceful shove against the door. A metallic groan erupts from the hinges as the door crashes open.

My momentum has me following the door into the bathroom, unable to stop myself from stumbling into the woman in front of me. She lets out a high-pitched yelp of surprise as her hands fly up to my chest, halting my forward motion. I mutter apologies as I stand upright, and then my voice cuts out altogether as I take in the sight of her.

She's slender and tall, although still shorter than me by about six inches. Wet curls fall just past her shoulders. The dry ends reflect the light, revealing their shiny strawberry-blond hue. My gaze travels from her hair across the smattering of freckles on her fair cheeks to the striking cornflower-blue eyes staring widely at me. I take another step backward, which only serves me a better view of the black robe cinched above the curve of her hips. The velvet robe appears to be the buttery-soft kind. But I intuitively know that her skin is softer than that velvet, even without touching it.

What are you doing thinking about touching her?! I swallow hard and tear my eyes back up to hers. That doesn't help. Those vibrant blues stall my words all over again.

Come on, man! I tell myself. *You never act like this around women. Stop being an idiot!*

Clearing my throat, I turn to survey the door. The top hinge has come undone, the door hanging lopsidedly from the frame. But overall, I don't think it's badly damaged.

"Sorry about the door," I say, as though it was my fault that it acted up in the first place. "Should be an easy fix though—you won't have to replace it."

She finally speaks, and her voice is even more adorably sweet than the muffled sound through the door had let on. "Thanks for the rescue. I was really starting to panic about living out the rest of my days in a bathroom. The thought spiral was getting grim."

I huff a laugh, which causes her to smile shyly. Which does not help the "Clark-acting-like-an-idiot" matter at hand. I'm suddenly very unsure of what to do with my hands, awkwardly shifting them from my pockets to crossing my arms to leaning one hand against the counter like a moron. I stand up straight and let them drop to my sides.

"I can replace the hinges on the door tomorrow. But I should take it off the frame in the meantime so it doesn't cause more damage hanging there," I finally say.

"Okay," she responds. "If you don't mind, I'm going to go to the bedroom and change while you take the door down."

I do mind. But I can't very well admit that I'd like to continue staring at her in her robe. To her or to myself. "No problem."

I hear the bedroom door click shut as I make quick work of the still-attached hinge, safely removing the door and propping it against the wall. The woman is still in the bedroom, so I move to the living room to wait for her. I give my head a shake, trying to dislodge the invisible string pulling me to her.

She enters a minute later, but her new outfit is somehow worse than the robe. Navy blue leggings stretch like a second skin across her long,

long legs. My eyes follow the lines of her legs up to her fitted, pale blue t-shirt that reads, *Botany Plants Lately?* I'm a sucker for bad puns and, apparently, for this stunning woman.

Once again, the connection between my brain and hands misfires. I clasp them in front of me briefly before feeling like I'm standing in church. I settle on crossing my arms across my chest as casually as possible, which is minimally casual.

"Thanks again for the help," she says. "I know it's late, so I appreciate you coming out quickly. The door opened and closed just fine earlier today—I'm not sure what happened."

"The combination of steam from the bath and heat from the lamp may have caused the wood to expand. And the doorknob and hinges aren't exactly new. It was the perfect storm of unfortunate coincidences," I say. "What time should I come back tomorrow to install the new hinges and doorknob?"

She shrugs. "I don't have much going on other than unpacking boxes. Whenever fits into your schedule is fine with me. I don't want to cause you any extra trouble—I'm just grateful for the help."

"It's no trouble," I shrug back. My impulses want to announce that I have all day for her, but instead I reply, "9:00 work?"

When she nods an affirmative response, I decide I'd better get out of here before Idiot Clark puts his foot in his mouth. I'm not sure what kind of spell this woman has conjured, because I'm generally a confident, prefers-to-be-left-alone man who's not flustered by women. And I definitely never feel the draw to get truly *close* to a woman. Which is exactly what her pheromone vibes are doing to me right now. I need to get out of here, fast.

I open the front door, but turn back and hold my hand out to shake hers. "I'll see you tomorrow morning—?"

"Clara," she says with a small smile as she places her hand in mine. "I'm Clara."

CHAPTER NINE

Clara

I push *brew* on my single-serve coffee maker, inhaling the scent of caffeine. This machine was one of the first items unpacked because I wasn't about to miss my morning cup of coffee. I stir in two vanilla creamer singles and take a sip. My brain appreciates the liquid energy, but my taste buds are missing the fancier machine at my apartment that makes mochas.

This will have to do, especially considering how little sleep I got last night. I thought I might have a hard time falling asleep in a new place, particularly being all alone. But that wasn't the problem.

Handyman Clark was the problem.

I barely spoke to the man, but somehow every detail of my fifteen minutes in his presence seared themselves into core memories. Even though half of those minutes were spent with a door between us.

It's not just that he's good-looking, though he certainly has all sorts of handsome features going for him. The full but perfectly trimmed beard. The bits of sandy brown hair poking out from under his baseball cap. The broad shoulders and tall stature that made even a taller-than-average woman like me feel short. It was too dark for me to get a good view of his eye color under the rim of his baseball hat. My imagination had a heyday filling in the blank with various shades last night.

But what really kept my mind racing was the deep timbre of his voice checking in with me through the door. Asking permission to break it down. Ensuring my safety by making sure I backed away first. Having the presence of mind to check that I was clothed prior to shoving the door open.

The firm chest muscles my hands inadvertently pressed against when he toppled into me may have also contributed to the insomnia.

I did *not* spend extra time in front of the mirror fixing my curls and applying light makeup in anticipation of Clark coming back over this morning. That was time spent in the name of having a productive day unpacking. Dress for success, you know.

Shoving a handful of Cocoa Puffs straight from the box into my mouth, I survey my new home in the morning light. I'm torn between the need to unpack and the itch to sit in the sunroom and write.

The foreign sound of the doorbell jolts me, coffee sloshing out of my cup and dripping down my arm. "Ouch!" I yelp, then quickly drop to my knees behind the kitchen counter, out of sight from the front windows. My watch reads 8:47 a.m. Apparently, Clark is the early type.

"Just a minute!" I yell as I reach a hand up to feel around the counter till I find a towel. I wipe off the coffee from my arm and the floor before standing again. *Pull it together, Clara,* I chide myself, rolling my shoulders back. *Just play it cool.*

When I open the door, all semblance of coolness flies right out as the crisp air flies in. Clark stands in front of me in faded jeans and a long-sleeve, hunter-green Henley shirt, toolbox in one hand and a hardware store bag in the other. Sans baseball cap, the morning sun provides me a perfect view of hazel eyes. Dark green rims with flecks of gold surround his pupils. The best work of my imagination last night hadn't come close to this green-gold perfection.

My own eyes widen, and my brain draws a blank on all the useful English phrases like "hello" or "good morning" or "come in." I simply smile up at him instead.

"I'm sorry I'm a little early," he eventually says. "I'm kinda a morning person, and I was eager to see—I mean, I wanted to go ahead and get that door fixed for you right away."

"Oh gosh, it's totally fine. Please come in," I reply, stepping to the side so he can duck in through the door. "Can I get you some water or coffee or . . . dry cereal?"

"Nah, I'm good," Clark responds, setting his tool box on the floor and following me to the edge of the kitchen counter. "I assumed you weren't attached to the existing 1980s doorknob style, but I wasn't sure what type of finish you'd prefer. I brought a few options." He sets three doorknobs on the counter: one brushed bronze, one nickel, and one matte black.

"That was thoughtful," I respond as I step next to him and study the choices. "I confess I haven't had time to think through hardware finish decisions for the entire cabin yet. Would have been the first thing I knocked off the list last night if the door hadn't conspired against my to-dos."

Clark chuckles. The sound sends happy shivers down my spine as I glance up at the crinkles around his eyes.

My eyes gravitate toward the matte black doorknob, so I pick it up and turn it over in my hands. "I think this is the one. The black seems to fit a rustic-but-cozy cabin vibe."

"I agree; that was my top choice," Clark responds.

I smirk up at him and quirk my eyebrow. "You would have said that about whichever one I picked, huh?" I tease, one hand on my hip.

He laughs again, and the happy shivers get out of hand. "No, I promise. I recently changed all the hardware in my house to matte black. It's a solid choice," he says, taking the doorknob from my hand. His fingers brush ever-so-slightly against mine, and I swear warmth slowly oozes its way from my fingers down my arm. Like when you take a drink of hot coffee on a cold morning and *feel* the heat travel down your esophagus.

Clark stiffens at the touch. Maybe I'm not the only one experiencing this attraction that is absurdly disproportionate to the amount of information we know about each other. He clears his throat again and reaches inside the bag to retrieve the matching hinges. "I'll, uh, get to work on this."

"I can help!" I chirp brightly, leading the way to the bathroom. "Thank you again for coming out last night and back today. I really don't know what I would have done without you."

My version of "helping" is pretty much sitting against the edge of the tub as Clark removes the existing hinges from the door frame. He pulls up his sleeves slightly in the process, and I notice tattoos on his left forearm that appear to continue up the full length of his arm. I tilt my head to better decipher the inky pattern. My best guess is tree roots, but I can't make out the exact design. A new mystery for my overactive imagination to mull over tonight.

"So, you just moved in yesterday?" Clark asks as he begins installing the new hinges.

"Yep," I respond, handing him the next screw he needs. I'm *helping*, not grasping for an excuse to brush my fingers against his again. "But I won't be living here full time. I live in Kansas City—well, in the suburbs on the Kansas side. But this cabin is going to be my place to get away and work in the quiet."

"Oh, really?" Clark says, standing up and turning to me. His hazel eyes darken momentarily with a look akin to disappointment. "What work do you do?"

"Ah, umm, I'm a writer," I say uncertainly. "I mean, I'm a copywriter and editor. I work for a company in KC that creates content for clients around the nation."

Clark's eyes narrow slightly. "Why would you need a quiet cabin to do that? Do you not work in an office?"

"Yes, there's an office—I have an office," I stutter. I guess there's no way around an admission at this point. "I hope to be a *writer* writer. Hence the cabin in the woods."

"Gotcha. Yeah, this place is certainly more inspiring than an office desk," Clark responds before moving to the detached door to fasten the corresponding hinge pieces. I watch silently, not sure how much more to share about my dreams. Something about Clark's thoughtful demeanor makes me want to tell him *everything*, but that's ridiculous.

He stands the door upright. "Could you hold this steady while I install the new doorknob?"

"Of course!" I jump up, happy to be truly useful. I concentrate on holding the door the steadiest that Clark has ever seen a door held—right up until I'm distracted by the flex and pull of the muscles in his forearm as he works. He stops suddenly and grabs the door to stop it from leaning, glancing up at me. I startle at being caught staring at him.

Easy there, Clara. You're acting like a total fool, I mentally sigh. But I notice a slight upturn of Clark's lips before he turns his attention back to the doorknob.

"So, how long have you lived here in town?" I ask, careful not to slack on my door-steadying job again.

"My whole life. Grew up here. I'm not sure I could hack the big-city life like you do." Clark replies, standing back to his full height.

"Oh, trust me, the suburbs are not exactly big-city life," I self-effacingly respond. Clark raises an eyebrow and looks around as though seeing beyond the walls to the town.

I giggle. "I suppose in comparison to here, it's a big city. But I'm excited to have a break from the hustle."

Clark nods thoughtfully. "Well, you'll certainly find some peace here. At least, I sure hope you do." We stare at each other for a beat before he drops his gaze. "I'm going to hang the door on the hinges now and then make sure the door jamb is lined up correctly, okay?"

"Yes, right, that's how I would do it too," I say with a nod, as though I've replaced hundreds of doors in my life. The corners of Clark's lips fight a smile, but he doesn't point out how obviously untrue my insinuation is.

I appreciate the shift of muscles in Clark's back as he lifts the door onto the hinges. It's not like I'm going out of my way to notice. But what choice do I have when those muscles are right there in front of me?

"Moment of truth," Clark says, moving to close the door.

"Wait!" I call out, putting my hand out to stop him. We both glance down to where my hand clasps his biceps. "Um, maybe one of us should be on the other side of the door before you close it, just in case?"

He tilts his head. "Let's take our chances." Clark doesn't take his eyes off mine as he pushes the door closed. I find myself irrationally hoping Clark is horrible at this handyman gig and the door is still broken.

"Would you like to do the honors?" he asks, gesturing to the doorknob and taking a step backward.

I breathlessly step past him, that first-sip-of-coffee warmth spreading from my head to my toes even without any physical contact. I reach out and turn the handle. The door pops open just like it's meant to. *Darn.*

"Amazing!" I say aloud, smiling over my shoulder at Clark. I step out into the hallway as he gathers up the old hardware and his toolbox. As he follows me out to the living room, I ask, "How much do I owe you for coming out? Do you take payment via Venmo?"

He appears caught off guard. "Oh, you don't owe me anything—it really wasn't a big deal."

"It was a big deal to me," I answer, and I swear his breath catches the same way mine does. "I mean, I'm grateful for the help. At least let me pay you for the new hardware."

Clark holds up his hands and responds, "Seriously, no need. Consider it a welcome-to-your-new-second-home gift."

I laugh, which brings the slightest of smiles to his face again. "In some ways, this cabin is nicer than my apartment back home." Reaching for a way to stretch his time here with me, I offer, "Are you sure you don't want coffee or anything before you go?"

The flecks of gold in his eyes catch the sunlight from the window as he studies me for a beat. "I guess I could—"

His answer is cut off by the loud ring of my phone. I jump at the sound, fumbling to pull my phone out of my leggings pocket, mumbling apologies. My mom's smiling face lights up the screen. I tell Clark, "Just one second, it's my mom, and she's been sick. Let me answer really quick."

"Hey Mom! Doing any better today?" I ask with more cheer in my voice than I feel about her interrupting this moment.

"Clara, honey, it's not good," my mom says. My body freezes in response.

"What do you mean? What's wrong?" I ask, voice now laced with concern.

"Your father tripped down the stairs and broke his ankle. They're taking him back to surgery shortly," she responds with tears. "But I'm still running a fever from the flu, so the hospital won't let me in to see him."

"I'll be right there, Mom. I'll leave right now," I say, already darting around the room to gather my shoes and purse.

"I'm so sorry, honey; I know you just made it to your cabin. I feel terrible pulling you away, but I don't know what else to do."

"Mom, don't feel bad. I want to be there—you and Dad will always come before the cabin. I'll drive straight to the hospital and call you when I get there." I awkwardly try to pull on one shoe while holding the phone with my shoulder. Clark reaches out to steady my elbow, and I glance up at him with appreciative eyes.

My mom gives me the information to the hospital and apologizes twice more before we hang up. I stand up straight and meet Clark's eyes.

"I'm so sorry. I have to go. My dad broke his ankle and is heading into surgery, but my mom is sick and isn't allowed to see him. I have to get home."

Clark nods at me. "Of course. Anything I can do?"

"No, but thank you." I give a disappointed glance around the cabin. "I guess settling in will have to wait." Clark leads the way out the front door, and I'm about to hit the lock button on the keypad when a realization hits me.

"Wait! My baby!" I rush back inside to get my new rubber tree plant from the sunroom. Clark is still waiting on the porch when I come back outside, shifting the planter to my hip so I can lock the door.

"A plant?" Clark raises an eyebrow.

"Not just *a* plant—my brand-new Ficus Tineke that I've been wanting forever and now finally have enough sunlight to keep alive," I tell him. "But I have no idea how long I'll be gone, so I can't leave her here alone. She'll have to survive on the minimal sunlight in my apartment for a while."

I turn back to lock the door, but the weight of the plant lifts from my hip.

"I'll keep it for you. My house has lots of light," Clark says.

My heart seizes with gratitude at the sight of my plant baby in his extremely masculine hands. It's most certainly gratitude, *not* attraction. I mean, maybe a mix. "That's really sweet of you," I respond. "Um, do you know how to take care of plants?"

He shrugs a shoulder. "I'll Google it. Don't worry about it—you go take care of your parents."

I resist the urge to throw my arms around him in a tight embrace. Although I may be the poster child for the physical touch love language, I know not everyone appreciates it. Especially from someone they've only met twice. Despite whatever raging chemistry vibes hang in the air between us.

Walking out to my car and his massive truck, I apologize three more times and thank Clark four more times. I climb into my Honda and punch in the hospital address. Before pulling out of the driveway, I take one final peek in my rearview mirror at Clark's face. A pang of disappointment shoots through me.

I guess my dreams will hang out in the periphery for a while longer.

CHAPTER TEN

Clark

"C'mon boy," I call out to Chase, opening the passenger door so he can jump into the truck. This is a job he can join me on—helping Davis repair one of his kayak storage racks. As we make the drive along the ridge to the riverbank, I make it a point *not* to think about a certain cabin at the top of that ridge. Or a certain cabin's new owner.

It's been over three weeks since Clara swept in and back out of town like a tornado. Sometimes I convince myself that I imagined her presence here, but then I see that dang plant sitting in my front window. Reminding me that it happened. Reminding me of *her*.

Although, Clara's abrupt exit was exactly what I needed to snap me out of whatever temporary trance I'd fallen into around her.

"You and Dad will always come before the cabin."

Clara's declaration to her mom was a slap to the face in the best kind of way. This is a temporary getaway for her, not a place she's putting down roots. Somehow in the twelve hours between busting open that bathroom door and watching her drive away, my heart had done some funny things.

It had a . . . feeling. Something I'm usually quick to shut down, not spend all night examining and encouraging. *I* had done some funny things, things akin to flirting. Had her mom not called, I might have accepted her invitation to a cup of coffee and stayed a while. Who knows what I might have shared with her under the influence of those periwinkle-blue eyes.

But now my inner walls are back up where they belong. I absolutely will not slip up again around her, not now that I'm prepared to keep her at arm's length along with everyone else. The only reason I ever drive past her cabin on the ridge checking for signs of life is solely due to her plant still in my possession.

I'd considered reaching out to Rhonda to try to get Clara's phone number. Rhonda's the only real estate agent in town—she had to be the one to sell the house to Clara. But small towns are cesspools for rumors, so I couldn't afford to let the town's biggest gossip make assumptions about why I wanted to contact Clara.

So I waited. And occasionally drove past the empty cabin, *not* thinking about strawberry-blond curls or freckles. Or a honey voice and bright laugh. Or dry humor delivering witty statements so casually I was completely caught off guard.

Or the electric feel of slender fingers gripping my biceps.

I'm definitely not thinking about those things as I drive toward my best friend—the only close friend I have left. Chase whimpers and nudges my arm, as if sensing my thoughts and reminding me of his presence in my life.

"Okay, *two* close friends," I tell him, ruffling his ears. He dances in the passenger seat as I turn down the road to Deer Floats. Chase knows exactly where we are, and it's one of his favorite places.

"Hey, it's getting cold now. You stay out of the river," I lecture Chase, knowing full well he's going to sprint to the water the second I open the door.

Davis calls out a greeting as I pull my toolbox from the back of my truck, Chase already chest deep in the river. "He's yours for the rest of the day," I say, nodding my head toward my soaking wet dog.

"Liar." Davis grins, knowing I never leave Chase for long. We rescued each other when we both needed it most and can't stand to be apart.

Davis claps me on the back. "Thanks for coming out. I need to get all the kayaks and canoes stored indoors before winter arrives. But turns out the combination of a preschooler and a toddler has a way of wrecking productivity."

Inside the main storage garage, we set to work repairing the broken kayak rack. Davis shares one story after another about Syd and the kids, but I mostly respond with one-word grunts.

"So . . ." Davis pauses, signaling a shift in conversation. "Still keeping that plant alive?"

I grunt again. "Growing two new leaves, I'll have you know. I'm perfectly capable of keeping a plant alive, thanks to some basic research."

A teasing grin spreads across Davis' face, which is right next to mine since he's holding the boards in place I'm about to screw together. I resist the urge to elbow that smirk right off his smart mouth. "Wow, really going above and beyond in this care-taking favor. The plant owner must be something special. Clara, was it?"

I glower at him. I never should have mentioned Clara to him. "It was the nice thing to do in the moment for someone who was panicking. I didn't realize it would draw out into a three-week-plus gig."

Davis clucks his tongue. "Keeping track of how long she's been gone, are we?"

His taunting is drowned out by the sound of my drill, which I allow to "accidentally" slip toward his hand as a warning.

Apparently, my reaction only convinces him that he's hit close to the mark. "I'm just saying, it wouldn't be the worst thing in the world for a good woman to *finally* catch your eye. You haven't even dated since high school. You don't have to get all moody about it."

I brace my hand on the board and give a firm tug, making sure the rack is now steady. "Whatever you think is going on is *not* going on. I got a call for someone who needed help, and I showed up to help. Like I do every day for people all over town who need house projects done. Or annoying friends who can't do basic repairs themselves."

"Ouch. I'm hurt," Davis deadpans. But the twinkle in his eye is still there. "You can keep telling yourself that, keep telling me that, but you forget—I'm one of the few people who *know* you, Clark."

And I'd like to keep it that way, I think but don't say aloud. I put everything back in its place in my toolbox and give a loud whistle to Chase as I walk back to my truck.

Davis follows me. "Come on, don't be like that, man. Is it such a bad thing if I want my best friend to be happy?"

"I am happy."

He crosses his arms and stares me down.

"I'm completely content. I've got Chase, I've got Pops to look after, the town to look after. And I've made peace with the fact that I can't get rid of you," I say with a smirk. "As you might recall from your front row seat to my life, I've been conditioned since childhood to be self-sufficient. I'm comfortable relying on myself, and I'm not going to magically change. I *don't* need a woman to be happy, Davis. Just let it be."

He's obviously unconvinced, but wisely drops it. We load the kayaks onto the repaired storage rack in silence. When we're done, I give Chase a thorough wipe-down with an old towel. I cover the passenger seat of my truck with a blanket that's stashed for this exact purpose. Chase's tongue lolls happily out the side of his mouth as he sits perched in the truck.

Davis gives him a scratch behind the ears through the open passenger window as I start the truck. "You know, Clark, it's okay to be content with what is, but it's also okay to want what could be."

I roll my eyes at him. "Thanks for that unsolicited wisdom."

He grins in response. "Can't help it if the sage advice flows out unbidden. Syd sure loves it."

I pull away from Davis and Deer Floats, Chase hanging his head out the window. I don't know how that dog isn't freezing. I drive the opposite way I came in, taking a different route home. Proving to Davis that I'm not drawn to the cabin on the ridge, not drawn to Clara.

Maybe I'm still trying to prove it to myself.

CHAPTER ELEVEN

Clara

I've died incrementally every day I haven't been able to go back to the cabin. It's all I think about lying in bed each night, trying to fall asleep. My perfect, cozy retreat, the writing desk in the sunroom calling me to take a seat. I'd barely been able to dip my toe into the oasis before reality slammed into me.

The past three weeks have been an exhausting blur of helping take care of my dad after work and on weekends. The handful of days I haven't gone to my parents' house have been spent working late into the evening at the office. I had to make up for the time I took off to be in the hospital with my dad and going to follow-up appointments. On top of my dad's physical needs, I've also pitched in to help with the Living Nativity preparation tasks he usually takes care of each November.

Madison repeatedly pushed me to take PTO days and delegate my assignments rather than catching up in the late evenings. But I can't bring myself to burden other people with my work. I'd rather abandon any semblance of a social life or time to myself.

Except each night, when I let myself replay a mental video montage of the hour of time I spent with Clark. Possibly even less than an hour of total time in each other's presence. But something about our interactions, about *him*, just won't vacate my short-term memory. So I relive it each night, sometimes wondering if I imagined the whole thing.

I'd failed at trying to explain to Mads exactly what it was about Clark that clung to my thoughts. Possibly because I couldn't quite nail it down myself. Sure, he was physically attractive—incredibly so—but that wasn't *it*. Or, at least, not the sum of it.

I nearly asked Dawn for his phone number, since she had to call him to send him to the rescue that night. But Dawn has been unsuccessfully trying to set me up ever since my college boyfriend broke up with me right before graduation. All the dates she'd arranged for me had been massive failures. Come to think of it, failure isn't a strong enough word to describe the disastrous dates accurately. Furthermore, calling them "dates" is an insult to the concept of a date.

Needless to say I'd never be rid of her meddling if she had the slightest hint of my interest in Clark. I can't even tell her it's only to check in on my Tineke. If she knew that I entrusted a plant to him, then she'd *really* clue in to my interest.

So I've waited, anxious to know if my plant is dead or not. Although, something about Clark's competence fixing the door, coupled with the kindness in his eyes when he steadied my elbow, has me believing he's entirely capable of keeping her alive.

It's Tuesday evening, and I'm pushing a shopping cart through the grocery store, picking up the final supplies we need for Thanksgiving. Unfortunately, Overland Park must be full of procrastinators, turning a grocery run into a fight through a battlefield.

My phone buzzes with an incoming call from Mom. I answer, anticipating her adding something to the shopping list.

"Hey honey, what are you up to?" she asks.

"Oh, you know, fighting the hordes for Thanksgiving groceries," I reply, only half kidding. The woman in the aisle next to me holds up a Mockingjay salute. I give her a smile of solidarity before reaching around someone to get the French-fried onions for green bean casserole.

"I wanted to tell you that your father and I talked about it, and we think you should go back to your cabin next week. Take some time off, work remotely, whatever you need to do. But go back down and enjoy a few days there," Mom says.

"But Dad's still recovering—I can't leave you on your own to take care of him, Mom," I counter.

"I'm not a total invalid!" my dad's voice yells in the background. My mom prefers to talk on speaker phone 100 percent of the time for reasons that remain a mystery to everyone. "I'm getting pretty good at navigating with the crutches, and your mom can take me to all the physical therapy appointments. You deserve a break, Care-Bear."

I spin the birthstone ring on my finger as I contemplate the option. My selfish inner voice screams, "YES!" But I'm worried about how well my parents will truly be able to navigate my dad's limitations without backup.

"Clara, I'm ordering you to go back to Noel," my mom says in her best drill sergeant voice. "If you attempt to come to our house next week, I will lock you out."

"I have a key, Mom."

"I'll install new locks."

"Like you'd know how."

My mom makes a *psssht* sound. "You need this, Clara. Your dad and I will be fine. We are grown adults, after all. And we have neighbors and friends from church who would be happy to step in and help if I need it. Arrange things with your boss for you to be out of the office and go take some time for yourself."

I enjoyed a lovely Thanksgiving Day with my parents, relishing the feast I helped Mom prepare. We even managed to continue our traditions of attending the Plaza lighting that night and visiting the giant Christmas tree in Crown Center on Saturday. Of course, my dad's temporary disabled parking pass helped make those activities much more feasible. It was pretty comical watching him putter around with his little knee scooter.

After spending all day Sunday preparing food for the week so my mom wouldn't have to worry about cooking, I'm finally making my way back to my cabin. The car fills with the sound of my voice singing along to one of my Christmas playlists on the drive down. I'm thrilled to have an entire week to get settled in and enjoy the Christmas festivities in Noel . . . maybe even reconnect with Clark? I plan to take Monday and Tuesday off, then work remotely the rest of the week.

It's pitch dark by the time I make it to the outskirts of town at 6:00 p.m. *This will be perfect to drive in and see the Christmas lights for the first time!* The anticipation sends a rush of adrenaline through me, and I can't help but grin as I turn onto Main Street.

My grin dies a slow, agonizing death as I idle down the street, searching every which way for signs of Christmas cheer.

There's nothing.

No festival. No shops. No decorative displays. There's not a strand of Christmas lights in sight.

There are no other cars around, so I'm not blocking traffic when I stop in the middle of the street. I give my eyes a firm rub, expecting Christmas to magically appear when I open them again.

Nothing.

My heart turns to a drum in my chest, beating with panic or disappointment or rage or all of the above. I pull a sharp left turn into the parking lot in front of Noland's, the small grocery store, determined to get answers—and food.

Walking through the doors of the small store, I grab a handheld basket and quickly fill it with basic food essentials to get me through the next few days. Confusion and frustration fight against my cheerful disposition as I walk the aisles, heated to a boiling point by the time I reach the check-out counter.

A woman who appears to be in her mid-forties sits on a stool, bits of gray streaking her dark brown hair with silver. It's tied up in a loose bun at the top of her head, and despite the dark circles under her brown eyes, she gives me a warm smile.

"Hi there, sugar. Did you find everything you needed?" she asks.

I glance down at her name tag—Emily.

"I did. Thank you, Emily," I reply, a waver in my voice. Maybe it's her warm smile or concerned eyes or my utter exhaustion from the past month that causes me to burst into tears. "Actually, no, I didn't find everything I needed."

Emily reaches a hand out to cover mine. "Oh my, I'm sorry. I'll help you find it—what are you looking for?"

"Christmas!" I blurt out between sobs. Emily's facial expression slips to confusion. Rightfully so. I compose myself, and everything tumbles out. "I bought a cabin here to use as a writing retreat because I love Christmas and I want to write Christmas movie scripts and I drove down from Kansas City today expecting to see a Christmas festival wonderland, but there's nothing. There's no Christmas spirit!"

I take a deep breath and blow it out. "I'm so sorry. I know I sound ridiculous. It's been an exceptionally stressful month, and I'm beyond worn out, and I was counting on a big dose of Christmas cheer as inspiration to pull me out of the funk."

Emily chews her lip before responding gently, hand still covering mine. "I'm sorry, hon, but we've never had any kind of Christmas festival. Who told you to expect that?"

I pause a moment, twirling my ring. "No one told me to expect it, I suppose. But I mean, the town is named Noel—I assumed there *had* to be some sort of big Christmas to-do."

"Ah," Emily responds, and I already know I don't like what she's going to say. "Well, the town is named after the surname of the man who founded it—pronounced 'Nole,' rhymes with hole. Not 'No-el.' I could see why you'd be confused."

I spin my ring faster around my finger, mind racing.

"What?! It's...but the town is spelled N-O-E-L. That's obviously No-el. What kind of false advertising is this?" I declare more as a statement than a question. "I want to file a complaint—who's in charge in this town?"

Emily fights a smile, which should make me upset, but makes her more endearing for some reason. "It's a small town, so our city council is limited and doesn't meet frequently. But we do have a mayor, and you're in luck—his office hour is on Mondays."

"You mean the mayor of the city only has office hours on Mondays?" I question, my big-city roots showing.

"No 's.' Hour, singular," Emily clarifies. "He has one office hour a week, Mondays from 10:00-11:00 a.m."

I'm too bewildered to respond. Emily pushes a button on the receipt machine to push out some blank paper, scribbling on it. "Here, this is the address of the mayor's office. And that's my phone number. You come back here and see me or give me a call any time you need something, sugar." She hands it to me and proceeds to ring up my purchases. I hand over my credit card without saying anything, too stunned to make conversation.

My manners overcome my disillusionment enough to thank Emily for her help. "By the way, what time does the coffee shop next door open in the morning?" I ask.

Emily frowns and gives a sad shake of her head. "I'm afraid it's closed for the season. Not enough people around town anymore to make it worth Becky's time keeping it open except during the summer tourist season. Most of the town will be closed up till April, at least."

Nodding my head in resigned acknowledgment, I carry my groceries out to my car. I fight back tears as I make my way to the cabin, punching in the code to unlock the door and carrying the bags inside.

The fatigue of the past month, combined with the despondency of Emily's revelations, drive my steps to the bedroom. I quickly change into flannel pajamas and fall into bed. My mind is too disenchanted to entertain optimistic thoughts of seeing Clark again. I slip into a fitful sleep.

I wake the next morning with righteous indignation in my bones.

How dare they not get into the Christmas spirit?! Even if the town was originally named for some old guy named Noel-rhymes-with-hole, how could they not embrace the alternate pronunciation, at least during the Christmas season?! This is outrageous.

My adrenaline is pumping, courtesy of my ranting thoughts, plus two cups of coffee. I stomp up to the door of the small office space in an otherwise abandoned commercial building. I glance at the sign on the door: Office of Mayor C. J. Noel.

Of course, nepotism would be the only reason a slacker, who only deigns to see people for an hour a week, could be voted as mayor of this town.

I'm notoriously terrible at conflict (i.e., I avoid it at all costs). So, I pause to huff out a breath and gird up every ounce of displeasure I can muster. Whipping the door open, I square my shoulders, raise my chin, and call out loudly, "Excuse me? I'm here to file an official complaint."

The rest of my words die off when I make eye contact with the mayor.

With him.

Clark.

Chapter Twelve

Clark

"Clara?"

A tangle of thoughts bursts through my mind at the sight of her standing in my office. Confusion about why she's here. Agitation at seeing her again *here*, in my context as mayor. Unbridled pleasure at the sight of those strawberry curls I've been trying not to dream about.

My eyes drink her in until I remember the walls, and I shut down my reaction to her. The phrase "file a complaint" finally registers in my mind, pricking my annoyance.

"What are you doing here?" I ask, rising to my feet and rounding my desk. Chase follows my movement from his spot by my chair, but I motion him to sit. I don't know if Clara is comfortable around dogs or not.

"I, I'm just . . . what are *you* doing here?" Clara asks, looking thoroughly bewildered.

"This is my office."

Clara whirls around, peering toward the door. She spins back to me. "But you're Clark. You're . . . you're the mayor? *You're* C. J. Noel?" she finally pieces together, spitting my last name like it's distasteful in her mouth.

I raise an eyebrow. Now I'm the one who's bewildered. *Why's she acting so weird?*

"Yes." I keep my answer simple.

"But, I thought you were the town handyman."

"Also yes. I'm both."

Her eyes travel down to Chase by my side. "You have a dog in here."

This is far beyond weird.

"Yes, I have a dog in here."

"The mayor of the town keeps a dog in the office during his one hour a week on duty. And you're him. The mayor of *Noel.*"

I glance down at Chase, who whines and paws at the floor, begging to go over to Clara. Like he senses her discomfort.

Which, honestly, wouldn't take an intuitive dog to figure out. She's *obviously* spiraling. Her cornflower eyes are wide as saucers, and the color has drained from her face. It makes her freckles stand out even more.

"I'm so stupid," she whispers so softly I barely hear it. "I can't believe this. This, this is just . . ." the volume of her voice creeps up with each word until she practically yells, "I've been hoodwinked!"

She turns on her heel, moving to march right out of my office, but Chase lunges and cuts off her exit. He stands directly in front of her, wagging his tail and giving her his irresistible puppy eyes. He raises a paw in the air but waits for her to initiate touch with him.

Clara reaches a hand down for Chase to sniff, letting him smell her before scratching him. Chase takes it as an invitation to nudge his head under her hand, demanding ear scratches and chest rubs.

Thankfully, Chase's distraction gives me the seconds I need to collect myself enough to respond. "Clara, what are you talking about? Why did you come in here? And how were you hoodwinked? Also, who even uses the word hoodwinked anymore?"

My line of questioning apparently reinfuses the bluster that Clara had lost in the shock of seeing me. She pivots back to face me with renewed agitation on her face.

"I came in here to file a complaint against your city, Mayor Noel. I was *hoodwinked* into believing that this town of No-el would be brimming with Christmas cheer. That I was purchasing a property in a city that would celebrate its Yuletide roots," she says. The fire blazing in her eyes could easily ignite a Yule log.

It takes everything in me to tamp down the attraction to that fieriness burning through me. I focus instead on the insult of her words.

The insult against my family name, against my management of the town.

"Imagine my surprise when I pulled into town last night and found zero Christmas spirit. Not a trace! How dare a town called 'No-el' not celebrate Christmas! It's just . . . *wrong*!" Clara finishes, arms crossed and glaring at me.

I narrow my eyes back at her. "First of all, this town isn't called 'No-el.' My ancestors founded and named the town, and our last name is pronounced 'Nole.' Second of all, we don't advertise any kind of Christmas festivities because we don't *have* any Christmas festivities. Every generation of the Noel family has guarded against the town being turned into some sort of gimmicky, holiday tourist destination. Any expectations to the contrary you may have had were your own. *My* town is not to blame for your assumptions."

"But that doesn't make any sense," Clara accuses. "Everywhere I turn in this city, businesses are boarded up and closed. The town looks *dead*."

I try not to flinch, but the barb hit its mark. My defenses spring into place, triggered by the fear that I'm failing at my one job as mayor—holding this town together.

"Even if your dear ol' ancestors didn't want to host any Christmas festivities, why not embrace the opportunity to draw more people now? It could breathe life back into the town again, boost the economy for an extra couple of months of the year."

Clara maintains her glare in my direction, jutting her chin and straightening to her full height, trying to make her point. Her thumb wildly spinning the ring on her index finger is the only crack in her composure. But I was born for stubborn stare-downs. I cross my arms and mirror her stance without answering.

Chase's head jerks frantically back and forth between us, unsure which of us needs emotional support more. Even though it's clearly Clara.

Her chin quivers, and she turns away muttering, "I can't believe this. Can't believe it's you." She hurries to the door and flings it open. Halfway out, she fires back over her shoulder, "I want my plant back, *if* she's even still alive!"

Then she's gone, Chase whining as he watches the door close. He scratches his paw against my leg, trying to comfort me.

"I don't need it, boy. I'm just fine."

At least, I'll keep insisting to myself that I am.

CHAPTER THIRTEEN

Clara

I close the front door behind me and scream into the emptiness of my cabin.

I'm such an idiot, I tell myself as I yank my shoes off.

Pacing the living room, I dial Dawn. "You could have told me that this stupid town is called Nole, not No-el, and that there is exactly zero Christmas atmosphere here!" I scold the second Dawn answers.

"Umm, whoa there tiger, what in the world are you all feisty about?"

I take a deep breath. "Dawn, when you sent me the listing for this cabin, had you bothered to do any research at all about the actual town of No-el? That there is no Christmas festival? That it's actually pronounced 'Nole'?"

Dawn hesitates. "I mean . . . no."

"Dawn!" I yell, exasperated.

"Well, neither did you!" she defends.

"But you're the real estate agent. You're supposed to know all this important stuff about properties!"

"Yeah, but you're the buyer! People looking to buy houses usually do some reconnaissance about where they're buying!"

Another deep breath in, out. Maybe I should have known to do more research on my own since Dawn is fairly new to real estate. Then again, I'm brand new to property ownership, so how was I supposed to know that I should Google the pronunciation of the town's name?!

"There's really no Christmas festival?" Dawn asks, contrition in her voice.

"No. There's nothing," I sigh.

"I'm sorry, Clara. I messed up. I should have investigated before I pitched the property to you," Dawn says.

I sigh again. "It's okay, Dawn. It's not your fault. And the cabin itself is still amazing. Perfect, even. I just . . . I just need to adjust my expectations now, that's all," I reply, not wanting her to feel guilty.

Dawn's on her way to meet a client, so I reassure her again that I'm not upset before hanging up. She's not really the one I'm upset with, anyway.

I'm upset with myself. Upset that I constructed this fantasy of writing Christmas stories in a cabin in a picturesque Christmas town without bothering to see if it even *is* a Christmas town.

Upset that I've spent the past month daydreaming about Clark, thinking there was some sort of connection between us, something remarkable about *him*. But he's C.J. Noel—descendant of the Nole scrooges, an anti-Christmas crusader.

Not to mention, his cold response to me this morning made it perfectly evident that he hadn't given me a second thought since I left. This was clearly one-sided on *my* side.

I'm such an idiot.

Thankfully, rage is the perfect productive energy. I have my boxes unpacked and everything put away in record time. I even hang up the Christmas decorations I brought with me, complete with a mini tree by the fireplace hearth.

At 5:00 p.m., I decide to make my own cocoon of Christmas cheer and put my writing desk to use. That's the whole reason I bought this cabin. Even if the rest of the town doesn't want to celebrate the season, I can still create my own inspiration.

I put my velvet robe on over my clothes and turn on strands of Christmas lights in the sunroom. Then, I make an extra-large cup of hot cocoa, complete with a heaping pile of whipped cream. My "Chill Christmas" playlist streams through my Bluetooth speaker, and I settle into the chair at my writing desk, glasses perched on my nose. The cursor on my laptop screen blinks at me as my fingers hover over the keyboard.

The chime of the doorbell jolts me out of my staring contest with the computer. Unless a neighbor is picking a peculiar time of day to welcome me to the neighborhood, odds are I know who's ringing that bell.

I sulk and make him wait an extra minute before I amble to the door, confirming my suspicion with a peek out the window on the way. I unlock the deadbolt and open the door a crack.

"My Ficus!" I exclaim, opening the door and pulling the plant inside. Consequently, I've pulled Clark into the cabin as well. "Don't let her get too cold!"

"It's fine; it was only outside for a minute walking up from the truck," Clark says. He's still wearing the same gray Henley shirt that he had on this morning, but now a backward baseball cap makes him look more casual. Not that jeans and a Henley shirt are typical business attire for a mayor.

I inspect the plant with concern. I'm pleasantly surprised to see an impressive amount of new growth. Clark hands me a bottle of plant fertilizer—my *favorite* brand of fertilizer. "Here. I researched, and this was the fertilizer most people raved about. It's what I've been adding to the water."

"It *is* the best," I murmur. I stare at Clark.

"Don't look so shocked—it's not that hard to keep a plant alive. I watered it a couple of days ago, so it should be good for another week or more."

"Thank you," I remember to say, setting the plant down on the coffee table in front of the couch. I straighten and shift awkwardly on my feet, unsure of what else to say. My awkwardness is equally matched by Clark's eyes darting a crisscross pattern from me to anywhere else in the room and back on repeat.

"Well, you have the plant. I'll just be going," Clark says, turning to leave.

"Clark, wait," I stop him. "I'm sorry about getting worked up earlier. I don't want you to be upset with me."

He simply nods, hazel eyes not truly meeting mine.

"I guess I don't understand why a little holiday celebration would be so bad," I press. "Christmas is kinda my thing. I could help. I'd love to help."

Clark closes his eyes and sighs. "It's . . . not worth it, Clara," he responds. "I've lived here my whole life—generations of my family have lived in this town since the beginning of its existence. Please, can you just trust me and drop it?"

My heart stings.

Blinking rapidly, I try to prevent Clark from seeing the watery hurt in my eyes. I pretend to pick lint off my robe. *Gosh darn it—why didn't I take the robe off before I answered the door?!*

I skirt around him to open the front door. "Thanks again for taking care of my plant. Goodnight, Clark."

For a moment, he looks as though he might say something more, but doesn't. He murmurs, "G'night," on his way out the door, and I lock it behind him.

There's no explanation for the salty tears streaming down my cheeks, for the ache in my chest. Clark and I barely know each other. There's no reason for me to care this much about his rejection of my offer to help. There's no reason to care this much about *any* of his thoughts.

An idea cuts through the ache like a spotlight through the night sky.

I'll *show* him how I could help, how great it could be. I smile and give my hands a small clap before springing into action.

My eyes are slow to open the following morning. I stayed up far too late rewatching my favorite Heartmark Christmas movies, taking meticulous notes about every detail of the perfect Christmas festivities pictured. Then I did some Internet sleuthing for real-life Christmas towns, noting all the best and most feasible ideas to implement in Noel.

I may not have slept enough, but I have a compelling case to present to Clark now. Real evidence of what's possible. A vision of what could be.

After a bowl of cereal and a cup of coffee, I take a short bath, only long enough to wash my hair and freshen my curls. I dress in dark jeans and a deep turquoise sweater—no leggings today for my business proposal.

I break down and text Dawn to ask if she still has Clark's number, making up an excuse about something needing to be fixed. I cross my fingers that she won't read into it. I'm relieved when she sends the number back shortly later without any commentary.

Thinking confident, breezy thoughts, I send a text to Clark's number.

ME

Hi, Clark, this is Clara. I was hoping to talk to you. Where might I be able to find you today, since it's not a Monday between 10—11 a.m.?

I stare at my phone to see if he'll respond right away, nervous when he doesn't. *Maybe I shouldn't have made the office hour dig?* I walk to the sunroom and stare out the windows, sit in my oversized chair, stand up and rearrange things on my desk, walk circles around the room.

Ping. My phone finally sounds.

CLARK

I'll make an office hours exception and meet you there. 15 min?

ME

Sounds good!

I take a moment to review my list, twirling the ring on my finger. *Maybe I should have typed it up instead of giving him a handwritten note?* I dismiss the doubt and stand in front of the bathroom mirror.

"You can do this, Clara," I tell my reflection. "You are the queen of helping people. You can help this town."

Fifteen minutes later, I walk from my car back to the mayor's office—Clark's office. I open the door, and the dog comes barreling toward me like he remembers our short encounter yesterday.

"Chase! Settle down," Clark admonishes, but I squat down to give Chase some proper love.

"He's fine—more than fine, he's a sweetheart," I say, slipping into that baby voice everyone uses talking to adorable children and animals. "Aren't you the sweetest boy?" In response, Chase's tail switches into high-gear windshield wiper mode.

"So, what did you want to talk about?" Clark asks, interrupting my moment with Chase.

I pull the file folder from under my arm and take out my list. "I stayed up last night doing research. Here's a list of easy things the town could do to create a small but inviting Christmas festival. I looked up events held by other cities with similar demographics to Noel, to get a realistic comparison." I even pronounce Nole without choking.

Clark accepts the list from my outstretched hand, but doesn't look at it. He maintains steely eye contact with me as he says, "I thought I told you to drop it."

My heart manages to drop to my stomach and simultaneously clog up my throat. Nothing in his hazel eyes is sparkling right now. Chase nuzzles my hand with his nose, and I absentmindedly stroke the soft fur between his eyes.

"Clark, I . . . I want to help. I thought if you saw an actual plan, you might see how amazing it could be. I even have screenshots to show you to see the vibes of the—"

"It's not gonna happen," Clark cuts me off. "I already told you that."

I swallow back the lump in my throat, willing myself to keep my composure. *Don't cry, don't cry, don't cry.*

"But if you'd just consider some of the ideas," I try again, motioning toward the paper in his hands.

The paper that he crumples and throws in the trash can behind him. "I appreciate that you want to help, but we don't need your help. We don't want a Christmas festival here."

Get out, get out, get out! my mind yells. My feet listen and slowly back away from Clark. There's no chance of hiding the tears in my eyes or the shock on my face. Trembling that started in my hands spreads throughout my body as I whisper, "I was so wrong about you."

And then I flee.

Chapter Fourteen

Clark

Clara's face haunts my thoughts for the rest of the day.

She'd come into the office filled with spunk, sparks of hope in her eyes. But she'd fled with devastation, tears in her eyes.

Because I'd been a jerk.

I didn't *want* to hurt her, to crush her like that. But I didn't know how to get through to her, to stop her from chasing this fool's errand. Noel is never going to be a Christmas town. It's just not.

And I didn't know what to do about that *feeling* she kept stirring up in my heart. When she'd answered the door last night, she was wearing the same robe from the first time I saw her. One look brought the warmth of our first encounter crashing like a tidal wave over my internal walls. That yearning to be closer pulled at me. To learn everything there is to know about her, to spill all of who I am out to her. I didn't know how to cut that sensation off. I was unprepared to deal with it because I've never experienced that draw to a person before now.

So I crumpled the paper. And regretted it the instant I saw the trust in her eyes splinter.

But I couldn't take it back, couldn't take the risk.

"I was so wrong about you."

Clara whispered the words so quietly, she may have thought I couldn't hear. But I heard. And I still hear them, words playing on a loop through my mind, no matter what task I distract myself with.

As I install a new storm door for Davis' parents, I swing between berating myself for being so cruel to Clara and exhorting myself to keep forcing distance between us. For his part, Chase is giving me the dog equivalent of the silent treatment. He nearly lost his mind this morning when Clara left, whining and barking and pacing and scratching up my door. He's been aloof today, punishing me for being a bad dog.

I've finished up the storm door when I receive a text from Rhonda.

Rhonda: Don and Kate are moving to Bentonville and putting their house on the market. Can you meet me there today or tomorrow to make a punch list of repairs to make before listing?

My fist involuntarily clenches around my phone. *Not another one.*

I rub my temples with my free hand, eyes closed. Chase nudges against me, and I open my eyes to see him staring up at me. "Oh, you've decided you love me again?" His tail gives a small wag, so I reach down to scratch his ears before responding to Rhonda to set a time.

While my text messages are open, my thumb hovers over Clara's name. *Maybe I should text her and apologize for being rude?*

The tug I feel to reach out to her is enough to make me lock my phone instead.

CHAPTER FIFTEEN

Clara

I shut myself in my cabin and ugly cry until every trace of moisture has left my body.

Maybe I should pack up and go home. Forget the week here. Retreat from my retreat.

My cheeks are blazing, so I step onto the back porch. The chill in the air calms the flush. Although trees have lost their leaves, there are enough evergreens to provide privacy around the lot.

I still don't have any porch furniture, so I sit down on the edge of the small deck. Even though it's the middle of the work day, I decide to call Madison. My solo brainpower isn't enough to compute this situation.

She answers, "Clareeeey, why are you calling me right now?" *Oh dear.* Mads only calls me "Clarey" with the drawn out "e" when she's annoyed.

"What's with the attitude?" I ask.

"Well A of all, it's supposed to be your day off, so you shouldn't be calling me during work. B of all, stinking Michael knows I'm your best friend. He keeps coming to ask me all his dumb questions and trying to wriggle his way out of assignments since you're gone. And C of all, I don't want to admit that I miss having you at the office," Madison ticks off.

I smile, grateful for the distraction that is Madison Wheeler. And her mash-up of list phrases.

"I'm calling because this trip is swirling the drain of nightmare territory, and I need your help processing through it," I tell her.

"Ooo, I love a good processing sesh—lay it on me."

I fill Madison in on every detail of the past two days, and she interjects with all the appropriate displays of supportive emotion and outrage. "I'm honestly tempted to wave the white flag and come home today. Forget working remotely the rest of the week. What's the point of being here when my inspirational setting has devolved into gloom?"

Madison scoffs, then says. "Firstly, dramatic much?" I harrumph before she continues. "Secondly, don't you dare, Clara Jane Sullivan. Just because McGrinchie or the town doesn't want your help, that doesn't mean you give up on *your* dream. Do you still want to write Christmas movie scripts?"

I sigh. "Of course I do."

"Do you still love the cabin itself?"

"Well, yes. It's precisely the cabin in the woods getaway I'd imagined."

"Do you still love Christmas?"

"Now you're just being ridiculous, Mads."

"Answer the question."

"YES, I still love Christmas!"

"Then stay there and make your Christmas dreams come true, Clara. He-who-does-not-deserve-to-be-named shouldn't ruin that for you," Madison finishes decisively. She abruptly ends the call when Michael comes back into her view, throwing herself on the land mine to save me from having to talk to him.

Wrapping my arms around my knees, I mentally survey my options again.

One: Admit defeat and leave, never to return again. Surrender the cabin to the forces of entropy. I've invested in a future haven for woodland creatures.

Two: Withdraw to lick my wounds, but return eventually to utilize the cabin as a hermit in solitude.

Three: This is my property, gosh darn it! Claim what's mine, and make it *mine*.

My eyes flash with new resolve as I settle on option number three, thanks to Madison's pep talk. *Aunt Gloria didn't give me this money so I could sink it into a cabin that I never use. Never realize my dreams.*

A rude, grumpy mayor can't ruin this place for me. Forget him and his unforgettable eyes.

I stand up and take in my surroundings. Around the perimeter of the cleared yard, there are three pines that have clearly waited their whole lives to be Christmas trees. One particularly adorable one is only three feet high. The others are taller than me, but less than seven feet.

You may not want Christmas, Mayor Scrooge, but you're not the boss of me.

I immediately head to the grocery store, glad to see Emily at the checkout counter again. I'm even happier when I see a mini Christmas tree on top of the register next to her. Christmas music is playing over the store speakers. *Maybe not everyone in this town is as grinch-y as Clark makes out.*

I beeline to Emily, even though she's in the middle of talking to a young woman who looks to be around my age. She has highlighted blond hair, light brown eyes, and the longest eyelashes I've ever seen. *Was she born with those, or is there some miracle eyelash serum I don't know about?*

Emily sees me coming and calls out a greeting. "You're back! I didn't even catch your name last time, sugar."

"Oh, I'm Clara. Clara Sullivan," I say. "And I'm glad you're here again—do you work most days?"

"Honey, I work here every day," Emily laughs. "My husband's family owns this store. Paul handles all the inventory, stocking, and finances, but I do all the caring about people up front." Her gaze assesses my face. "Speaking of caring for people, I can't help but notice your eyes appear to have shed a tear or two recently. Everything okay, Clara?"

Instant heat flames my cheeks. In my zeal to enact my newest plan, I didn't take time to freshen up my makeup or even glance in the mirror. Here I am, standing by the woman who should be hired for *every single* mascara commercial, and I likely have black smears on my splotchy cheeks.

"Oh, yes, I suppose I . . ." I trail off, floundering for an explanation. Emily and Gorgeous Eyelash Woman gaze at me with such sincere concern, I settle on the truth. "I recently had an unpleasant conversation with the mayor. A couple of unpleasant conversations, to be precise."

Emily gives a hearty guffaw. The other woman regards me with compassion as she says, "Oh goodness, I'm afraid Clark doesn't always make the best first impression."

I don't bother to explain that this wasn't my first impression of Clark. That my *first* impression of him was rather captivating. That the dissonance between my first impression and most recent impression is what caused these puffy eyes.

"I'm Sydney, by the way, but everyone calls me Syd," she offers. "My husband is best friends with Clark, and I've known him my whole life too. Sometimes you have to take Clark with a grain of sugar to counterbalance the gruff exterior."

"Gruff is one word for it," I mutter under my breath.

The two women exchange a look before Sydney speaks up again. "I'm not making excuses for him by any means. He's always come off a bit rough around the edges. But he's . . . well, he's been through the wringer in a lot of ways. He lost his parents and older brother a while back. Plus, he carries the weight of his family's legacy in the town in ways he maybe shouldn't. With so many people moving away from Noel lately . . . let's just say Clark's gruff exterior has been *extra* gruff."

Sydney's words poke holes in my Madison-inspired resolve to write Clark's name in a metaphorical burn book. Knowing he has a tragic backstory behind his behavior would normally make me want to do whatever I could to help him heal and be happy. I *love* helping people get better. But there are still yellow "slow down" lights going off internally regarding Clark. I decide not to delve into those emotions yet, refocusing on my original mission coming in today.

"Emily, do you sell any Christmas lights? Or is there another store in town that does?" I ask.

"We're the only store in town, aside from the small hardware and auto parts store. We don't carry an abundance of Christmas stock, but I'll show you what we do have," Emily offers, coming out from behind the register.

"Thanks for the groceries and the adult conversation, Emily," Syd says. "I'd better get back home before Addie wakes up from her nap.

She'll throw a fit if Davis is the first one she sees upon waking." Syd smirks at Emily and turns to me. "It was nice to meet you, Clara. I hope I'll get to see you again soon."

"Oh, thank you," I respond. "I live in Kansas City, but I got a cabin here to come stay a couple of times a month. Or at least that was the original plan."

Syd smiles warmly, "Well, feel free to get my phone number from Emily—I'd love to hang out whenever you're here. I'm always looking for more friends my own age."

"And what am I, missy—geriatric?!" Emily mock-scolds Sydney.

"You are like my wise older sister, Em," Sydney replies, a twinkle in her eye. "My *much* older sister."

Emily laughs as Sydney leaves, then leads me to the back corner of the store. She wasn't kidding about the minimal Christmas stock. *Did some Ghost of Christmas Past cast an anti-holiday curse on this town?!* I silently wonder, gritting my teeth.

"I'll take all the lights you have," I tell Emily, who raises her eyebrows in surprise. "Do you sell any extension cords?"

As Emily scans my purchases, she prods me. "I didn't want to say much in front of Syd, seeing as how you hadn't met her before. But since you and I go way back, you care to tell me more about your unpleasant conversations with Mayor Noel? Have anything to do with the town not being No-el?"

I blow a breath out the side of my mouth, fluffing the curls on my cheek. "Something like that."

Emily continues scanning silently, a quirked eyebrow the only sign she expects more of a response.

"I might have expressed my displeasure at the lack of Christmas spirit in town," I begin. *Beep, beep* goes the register. "And I might have offered some suggestions to, you know, imbue a dose of Yuletide cheer into the city."

"Ah," Emily responds. "Say no more; I can imagine how the rest of the conversation went. And why the splotchy eyes."

I avoid eye contact as images of my morning conversation with Clark play on the IMAX screen of my mind against my will. Emily takes my credit card and swipes it through the register. She taps my card as she waits for the receipt to print, then hands both to me.

She traps my hand in both of hers, forcing me to meet her gaze. "I hope you'll keep your original plan to come to Noel regularly. And that will mean interacting with Clark. It's a small town—there's no way around it. Just . . . don't write him off, okay? Or, at least, don't write the town off."

Something about the way Emily says it makes me think that maybe this whole community, not only Clark, might be hurting in ways I don't understand yet. Emily's kindness makes me want to understand.

Three cups of hot cocoa, two bowls of Cocoa Puffs, and countless frustrated outbursts later, I plug in the chain of extension cords, illuminating my backyard with bright, multicolored light. A satisfied grin spreads across my face at the glow. The three pine trees are wrapped with strand after strand of Christmas lights, throwing a beacon of holiday joy into the dismal atmosphere of Noel.

A beacon of joy. Maybe that's exactly what they need. What *he* needs.

"All right, Clara. We're playing the long game," I tell myself out loud, rubbing my hands together.

No-el to the rescue.

CHAPTER SIXTEEN

Clark

"**Y**ou wanna know where being your best friend gets me? Sleeping on the couch, that's where." Davis' grouchy voice pierces my ear.

I switch my phone to speaker and set it on the counter, not wanting Davis' bluster bursting my ear drum. I put my bowl into the microwave and start it. Every Sunday I make a big batch of food to eat for dinner all week, and it's chili's turn in the rotation.

"What are you talking about?" I ask, though I don't think I want to know the answer.

"I'm talking about how I—being the greatest, most loyal friend in modern history—didn't mention anything to Syd about you meeting Clara when she first moved here. And now I'm in the biggest doghouse in modern history," Davis grumbles.

"Wait, how could you be in the doghouse about not mentioning it unless you *have*, in fact, mentioned Clara to Syd?" I narrow my eyes, even though Davis can't see my expression. Hopefully, he hears the annoyance in my voice.

"Because Syd met Clara for herself today."

"Oh, no."

"Yeah, oh no. And when Syd came home from Noland's to tell me about it, I made the mistake of not acting like this was the first time I'd heard of Clara."

"Uh-oh."

"Uh-oh is right. It was exactly 3.2 seconds before Syd had pried the whole story out of me. Now I'm being punished for not telling her about something as monumental as a new woman in town turning your head," Davis yammers.

"She did not turn—"

"Stop trying to deny it, you idiot," he interrupts. "And to make matters worse, you apparently were idiot enough to be a total jerkwad to Clara, who came into Noland's looking like she'd been crying all morning, according to Syd."

"Shoot," I sigh. Chase whines next to me. I swear he understands every word of the English language.

"So now I get to sleep on the couch, courtesy of my loyalty to you," Davis finishes.

"Sorry about that, man," I respond. I am genuinely sorry to be the cause of a fight between Davis and Syd.

"Oh, don't you worry. You'll get yours. Consider yourself warned for the next time you see Syd." Davis adds, "Anything you want to tell me about some dummy I call my best friend being mean to the newest resident of Noel?"

"Clara is not a resident of Noel—she lives in Kansas City and only intends to come here to visit," I clarify.

"Technicality."

I growl at Davis. Chase growls at me.

"Good boy, Chase," Davis calls out. I take the phone off speaker and return it to my ear.

"I have nothing I *need* to tell you," I say. "But because you're the nosy type who doesn't know when to back off, Clara came here expecting the city of No-el to be the North Pole. She got all huffy when she discovered the truth. Then she decided that *her* disappointment was reason enough to justify a complete overhaul of everything the town stands for. She brought me a list of all the ways we could make Noel a Christmas festival destination. I simply informed her that it wasn't going to happen."

"You *simply* informed her?"

"I *firmly* informed her," I add, annoyed.

"You idiot."

"You know, for claiming to be my best friend, you're sure insulting me an awful lot tonight," I chide, annoyance rising. Removing my bowl of chili from the microwave, I stalk over to the kitchen table but don't bother to sit down.

"I am your best friend, and that's why I'm telling you to stop being a moron, Clark. Recognize a good thing when you see it for once," Davis fires back.

Chase barks twice, apparently not liking the expression on my face.

"See, your other best friend agrees with me," Davis says, a lighter tease in his tone of voice.

"Need I remind you that you haven't even met Clara?" I tell Davis. "You can't be so positive that she's a good thing without even knowing her."

"First of all, it's a short matter of time before I meet Clara, because Syd is convinced that Clara is going to be her next bosom friend," Davis says.

"Her . . .what?" I interrupt.

"Syd's on an *Anne of Green Gables* kick again," Davis continues, as though this explanation is entirely sufficient. "But second of all, I don't need to have met Clara to recognize when something good has happened to you. Even if you're too dense to see it."

"You've reached your insult limit for the night. This conversation is over."

"I'll continue the stream of insults in my dreams tonight. The gaps between the couch cushions will provide constant inspiration."

"See you in your nightmares, then," I say before ending the call. Chase gives me a look so laced with disappointment, he appears eerily human for a second.

Should I apologize to Clara? I wonder to myself. Taking a bite of my lukewarm chili, I find my appetite has disappeared.

Sure, I'm a man who enjoys my privacy and doesn't need a lot of friends. Some might call me grumpy from time to time. But I'm not usually downright rude. Not like I was to Clara today.

I sigh.

Whistling to Chase, I slip on a fleece jacket and head out the front door. Moments later, we're driving up the steep road to the ridge on the edge of town.

As we near the driveway to Clara's cabin, there's a conspicuous glow piercing the night sky. "What the?" I question aloud, slowing down.

A kaleidoscope of colors floods the air around the cabin. The unmistakable shine of Christmas lights. Hundreds of them. Possibly thousands.

"That woman," I grumble. I step on the accelerator and drive right past her driveway. Drive right home without stopping.

CHAPTER SEVENTEEN

Clara

"Would you say that each member of your team is equally deserving of a holiday bonus?"

Mr. Douglas, my boss, stares at me, waiting for my answer.

It's end-of-the-year review time. While I'm thankful for my glowing personal review, I don't enjoy the part where I have to give feedback about the copywriters on my team. Particularly one member of the team.

I squirm in my seat, eyes flitting away from Mr. Douglas' stare. Madison attempted to make me take a blood oath to be honest about Michael's less than stellar job performance. But just this morning, he'd come into my office with tears in his eyes, asking for my help with his final article of the month. His childhood dog passed away, and he was too broken up over it to concentrate.

"Umm," I hum, spinning my ring. "I, uh, yes, I think all the members of my team have done their part to earn the holiday bonus," I finally confirm. I can already picture Madison's disappointed rage face.

"Okay, thanks for your help, Clara," Mr. Douglas wraps up. "We appreciate your exemplary contribution to the company, as always."

I murmur appreciation before leaving the office, heaving a sigh. Unlocking my phone reveals I have a text from Madison waiting for me.

MADS

And????

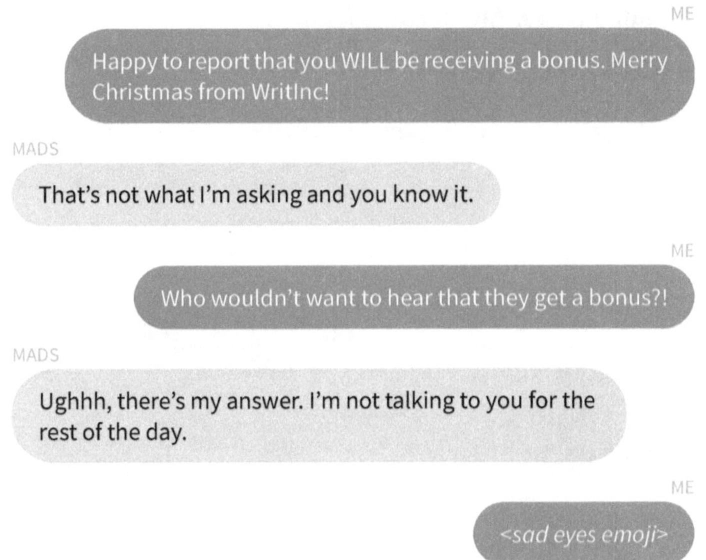

Returning to my office, I scoot past my Tineke plant to sit down at my desk. Although I'm grateful to have a private office and not a cubicle, it's still tiny. The plant is too large for the small space, but my office window gets better light than any room in my apartment. When I left Noel two days ago, I wasn't sure I could bring myself to go back before Christmas, so she came home with me. I certainly wasn't going to ask *him* to take care of her again.

I'd gathered up enough gumption to stay in Noel for the rest of my planned week, although working remotely proved to be less efficient than I'd anticipated. I wound up having zero time to start writing a Christmas movie script, but I did enjoy the view of my Christmas lights from the sunroom while working. I also enjoyed a few more conversations getting to know Emily when I craved people time and returned to Noland's for random groceries. Her kids—a son in tenth grade and twin daughters in ninth grade—supplied her with a never-ending well of dramatic tales to draw from. She liked to associate each story with an individual strand of gray hair.

Emily gave me Sydney's phone number too, but I ran out of gumption to contact Syd on this trip. I didn't know how to handle conversation with the wife of Clark's best friend just yet.

My phone dings. Anticipating another scolding from Madison, I open it with an eye roll at the ready.

McSCROOGE

> Why would you leave your Christmas lights on when you're not in town?

Madison may have changed Clark's name in my phone first thing when I got to the office.

ME

> Why were you at my cabin??

McSCROOGE

> I wasn't. The glow party is visible from the road.

ME

> Why were you driving past my cabin??

McSCROOGE

> Stop evading the question. Why are you wasting electricity running lights when you're not there? Are they on all day?

I'm not the one evading a question here. Why was Clark driving past my cabin?

ME

> There's this genius new invention called the smart phone that allows you to control a power switch remotely. Of course I'm not leaving them on during the day. They're on a timer that I can control from my phone.

ME

> And maybe leaving behind a dose of Christmas cheer in your precious town is worth a higher utility bill.

Clark doesn't respond right away, and I find myself unable to do anything but stare at my phone, waiting. Maybe I shouldn't have prodded his anti-Christmas sentiments. A realization flashes through me with fury.

> Don't you dare unplug them.

> Annoying the town with your disco party is not worth your hard-earned cash.

Before I can fully think through my actions, I hit the call icon next to McScrooge's name.

"What are you doing calling in the middle of a perfectly adequate text conversation?" he answers gruffly.

"I'm making sure you're not on your way to unplug my Christmas lights, that's what I'm doing," I respond, heart racing. *I can't believe I just called him.*

I *really* can't believe he answered.

Although he's not answering my accusation now. "Clark . . . Don't. You. Dare unplug my lights." The sound of Chase barking is the only response on Clark's end.

"I will look up the police department and contact them about a trespasser," I threaten.

"Oh yeah? Who do you think Larry is going to side with? You, or me—the guy he's known since first grade, who also happens to be the founding father's descendant and current mayor?"

"Wow, really inflating that self-importance, aren't we? I'll do some digging into your genetic connection to George Washington and see what turns up."

"Har har."

"Clark? Stay away from my cabin."

Silence. Then a huffed, "Fine. I'm turning around."

"Now, if you're done plotting felonies, I need to get back to work," I say.

"Unplugging unwanted Christmas lights is hardly a felony," he grumbles. Barking sounds again, and I hear a muffled, "Stop it, Chase."

I can't help but crack a smile as I respond. "I'm sure trespassing and property damage could be inflated to amount to a felony. I am a writer, you know—I could be exceedingly convincing in my police report."

"You clearly don't know how small towns work."

"Besides, texting while driving is also illegal in some places. And I caught you in the act," I chide.

"You know, there's this genius thing called a smart phone that lets you voice to text," he retorts.

We're both silent for a long pause. Just as I'm opening my mouth to say goodbye, Clark clears his throat and asks, "When are you coming back to the cabin?"

Surprise has knocked the words right out of me, but Clark rushes to fill in my silence. "I didn't know if you needed someone to water the plant if you'd be gone a while."

"Are you trying to trick me into giving you permission to be on my property so you can conveniently disable the Christmas lights?" I ask, giving in to a small smirk.

"What?! No!"

"Kidding. But no, I brought her back with me this time. She's sitting right here next to me in my office. Taking up way too much of my personal space."

"Oh."

"Thanks for thinking of it, though," I say, taking a baby step to test out this bridge he seems to be rebuilding between us.

"Well, next time you can leave it here. I already know the watering drill." Clark clears his throat and abruptly says, "Take care, then."

"You too—" the words are barely out of my mouth before the call has ended.

What in the Magic Eye illusions are you, Clark Noel?

I think about the books of optical illusions my parents always had at the house. It's the perfect metaphor. I just can't bring the true Clark into focus. There's obviously a cohesive image below the surface-level mess of colors and patterns. But it's not making sense yet. He's not making sense.

And gosh darn it, there's suddenly nothing I want more than to figure out the hidden picture beneath Clark Noel's confusing exterior.

A teardrop trickles down my cheek, closely followed by the gathering stream.

Magical snow slowly falls from the rafters, gathering in small drifts between twirling pointe shoes.

The Snow Pas de Deux has always been my favorite scene in *The Nutcracker*. I'm sure that was directly influenced by Aunt Gloria's opinion—it was her favorite to perform, even more than the Dance of the Sugar Plum Fairy.

It's our first time to watch the ballet without Aunt Gloria sitting next to us.

As the curtain falls for intermission, I can tell my parents are wiping away the same tears I am. Madison pats my arm in support—she took our fourth ticket tonight in Aunt Gloria's place, an invitation I know my parents will offer for as many years as she accepts.

I excuse myself to use the restroom, grateful to stretch my limbs and collect my emotions. My parents and I had enjoyed all of our usual Christmas festivities in the past few weeks. We hit up every major lights display in the Kansas City metro. We took photos with the elaborate decorations at Union Station. We even went ice skating at Crown Center—Dad enthusiastically cheered from a bench. Activities that historically included Aunt Gloria as our fourth. I know we'd all equally smiled at the memories and cried at the loss.

As I dry my hands, I study the tanzanite ring Aunt Gloria gave me on my sixteenth birthday. We were as close as an aunt and niece could be, even after I abandoned ballet lessons in eighth grade. I'd inherited her lithe ballerina frame from my dad's genetic pool, and I trained at the ballet school where she was an instructor from the time I was itty-bitty.

But Aunt Gloria recognized my heart was filled with stories and words more than fouettés and échappés before I was brave enough to admit it. She encouraged my parents to enroll me in a creative writing course in lieu of ballet class. Aunt Gloria always understood me, always supported me. Even in her passing, she understood and supported me with the gift of the writing cabin.

I return to my seat right before the curtain rises. As the dancers travel to the Land of Sweets, I picture all the worlds, all the princes, all the love stories I've dreamed up over the years. It's time to use the gift that Aunt Gloria gave me to the fullest extent. It's time to write one down, finally.

CHAPTER EIGHTEEN

Clark

Thwap! Chase's tail slaps me across the face as he hangs his head out the window.

"Dang it, Chase, sit down!" I scold halfheartedly. "You know you're gonna have to move to the back once we pick up Pops. And we can't have the windows down."

I'm picking up Pops on our way to Davis and Syd's house for Christmas Eve festivities. They've been kind enough to allow Pops and me to crash their family celebration with their parents and siblings for the past few years. Davis and Syd do a special Christmas morning tradition with only their kids, but they open up the house to the whole gaggle of us every December 24. Their kids are the youngest out of the cousin crew on both sides. Being at their place allows them to put the kids to bed and continue hanging out with the grown-up crowd after 7:30 p.m.

Pops and Bev never had kids, and with my family all gone, we got absorbed into the Baker/Smith joint celebration. Christmas was never a big enough deal in our house growing up to mourn its loss. But it is nice to have a semblance of familial belonging on Christmas Eve. I always manage to stay busy with home projects on Christmas Day, making it a normal day like any other.

I pull into Pops' driveway, and Chase starts dancing in the seat next to me. Pops is already waiting on the front porch. *Stubborn man.*

"What are you doing sitting out in the cold, old man? That can't be good for your joints," I rebuke as I stride toward him.

"I don't need to hear another word from you about my joints, boy," he fires back, though he's slow to straighten fully upon standing. I wait next to the porch stairs, arm twitching to reach out to steady him. "And I don't need no help walking down two steps," he adds with a glare. He hands me a bag of gifts for the kids.

"Have it your way," I gripe back. But mentally I'm cataloging the stiff nature of his movements. Concern slices through me.

Chase leans out the window to lick Pops' face, earning a scratch behind the ears. He then obediently hops to the back seat of the truck, making way for Pops to climb in. I stand by the door, just in case. After placing Pops' bag of gifts next to mine, I close the door behind him.

"Now, what's this I hear about you telling off some nice girl a few weeks back?" Pops asks, no small amount of admonishment in his voice.

"Davis is a dead man," I growl.

"You'll have to kill off Sydney and Emily while you're at it," Pops adds, sounding smug. "I got an earful from multiple sources. They're under the illusion that I could talk any sense into you. We both know that ain't the truth."

I snort.

Pops continues staring at me, unnerving my peripheral vision. "You're not gonna let it drop?" I ask, eyes on the road.

He shakes his head.

Sighing, I surrender the bare minimum of information. "This new Christmas-obsessed girl, Clara, buys a cabin in town to use as her writer's retreat or whatever. Then, she gets bent out of shape when she finds out the town isn't the No-el, mecca of Christmas cheer, that she expected it to be. I just . . . set her expectations straight."

I glance over to see if Pops is satisfied, but his eyes are narrowed. "And made her cry?"

Groaning, I lean my head back against the head rest. "It's not like I set out to *make* her cry," I say. "I can't help it if she didn't like the facts. This isn't a Christmas town, and we don't *want* it to be a Christmas town, despite what she may think we need. I made sure she understood that, and that's all."

No response.

"I don't appreciate your judgy silence, Pops," I say, not daring a glance at him.

"I'm thoroughly acquainted with this town's historic aversion to Christmas," Pops says. "Any close friend of your grandad's knew all that. But I find it curious that you would need to react so strongly to a sweet, beautiful woman."

"I . . . what? What are you talking about, 'beautiful and sweet'—you haven't even met Clara," I stutter.

"I have my sources," Pops declares. "Sources who hypothesize there's more going on here with you than simply clearing up Nole/No-el expectations. Sources I'm going to have to concur with at present."

"We're done talking about this. Let's go enjoy our Christmas Eve," I say, pulling into Davis' driveway.

"Yes, let's," Pops quips, an ornery twinkle in his eye.

Four hours later, I unlock my front door and let Chase run inside ahead of me. I arrange plastic containers of leftovers in the fridge, grateful I won't have to cook for the next couple of days. Before letting the kids go wild opening gifts, we'd enjoyed a full Christmas dinner with smoked turkey, ham, and endless sides. I stuffed myself with more food than I'd normally eat, just to keep my mouth full and avoid answering leading questions.

Aside from some sly side remarks, Davis and Syd were considerate enough not to grill me about Clara openly in the presence of their families. But there had been several near-misses with Pops. Pretty sure he was intentionally trying to out me.

Not that there is anything to out. I have no underlying feelings for Clara.

Then again, my success rate at convincing myself of such is slowly nosediving.

I shouldn't have texted her that day after she left. Ever since she called me unexpectedly and I'd listened to her sugar-spun voice again, I haven't been able to get that voice out of my head. Or those corn-flower blues—eyes I'd seen light up with laughter and pool with pain. I'm not sure which version tormented me more.

Taking a seat in my leather "thinking chair," I close my eyes, trying to slow my thoughts. Chase is still amped from all the chaotic attention he received from the kids tonight. He tries to engage me in tug-of-war with his rope. When I don't play along, he goes full-on zoomies mode and races imaginary competitors around the room.

My thoughts are running similar circles. I've tried every trick I can think of to put Clara out of my mind. I kept myself busy so I'd have less time to think—unsuccessful. Then, I attempted to discourage my mind from dredging her up by listing out things I don't like any time she popped into my head—wildly unsuccessful. Drowning out my inner monologue by listening to loud music at all times was my most recent failure—couldn't handle it because I enjoy silence too much.

I lean my head back against the chair and stare at the ceiling. There's something about Clara that keeps reeling me back toward her. As attracted as I am to her gorgeous appearance, it's not about her looks. It's something about her sweetness, her eagerness, her spark. I'm a fish caught by the hook—I swallowed the shiny bait, and now I'm desperately trying to swim away before I'm a goner.

I can't be a goner. I enjoy my solitary life too much—I *need* my solitary life too much. I wouldn't fit with Clara. She wouldn't fit with me. She'd get sick of a relationship with me so fast, it's best to not even go there. For her sake, more than mine.

But all my mental thrashing hasn't snapped the fishing line yet.

I don't think through what I'm about to do before my feet are moving, carrying me back out to the truck. Chase happily tags along, settled and content next to me as we drive the winding road.

Killing the truck engine, I whistle for Chase and close the door as quietly as possible. The multicolored glow of Christmas lights may as well be a searchlight beaming the cabin's location to the entire town. I know she's not home, and I also know she doesn't have any security cameras, so she'll never know I'm here.

Chase leads the way around the back of the house, drawn to the bright lights like a mosquito to a bug zapper. We need a lot of those in the Arkansas summers.

I round the corner of her cabin and bark out a laugh before I can stop myself. Lord knows how many strands of lights that fiercely determined woman strung up out here. There are three evergreen trees covered in more lights than they have pine needles.

Clara doesn't have any furniture on the deck, so I ease myself down to sit on the edge, taking in the bright view. I have to hand it to her; as I sit here in the festive glow, there's a flicker of contentedness that flashes through me.

Dad would have hated this. It's not as though my family forbade private Christmas decorations in town—heck, Davis and Sydney's house was decked out with lights and a huge tree. We even had a small artificial tree growing up. It was the overdone public displays that got shot down before they could even be suggested.

"This isn't some holiday circus town." I can still hear my grandad's cranky voice. *"We're an upstanding city full of salt-of-the-earth people. The Noel family name will not stoop to tourist trap nonsense."*

Noel family men had a long history of strong opinions and dogged bullheadedness. At least I came by it honestly. But we also had a long history of taking care of this city, the *people* of this city, doing all we could to help it prosper. My grandad was the mayor responsible for enticing Byers to build a plant here back when my dad was a teenager.

Dad also served a long stretch of time as mayor, though he found his success working as a financial planner for the northwest Arkansas region rather than working with Byers. I'm sure Dad intended for my older brother, Sam, to take a turn at the mayor helm one day. I can't imagine the disappointment he'd feel knowing we'd lost the stability of the Byers plant on my watch.

Scratch that—I can *exactly* imagine his disappointment. I'd experienced enough of it throughout my life to describe its precise flavor and texture without having to taste it now.

I lose track of time sitting out in the cold on Clara's deck. Chase explores the area in the kaleidoscope of lights as I silently watch. I picture Clara out here, curls piled on top of her head, intensity in her blue eyes, wrapping strand after strand around the trees. I imagine her dangerously perched atop one of the stools from her kitchen to reach the highest boughs of the taller trees. I'm hit with a pang of regret that I wasn't here to help her.

"Snap out of it, man," I tell myself, Chase's ears perking up at the sound of my voice. He rushes over and nudges his head through the crook of my arm propped against my knee. "We can't let her in, boy," I tell Chase, who whimpers.

"I'll be civil. But we gotta keep our distance."

Chapter Nineteen

Clara

Our company onboarded two major clients in January, so I was far too swamped to make a trip down to my cabin. But my boss promised I could take two days off to make a long weekend possible at the beginning of February. I've never been more excited about a break in my life.

Driving south down the highway, Tineke strapped into the passenger seat, my mind jitters with thoughts of Clark. No matter that I hadn't seen him for nine weeks or that the last time I did see him was unarguably awful—I couldn't seem to evict him from my thoughts.

I'd shared as much with Madison, who responded with a disapproving lecture about boundaries and toxic people. Then again, she's the one who refuses to kick out the roommate whose most recent hobby resulted in the tent fumigation of their house. So my kettle is no blacker than her pot.

Still, my stomach churns as I turn off the highway onto the road that will lead me into Noel. I'd decided to get together with Sydney this time around—I even texted her before hitting the road so I couldn't chicken out upon entering the Noel city limits.

Pulling into the driveway, a peace settles in my chest as the cabin comes into view. It's as quaint as I remember it, nestled among the bare trees. I take my Tineke from the front seat and hurry to unlock the door and get her inside. I'm grateful that the previous owners had installed a smart thermostat, enabling me to turn up the heat prior to my arrival.

Two months' worth of dust provides a misty coating on the furniture, but otherwise, everything looks undisturbed. I make my way to the sunroom, and my heart drums with displeasure as I notice the bare evergreen trees in the back. Not only did McScrooge go against his promise not to unplug my lights, he'd removed them completely.

How dare he?!

I unlatch the sliding door and step outside, nearly tripping over a plastic storage tub. A note taped to the top reads:

I swear I didn't take these down until January 1. All of Noel beheld the twinkling glory of your lights the whole season. I didn't want you falling off a stool trying to unwind them from the trees, so I took the liberty of removing them for you.
Syd will confirm my story.
Clark
P.S. Seemed like you needed a place to sit to properly enjoy the backyard.

Jerking my head up, I notice a beautiful wood rocking chair to my right. I step closer to run my fingers along the back of the chair, smooth to the touch. I brush a few leaves off the seat and ease myself into it, settling in to the effortless rocking motion.

There's a new splash of color on the Clark Noel Magic Eye image, and I'm more confused than ever.

Who are you, really? The charming, thoughtful hero I thought you were the first night, or the ruthless, grumpy Grinch from the mayor's office?

It's the mystery I'd equally love to solve and love to avoid.

After a quick supply run to Noland's—complete with a huge welcome-back hug from Emily—I spend the evening holed up in my cabin. Christmas may be officially over, but I still queue up my "Christmas Piano" playlist, hoping it will provide inspiration for a perfect movie script.

I've imagined countless couples falling in love at Christmas over the years, dreamed up innumerable fictional holiday settings—you'd think everything would overflow right out of me. But maybe the plethora of options floating around in my mind is precisely what keeps the blank screen staring back at me.

Just start something, Clara. Write something bad. Something bad is at least something.

I pause to make a cup of hot cocoa, adding a dash of cinnamon to the whipped cream. But even my festive drink does nothing to squeeze the creative juices out of my brain.

I give up and run hot water in the bathtub instead. Soaking in suds, pumpkin spice scent filling my nostrils, I'm transported back to my first night here. The warm bath, the broken door, the broken-*down* door. The magnetic man who stumbled into me.

"Ughhh," I sigh before plunging my head below the bubbly water.

I follow the directions to Sydney's, pulling up in front of a two-story house that's far more modern than the rest of the town. Syd flings open the front door before I can knock, a miniature version of Sydney peering from behind her leg.

"Clara! I'm so happy to see you again!" She beams, pulling me into a hug. She gestures me inside. "This little angel is Addie, and somewhere around here is Davis Jr. We call him Junior. He's probably dismantling furniture or training an animal he snuck into the house. You'll meet him when he comes out in search of food."

I laugh, bending down to Addie's eye level. "Well, hi there, you little cutie." She rewards me with a huge grin, showing off four tiny teeth.

"I've got some decaf coffee brewing, but I've also got tea if you'd prefer," Syd says, leading me deeper into the house. My eyes sweep the space. It's lived in with ample evidence of young children, but also classically modern with warm, homey touches. "Wow, you really have an eye for design, Syd!"

"Hey, how do you know I'm not the decorating mastermind?" a voice booms from behind me. I twirl around to a grinning man. His appearance is similar to Clark's, with a matching beard. Although, his hair is more sandy-blond than brown. "I'm just kidding—my beautiful bride is responsible for all the beauty here. I'm Davis." He holds out his hand to me, and I shake it firmly.

"Clara."

"I know." He winks, and warmth spreads through my cheeks. Syd mentioned that Davis is Clark's best friend, so did he know about me because of Syd, or . . .

"Syd told me you were coming over. She's been beside herself with excitement all day. A kid at Christmas," Davis winks at Syd now, who slaps him across the arm.

"Hey! It's not every day a woman my age moves to town!" She laughs, then turns to me. "At least, I assume you're around my age. Despite the two kids, I'm only thirty-one, but my apologies if you're a fresh college grad young'un."

I laugh again. "I recently turned thirty, so you're spot on. And seriously, I love how you've decorated your house."

Davis wraps an arm around Sydney's shoulders. "She's a decorating genius, this one. Any house in town that's marginally in style is due to Syd's magic." He beams a smile down at Syd, who grins back at him.

"He exaggerates, but I did major in interior design. There hasn't been a ton of opportunities to use it here in Noel, but I do enjoy helping people decorate their spaces. And Becky let me design the interior of her coffee shop when she opened it. That was super fun."

"And it turned out amazing," Davis chimes in. He leans over to kiss Syd on the cheek, and it's impossible not to smile at them. "I'm going to make myself scarce so you two can talk, but I'll be back to pick you up for dinner at 6:00."

We walk into the kitchen as Davis heads out the front door. Sydney hands me an off-white clay mug with a leaf imprint design in sage green. She takes one for herself that has turquoise swirls cascading from the handle diagonally down the mug. She holds up the coffee pot like a question, and I nod. Then I say, "These mugs are beautiful. Did you make them?"

"Goodness, no!" Syd laughs. "I have a good eye for *other* people's designs, but I don't have a crafty bone in my body. A lady here in town, Pearl, makes hand-thrown pottery. I bought them from her. She used to travel to different craft fairs around the region, but I'm not sure if she still does that or not."

"I need to get her info from you. These would make great birthday gifts for my parents this year," I say, pouring some hazelnut creamer into my coffee.

"I'll text it to you," Syd responds, leading me over to the living room. Addie is still superglued to her, and I'm impressed by Syd's ability to maneuver the house with a small human attached to her leg while carrying hot coffee. "We've got about thirty minutes of distracted conversation before Addie will go down for her catnap, and then we'll be able to focus."

I glance around the room. "There's another child running around that you're not worried about?"

Syd waves a hand. "Eh, he'll turn up soon. It's almost feeding time. Thank goodness he hasn't figured out how to unlock the doors yet, so he can't have run off."

On cue, a voice shrieks, "Timber!" It's followed by a loud crash from upstairs, but not a "something shattered" crash. More like a "blocks fell and scattered all over the floor" crash.

"Speak of the devil." Sydney smiles with an eye roll. "Don't worry; as soon as we figured out Junior's curious nature and rough-and-tumble tendencies, we padded every hard surface in his room. And secured his dresser to the wall. And every other safety precaution we could think of. He'll make a lot of noise and a lot of messes, but he can't hurt himself in there."

We settle in to easy conversation, frequently interrupted by Addie showing me treasures or giving Syd kisses. She tells me about how she and Davis grew up together but didn't fall in love until they were away at college at the University of Arkansas. "I guess seeing each other in a different environment is what we needed to realize we were always supposed to be together," she says.

Sydney asks about my family, and I tell her about my parents and Aunt Gloria. I fill her in on how I ended up with a cabin here in Noel, even cautiously admitting my dream of writing scripts for the Heartmark Channel.

"Oh, I *love* their movies!" she exclaims in response. "I watch all of them every year!"

Shock must show on my face because Sydney rolls her eyes. "What, you think the whole town hates Christmas just because Clark was grumpy about it?"

Mortification is definitely showing on my face now because Sydney gives me a wry smile. "Yes, my friend, I got the scoop on your interactions with Mayor C. J. Noel."

I cover my face with my hands, unsure of how to react. I love that Syd has so quickly and completely adopted me as a friend, but I'm uncertain how much to share about Clark with her. She doesn't act ruffled by my embarrassment at all, laughing as she stands up. "I think that's my cue to get Addie down for her nap so we can *really* talk. Feel free to help yourself to more coffee."

Pouring a second cup of coffee is exactly the task I need to calm down my spiraling thoughts. *How much should I admit to her? Syd is kind and fun to be around. I want to spend time with her when I'm here! But Davis is Clark's best friend. If she's already heard about my interactions with Clark, will what I tell her get back to him?*

I'm sitting on the couch again by the time Syd comes out, baby monitor in hand. "I'm giving Junior his iPad time, so we shouldn't be interrupted for a while." She sits down next to me, thanking me for her refilled coffee mug.

"All right, tell me your side of the story about your encounters with our dear mayor." Apparently reading my thoughts, she adds, "And don't worry, my lips are sealed. Just 'cause I'm friends with Clark doesn't mean I'm going to breathe a word to him about anything you tell me. Even if I pried his version out of Davis." She ends with a wink.

I blow out a long exhale. "I don't know what to say. I'm not really sure how to summarize my interactions with Clark."

"Then give me the long version," Syd says simply, coffee mug cradled in her hands.

So I do. I tell Sydney all about my first time meeting Clark when he stumbled into the bathroom. I tell her about that odd draw I felt to him the first night and following morning, about me leaving abruptly and Clark taking the plant from me. She has a soft smile on her face as she listens, like she recognizes the man in the picture I'm painting.

Then, I tell her about my misguided expectations for the town and my angry encounter with Clark at the mayor's office. I tell her about my shock at finding out he was the mayor, my disappointment when he told me to drop the idea of a Christmas festival. Syd has a sympathetic smile on her face, like she also recognizes *this* man in the picture I'm painting.

But when I get to the part of the story about Clark crumpling up my list of ideas, Syd jolts upright, mouth in a shocked "O" position. "He what?! He crumpled up the paper?! Okay, Clark can be grouchy, but that's harsh even for him. Something must have *really* gotten under his skin. Not that I'm excusing it."

I finish the story with our brief phone conversation, Clark's offer to take care of my plant again, and returning here to find the stored Christmas lights and rocking chair on the deck. "I don't know what to think. It's like a Jekyll and Hyde scenario, and I don't know which version is the real Clark. Or if he's some bewildering mixture of the two."

Sydney worries her lip as she regards me, the posture of someone carefully formulating a response. "Clark is certainly a . . . unique character. He truly is a kind, generous, steady man. But he does have a surly side that gets the better of him sometimes." She pauses to take a sip of coffee, but I'd wager a guess that she's stalling to think. I wait.

Syd taps her fingers on her coffee mug and dives in. "Clark hasn't had an easy go. I know you're from a big city, but try to put yourself in his shoes. The child of a small town's founding family. A family that has been pretty much in charge of the town across generations. That comes with some certain expectations and pressure that would get to any kid.

"On top of that, Clark always had a strained relationship with his dad. Clark's older brother, Sam, was the poster child of favored elder sons. Sam was a carbon copy of their dad and opposite from Clark in every way. Clark never could live up to his dad's expectations of what a Noel man should be—the exact type of guy that Sam was."

Syd pauses, thoughtful again. "So Clark struggled in his role, in their relationship, even before the accident."

I blow out the breath I've been holding. "What happened?"

"Car accident. Clark's parents and Sam were riding home together from a conference in Fayetteville, and a drunk driver swerved into their lane and hit them. All three were pronounced dead at the scene. Clark was only twenty years old at the time," Sydney explains sadly.

I draw in a sharp breath. *Poor Clark. No wonder you're so grumpy. You're hurting.*

"Clark moved back here to Noel full time, trying to cope with the loss of his family. Trying to cope with the confusion of losing a family that didn't love him very well to start with. In some ways, Noel rallied and helped him through it. But in other ways, the town placed an additional burden on Clark because of who he is," Syd says.

"The last remaining member of the Noel family," I conclude. She nods.

"Clark *hates* being the mayor," Syd comments with a huffed laugh. "When Clark turned twenty-eight, the town voted him in as mayor against his will, and I'm sure they'll re-elect him this year."

I shake my head. "Can't he decline?"

Syd smiles. "Technically, yes. But he still has enough lingering sense of Noel family obligation that he doesn't. And he truly does want to see the town prosper, wants to see families here thriving. So, when the Byers plant closed last year and people lost their jobs, it was like a gut punch to Clark to see so many families forced to leave."

"He feels responsible, doesn't he?" I observe. Syd simply taps her finger to her nose.

I sigh. "Well, that sure explains a lot about why he's complicated. But that doesn't un-complicate him!" She laughs in response.

"I'm not saying that Clark wasn't wrong for treating you the way he did—he was absolutely wrong. Believe me, he heard an earful from me about it. But . . .there are reasons why he is the way that he is. Painful, complicated reasons."

I silently contemplate everything Syd has told me, staring into my coffee mug.

"Then again," Syd drawls, a lighter teasing tone in her voice, "I can't say I've ever seen him get *quite* this worked up in response to anything. I suspect you might bring out some heightened reactions in him, Clara Sullivan."

I aim a throw pillow at her as she laughs. I'm surprised at how Sydney has put me so at ease, especially talking about something so personal, so complex. Sydney's the type of friend you instantly feel like you've known forever. The type of friend you *hope* you'll know forever.

When Addie's cry sounds through the baby monitor, we both stand. "I'll take the coffee mugs to the kitchen while you get her up," I say.

"This is perfect timing," Sydney responds. "My parents should be here in about thirty minutes. I'll help them get dinner set for the kids, and then Davis will be back to pick us up."

"Where are we going?" I ask.

"There are only two options now," Syd says. "A pizza place and the bar down by the river are the only restaurants staying open through the winter months this year. We're heading to Deer River Bar—prepare yourself for the true small-town experience, friend."

Chapter Twenty

Clark

I pull into the parking lot of Deer River Bar and turn off the engine. Davis invited me to join him and Syd for dinner and wouldn't take my "no" for an answer. I'd dropped Chase off with Pops for the evening, figuring Pops could benefit from the company as much as Chase would appreciate not being left home alone.

The sinking feeling in my stomach sinks deeper every time I visit Pops. He's had a defeated air about him ever since we moved his bedroom down to the main floor, even though he tries to hide it. The colder weather combined with the arthritis has him hobbling around worse than ever. Of course, he's too stubborn to use the cane his doctor suggested.

At least Pops has been taking the medication the doctor prescribed him, although doctor's orders were that regular movement and activity coupled *with* the meds would be the most effective. Pops doesn't seem interested in following those orders, though.

Maybe Chase can convince him to throw the ball or play some gentle tug-of-war. Anything to get Pops using his hands and moving around.

Sighing, I get out of the truck and walk up to the bar. Looks pretty busy tonight, though that's not a surprise when the pizza shop is its only competition. The other restaurants in town decided they couldn't recoup operating costs to stay open all winter. It's a fact that looms over me, alongside the growing list of families who have checked out of Noel.

I open the door to a cacophony of noise. Lively conversations, cooks calling up orders, the clink of glasses at the bar, and boots clanking on the small dance floor. All mixed with a twanging undercurrent of country music. This crowded bar is just about the last place I'd like to be tonight. But Davis pestered me with a bunch of guilt-ridden comments about mingling with the town, staying connected with the people who have been loyal to me my whole life.

Manipulative excuse for a friend.

Scanning the tables, I see Davis right as he calls out "Clark! Over here!"

I take a step in his direction but come to an abrupt stop. Because Davis and Syd aren't alone at that table. A third seat is taken by the in-the-flesh version of the phantom woman haunting my dreams. One of the can lights in the ceilings is placed just so over Clara's head, illuminating her strawberry-blond curls with a glowing halo.

By the saucer size of her eyes and blanched skin, I'd place an all-in bet that she also had no heads up about my presence tonight.

I snap my eyes back to Davis, meeting his bemused expression with my best *"you're a dead man"* scowl. Syd has the audacity to swivel in her seat and full-on grin at me, eyes dancing with delight.

Since Davis has already drawn attention to my entrance, I can't turn around and walk out without it being obvious. The thought still crosses my mind, but then I remember my vow to Chase that I'd be civil to Clara. Booking it out of the bar at the mere sight of her probably wouldn't qualify as civil.

I make my way over to the table, taking the empty seat between Davis and Clara. "Davis, Syd," I greet with a stiff nod. Then I turn my attention to the exact person I've been trying to steer it away from. "Clara, good to see you again. When did you get back to town?"

She swallows hard. The resulting twitch of her lips and bob of her throat does *not* aid my efforts to absolve my thoughts of her. I know exactly what I'll be thinking about all night now. That and the way her navy blue shirt makes her eyes pop even more than they already do on their own.

"Clark, hi," she answers softly, her eyes flitting briefly to Syd's. Clara clears her throat and continues, "I got back yesterday. Just here for a long weekend, so I'll be going back to KC on Monday." Her eyes have been shifting around, not daring to look me straight on for more than a split second at a time.

I notice her twirling that ring on her finger as she exhales a deep breath. Her eyes finally find mine and stick. "Um, thank you for getting the lights down for me. And for the rocking chair. It's absolutely gorgeous."

She tucks a curl behind her ear, and my eyes follow the movement. Now it's my turn to swallow hard, momentarily wonderstruck into silence.

Get a grip, Clark!

"Uh, you're welcome," I half speak, half grunt. I want to tell her that it's a Pops original chair, but that would require explaining who Pops is. And that's more words than I trust myself speaking right now. A quick glance around the table confirms that Davis and Syd are living their best lives in this moment.

"We were filling Clara in on what's good to eat here," Syd chirps, filling the awkward silence. Well, Syd and Davis aren't acting awkward at all. The awkward silence for the *other* half of the table.

"Just don't order the soup of the day. You'll regret it later tonight," I offer, making an attempt at conversation.

Clara smiles, first at me and then at Sydney. "That's what Syd told me. Something about a pot full of questionable leftovers and living on a prayer. Davis tried to dare me, but I don't think I have the gamble in me tonight."

Watching Clara smile, listening to her talk about Davis and Syd like old pals of hers—something about it hits me, hard as a sucker punch. I hope I didn't visibly flinch.

I cross my arms on top of the table, trying to ground myself. "The burgers are fail-safe, and pretty much anything fried. You can't come here hoping for diet food," I add, and Clara bursts out a laugh.

Good lord, I'd do anything to hear that laugh again.

NO! No, you wouldn't, Clark. Her laugh is no different from Sydney's or Emily's or any other woman's in this town.

How long are you gonna keep lying to yourself?

I'm saved from my crippling inner dialogue by Jake coming over to take our order. He's a junior in high school, but because his dad owns the bar, he gets roped into working here most weekends. He's been slightly less enthusiastic about life lately. Understandable, since multiple of his friends have moved away. Considering that Noel already has to combine with a few nearby towns to share a high school, each student who moves on leaves behind a noticeable absence. I'm not sure how I would have coped if Davis or Beau had moved away during high school. I'll leave an extra-large tip for Jake tonight.

Syd orders chicken tenders, Davis gets the fried catfish, and I ask for a bacon cheeseburger plain. I try to ignore the skip in my heartbeat when Clara copies my order. When Jake takes our menus and leaves the table, Clara speaks up first, asking me, "Where's Chase tonight?"

"I dropped him off at Pops' house on the way here so he wouldn't be alone," I answer. Clara props her chin on her hand, leaning forward and listening intently as Davis and I take turns explaining the legendary Bill "Pops" Allen. It's the perfect opportunity to explain why her porch rocking chair is extra special.

"How was Pops when you saw him today?" Davis asks.

"I don't know. Not great." I sigh, rubbing a hand across my beard. "'Course, you never get a straight answer from him. But he's not moving too good, and I'm not sure that anything is motivating him to change that."

Clara's brow furrows adorably. "What's wrong?"

"Pops has arthritis that's slowly getting worse. Mentally, he's still sharp as a tack, but his joints, not so much," I explain. "Ever since Bev passed a couple years back, he hasn't been motivated to take care of himself."

A spark lights in Clara's eyes, and she purses her lips. "We have to help him!" She exclaims it so earnestly that I'm bowled over by the urge to wrap her in my arms against my heart. I shake my head to clear the thought.

Clara mistakes my head shake as a negative reaction to her suggestion and doubles down. "Even if he acts like he doesn't want help or doesn't want to take care of himself, that doesn't mean we listen. Not if we care about him. We find a way to help, anyway."

The multiple uses of the word "we" in that sentence have me thinking about doing a lot more than just pulling her against my chest now.

Syd chimes in to back Clara up. "Clara's right. Pops is way too special to let him decline so quickly, cantankerous as he may be. Can we get him started making furniture again?"

Davis answers. Which is good, since I don't trust my mouth to not say out loud the thoughts swirling in my mind. "I don't know that Pops could manage making furniture anymore. That's a lot of heavy lifting, not to mention dangerous machinery. I don't think it would be safe."

We pause the conversation as Jake sets our plates of food in front of us. Syd offers the ketchup bottle to Clara, but she declines. "Can't taste the char of the burger if it's watered down by a bunch of condiments," she says before taking a huge bite. I take a bite of my own ketchup-less burger to hide my small smile.

"Now, back to Pops," Clara says before she's completely swallowed her food. "Could he make something smaller scale? Wood signs or trays or something similar?"

I think about the carved blue birds on Pops' night stand. "He used to do some whittling, made animal carvings way back when. It's been a long while since he's done that, though. I'm not sure he'd be interested in picking it back up."

"Well, it's worth suggesting to him. Don't give up before you even try, Mr. Cynical," Clara counters back. Davis snorts a laugh, trying to cover it up with a cough.

"Fine, I'll ask him," I respond evenly before shoving a fry in my mouth.

Clara gives a small, pleased toss of her head, which sends her curls bouncing and my blood through a broiler. I take a long chug of water.

Sydney keeps the conversation moving throughout dinner, asking Clara lots of questions about her life that I'm keen to hear answers to. If I didn't know any better, I'd think Syd is doing this mini deep-dive into Clara's life more for my benefit than hers. Actually I do know better, and I know for sure that's what she's doing. I try to work up some irritation toward Syd for meddling, but I'm secretly too pleased to learn more about Clara.

She talks about her job, her absent roommate, her best friend, Madison, and her upbringing with her parents and aunt. Clara's voice is hesitant as she talks about her dreams of writing more creatively, but Davis pummels her with question after question until she finally confesses.

"Watching Heartmark movies transports my mind back to my childhood, watching with my mom or Aunt Gloria. It's a sweet nostalgia that I want to provide for the next generation, I suppose," Clara concludes, a slight blush on her cheeks. Although she doesn't exude the same blatant eagerness as when she talked about helping Pops, there's a quiet joy radiating as she shares about her writing dream.

A hundred follow-up questions swell in my throat, begging to be asked. To understand more about what makes Clara tick, where this dream was born, how she plans to pursue it, what else makes her happy. I take a bite of my burger to stop any of them from coming out.

Clara turns the conversation around, asking Davis about running Deer River Floats. By the time Davis finishes telling her all the ins and outs of a river float experience company, we're finished with our food. Jake clears our plates, and without the distraction of the food, Syd's eyes bounce around the room enough to notice a few couples dancing.

"Oh this is the best song! Clara, do you know how to two-step?" she asks.

"Definitely not," Clara answers. "Please tell me we can still be friends if I don't enjoy country music."

Syd claps a hand to her chest like she's been shot. I roll my eyes at her theatrics.

"In the name of maintaining our friendship, I'll do my best to overlook your obvious lack of taste in music. You're lucky you're one of the few women my age in town." Syd winks, and Clara laughs good-naturedly. I frown, realizing the toll that Abby and Beau leaving must have taken on Syd.

Sydney continues teasing Clara, though. "Even if you don't listen to country music on your own, I insist you learn to two-step if you're going to keep coming around here. Davis can teach you—he's the best two-stepper in the county."

Davis puffs up his chest at the compliment from Syd, leaning over to kiss her on the lips. "Anything to impress my woman." Syd clasps Davis' cheeks and kisses him again. An uncomfortable heat flushes my neck, but Clara is simply smiling at them. Davis stands up and holds a hand out to Clara, which she accepts. I hear him explaining the "quick, quick, slow" basics to her as they walk toward the other couples dancing.

I should make conversation with Sydney, but I can't tear my eyes from the sight of Clara dancing with Davis. She may not know how to two-step, but those ballet lessons she mentioned taking as a child clearly set her up for success in any form of dance. Her movements are graceful as she follows Davis' lead around the floor, her furrowed brow the only indication that she's concentrating.

Davis is my best friend. He's happily married. I *know* that he has zero interest in Clara. Not to mention, I keep telling myself that *I* have zero interest in Clara. But the primitive part of my brain isn't processing that information. Instead, it's sending all sorts of "competitor moving in on woman" caveman instincts to my body. My heart is pounding, my breathing is shallow, my eyes are seeing red, and my grip on the water glass might leave my hand permanently cramped in this position.

The sound of Syd's snort forces me to glance over. She's not even attempting to hide the glee on her face. "Why don't you take me for a spin around the dance floor, Clark?" My attempt to turn her down with a scowl doesn't deter her. Thirty seconds later, Syd and I are also on the dance floor.

"I know you know how to do this, you big grump." Syd ribs me. I lead her through the steps, but my eyes can't help but find Clara every few seconds. The dance floor isn't large, so it doesn't take long for us to bump into Davis and Clara.

"Sorry, girl—I'm going to have to cut in on my hunk of a husband now," Syd proclaims cheerfully. She twirls herself out of my arms at the same time Davis twirls Clara into them with such finesse, there's no way they didn't rehearse this move ahead of time.

They're both manipulative excuses for friends.

Clara freezes, likely about to take flight away from this uncomfortable setup. I *should* take flight, *should* suggest we go back to the table. But that primitive part of my brain is locked in on the soft skin of her hand in mine. The blue of her eyes up close. Her pumpkin spice scent filling my nostrils.

After a split-second's hesitation, I resume the quick-quick-slow movements to guide Clara on the floor and keep her body close to mine.

"So, is the two-step a class you take in school down here?" Clara asks, voice breathy.

Her joke catches me off guard, and I laugh. Her eyes warm in response, crinkling at the edges as she smiles. *I could lose myself in those eyes.*

"You caught us—we forgo subjects like chemistry in the name of two-step fluency," I reply. A blush of pink shades the skin beneath her freckles. I wasn't purposely making a chemistry joke. But I'm earning an A+ in science class, given the bubbling reaction burning inside me, hotter and hotter the longer she's in my arms.

The music changes tempo as "Can't Take My Eyes Off You" by Lady A starts playing. Clara's hand tenses in mine as the surrounding couples sway to the slower beat. I ignore the alarm bells sounding in my mind and drop my right hand slightly lower to her waist, pulling her a touch closer to a more natural slow-dance position.

Clara relaxes slightly, following my lead. Her left hand slips down from its two-stepping position on top of my shoulder until her palm is resting on my chest. Her fingertips are gentle on my shoulder, but they may as well be lit sparklers for the heat they're shooting through my back and chest.

In sync with the song lyrics, I'm finding it difficult to take my eyes off Clara's. My attention is diverted to her mouth, however, when she licks and purses her lips. Like she's trying to stop herself from saying something, or *doing* something with those lips. The same way I am. The tension between us is inching into dangerous territory, so I clear my throat. "Um, it seems like you and Syd have hit it off."

My comment breaks the spell, and Clara blinks twice. She shakes her head slightly before glancing over at Syd and Davis nearby. There's no room for Jesus between them, and their googly-eyed expressions are more akin to high schoolers than a married couple in their thirties. Clara huffs a small laugh at the sight before returning her eyes to mine.

"Absolutely. Syd is full of life. And easy to talk to. I'm excited to get to know her even better the more time I spend here," Clara responds. Her voice starts off breathy, but gathers strength as she talks. "And Davis is a hoot, not to mention little Addie and Junior. I'm excited to spend more time with all of them."

I'm completely lost in her gaze, drowning in the deep blue sea of her eyes. "You're not wearing contacts," I comment without thinking, and those blue eyes widen.

Great going, man. Just admit to intensely studying her eyes. Subtle.

"I mean, ah, you were wearing glasses that night I brought your plant to your cabin," I stumble to recover. Unfortunately, there's no recovery from my initial comment that sounded more like a confession.

"Oh, yeah, I have twenty-twenty vision, but my eyes don't focus the way they're supposed to," she explains. Although her eyes appear perfectly focused on mine. "The prescription helps my eyes stay in focus so they don't get as tired. I always wear them when I'm working or reading, but not when I'm out and about."

I'm suddenly uncomfortably hot, chest tight. Maybe it's the lyrics to the song playing, maybe it's the intoxicating proximity of Clara's body close to mine. Maybe it's my blundering admission about staring into her eyes, maybe it's hearing her talk about my best friends like they're her friends too. Or, maybe the combination of everything finally breaks the gauges of my internal warning system.

You're already losing yourself. Back away, Clark!

I abruptly stop dancing, breaking off physical contact with Clara. "Um, I think I should go pick up Chase from Pops' place before it gets too late. Old man needs his rest. I'll see ya around."

The stunned expression on Clara's face—far too similar to the face she had when I crumpled her paper—grips my heart with guilt. But not enough to negate the urgent need to put space between us.

I toss some cash on the table for Jake and hightail it out of the bar.

Chapter Twenty-One

Clara

Christmas music is playing, my cozy robe is on, and a steaming mug of hot cocoa warms my hands. I slowly rock in the chair on my back deck in the quiet darkness. All perfect conditions for relaxation.

But I've never felt less relaxed in my life. And it's all Clark Noel's fault.

My mind was already overloaded with information leaving Sydney's house today. Hearing more about Clark's background, about all the traumatic elements that have added up to the man he is today . . . it made me want to hug Clark and punch some people simultaneously.

But then my mind tipped over the edge, watching Clark walk to our table. Davis and Syd obviously schemed the whole thing, but I'm not sure it went exactly according to plan. At least, I assume their plan didn't end with Clark beelining it out of the bar like the building was on fire after dancing with me.

I don't want to remember the strength of his hand on my waist or the sensation of his calloused fingers holding mine. I don't want to remember the way the flecks of gold in his eyes crowded out the green the longer he held my gaze. I don't want to remember the cold-plunge sensation washing over me when he dropped my hand mid-dance and ran away.

I don't want to remember. But it's all I can think about.

I sigh.

Slipping inside the sliding door, I lock it shut and take a seat at my writing desk. I have four different movie script files that I've created, only to stop a few pages in when I realize I hate them. I just can't seem to find the right inspiration.

Perching my glasses on my nose, I'm reminded of Clark's comment about me not wearing contacts. The thought of him peering that intently into my eyes makes me flush with warmth.

Clark's frowning face fills my mind's eye.

Opening a new document, I begin typing.

CHAPTER TWENTY-TWO

Clara

Two weeks later, I'm driving back to Noel. This is the first time I've made the biweekly trip I'd imagined when I purchased the cabin. But I can see it becoming a comfortable new groove. At home, I've been too swamped to get any writing done on the script I started during my last trip here. Between helping my parents repaint their basement and picking up Michael's slack at work, I've hardly had any free time.

I went to work early today so I could leave after a late lunch and make it to Noel at a decent time. But first, I made a quick detour to a neighboring suburb. Syd invited me over for dinner tomorrow, and I'm bringing some of the best cookies the world has to offer. A local baker was baking and selling enormous cookies out of her house until demand grew so large that she opened a storefront. With rotating flavors, my sweet tooth is always begging me to stop in for a taste. It's probably a good thing that it's a solid thirty minutes from my apartment, or I'd be there every day.

The puppy chow cookie is currently calling to me from the box on the passenger seat. It nearly has me convinced that taking one less cookie tomorrow wouldn't be such a bad thing.

I resist the temptation and slow down as I reach the Noel city limits. Arriving at my cabin a few minutes later, I unload the car and check on my Tineke plant. After giving her some water, I introduce her to her new siblings—a cheerful Pilea and a trailing Jade Pothos.

After heating up a can of soup for dinner, I make a cup of hot cocoa. I'm eager to get back to writing my script, and see where inspiration takes me. I even left my little Christmas tree set up by the fireplace hearth to keep me in the holiday mood.

I queue up some Christmas music and settle into my desk chair. The script slowly takes shape as I develop the story and characters. Renee, the female main character, is ambitious, charismatic, and tenacious—basically polar opposite from me. She buys a property in a town called Bethlehem, intending to turn it into a Christmas-themed bed-and-breakfast. Imagine her shock when she arrives and finds the town lacking Christmas cheer.

Sometimes our own lives provide the most accessible means of inspiration.

I know I've hit a stride writing when I glance up and over three hours have passed. I've filled in the details of Renee's plans for the bed-and-breakfast, and I find myself wishing that it was a real place I could visit. I think that's a good sign.

Leaning back in my chair, I stretch my hands overhead to pop my back. After a short soak in a bubble bath, I put on a pair of Christmas pajamas—it's only fitting. I fall into bed with a smile on my face, feeling accomplished and encouraged.

Chirp!

I'd just dozed off when a noise jolts me out of slumberland. I prop up on my elbows, glancing around the room. After a few seconds of intent listening, I lie back down, deciding I must have imagined it.

Chirp!

Now I know I'm not imagining things. I get out of bed and walk to the living room.

Chirp!

The sound has gotten louder and is coming from directly above me. Overhead, the smoke detector blinks with a low battery.

"Are you kidding me right now?!" I yell at the ceiling.

Flipping on the lights, I assess the situation. When I bought the cabin, I loved the way the vaulted ceiling made the tall, stone fireplace a statement fixture of the room. Having to change the battery in the smoke detector on that vaulted ceiling did *not* cross my mind.

I pull over a bar stool and retrieve my broom from the closet. Perched atop the stool, I'm hoping I can at least hit some sort of silence button with the broom. Holding the broom up as high as possible, I'm still well short of the ceiling. Huffing a breath, I climb down and search for something to extend the reach of the broom.

Ten minutes later, my attempts at taping a coat hanger and a spatula to the end of the broomstick have proved unsuccessful. The consistent *chirp* of the smoke detector is mere centimeters away from the edge of my sanity. I'll never be able to sleep like this.

My watch reads 11:15 p.m. I can't bother Syd this late, not with two young kids. I know what I should do. I just don't want to do it.

I groan.

Begrudgingly, I pull out my phone.

ME

Any chance you're awake?

I hit send and wait. On the one hand, I hope he's not awake and doesn't answer, so I don't have to cope with the mixed emotions of seeing him right now. On the other hand, my sanity.

McSCROOGE

Yes. Why?

I sigh, unsure if I'm relieved or disappointed.

ME

Any chance you have a tall ladder among all your handy-man gear?

McSCROOGE

. . . yes?

McSCROOGE

Am I about to be an accomplice to a crime?

ME

On a scale of 1 to 10, how open to that would you be?

McSCROOGE

I'm the mayor. Obviously zero.

ME

But you have the perfect character credibility to get away with it!

McSCROOGE

Clara . . .

ME

OK, OK, no crimes. The smoke detector on my vaulted ceiling has decided tonight is a convenient time to run out of battery. The chirping won't stop and I'm losing my mind.

McSCROOGE

I'll be right there.

CHAPTER TWENTY-THREE

Clark

Adrenaline courses through my system, not at all ideal for 11:30 at night. Syd told me that Clara was coming to town this weekend, but I certainly wasn't expecting to get a late-night SOS text from her.

I can't figure out if the adrenaline is the excited anticipation kind or the fight-or-flight variety. Pulling into Clara's driveway, I turn off my truck and pull my ten-foot ladder out of the truck bed.

Knocking on the door, I hear Clara call, "It's open!" I turn the doorknob and step inside, not at all prepared for the sight before me.

A barstool is in the middle of the room, with what appears to be a spatula attached to a coat hanger attached to a broom handle propped against it. Glancing left, I see Clara sulking on her couch. Her curls are tousled, and she's dressed in flannel Christmas pajamas, because . . . of course she is. She's holding the remnants of some sugary concoction in her hand, her shirt coated with a dusting of white powder.

A chuckle erupts out of me before I can stop it.

Clara's eyes narrow at me, and I quickly clear my throat.

"This is not funny, Clark," she says, trying to sound firm and sassy, but coming across unfairly adorable instead. Clara stands up and strides over to me. "It's important for you to understand that I am *not* a night owl. I need copious amounts of rest in order to be a functional human being, and that *thing* is destroying my chance at a full night's sleep."

In a stroke of excellent comedic timing, the smoke detector lets out a loud *chirp!*

Gesturing toward the bar stool situation, I say, "And this was your solution?"

"Pardon me for not having a ladder at the ready," she snipes back.

"I thought you were a Girl Scout?" I question with a wry smile.

Clara rolls her eyes. "I may have exaggerated that point."

I can't stop my lips from spreading into a true smile. "I'll get it silenced in no time. Do you have any extra batteries?"

"Oh shoot; I do not," Clara says sheepishly. "I'm going to need you to strike from the record my claim of Girl Scout preparedness."

I pull two batteries out of my pocket. "Good thing I brought some then."

The corner of Clara's lips quirk, mesmerizing my attention. Another well-timed *chirp!* interrupts the moment, and I move to set up the ladder. "You mind moving the bar stool out of the way?" I ask.

Clara does so, then she comes back to hold the ladder as I climb up. "I'll be fine," I tell her. "I climb ladders without supervision all the time. You can just relax."

"Nope, can't risk the lawsuit if you fall on my property. I'll hold it steady," she answers.

"As I recall, your 'holding items steady' skills could use some work," I quip. Apparently, the late hour has made me bolder than usual. That's the second time I've referenced the first time we met. Or first times, if you count the night and the following morning as separate occasions. I glance down long enough to see the color in Clara's cheeks, then quickly look away.

Or I really will fall off this ladder.

I focus on the task at hand, quickly changing out the battery and resetting the smoke detector. I put the old battery in my pocket to dispose of later, then climb down the ladder.

"There you go. No more sleep interruptions," I say once I'm back on the ground.

Clara's eyes are locked on mine, not the slightest bit sleepy.

"Well, now I'm wide awake," she sighs, turning away from me. She plops down on the couch and pats the cushion next to her. "Want a cookie?"

No, you don't. Leave now!

"Sure." I take a seat, and she holds a box over to me. Inside are the largest cookies I've ever seen—so big, I'm not even sure they should be marketed as cookies.

"This one is the rest of the puppy chow cookie I was eating. This is raspberry dark chocolate sea salt; that's confetti; and this one is ooey gooey butter cake," Clara explains, pointing out each option. "I was supposed to take these to Syd's house for dinner tomorrow night, but the smoke detector drove me to break them open early."

I break off a chunk of the butter cake cookie and take a bite. The sweetness is tempered by the abundant rich butter flavor. While the middle is the softest cookie I've ever tried, the edges have that perfect crisp texture. "That is . . . wow," I say, turning to Clara. Chewing another bite of the puppy chow cookie, she nods with wide eyes, as though "wow" is the only possible response.

"Kansas City's finest," she quips, then licks the powdered sugar off her fingers.

"How's your dad?" I ask, knowing I should go home yet unwilling to do so.

Clara's eyes scrunch up quizzically.

"The first time you were here, you left because your dad broke his ankle. Is he all healed up?" I clarify.

Her eyes soften. "Oh, yeah, he is. He doesn't even have to wear the walking boot anymore. The physical therapist gave him several exercises to work on at home, but he's done with the official sessions. Which he's elated about. Although, I think my mom misses the temporary handicapped parking pass they got to use. My dad is one of those stop-and-smell-the-roses types. Parking closer gave him less time to get distracted by the world around him."

I give a small smile before eating the final bite of cookie in my hand. *Time to go, Clark. You're playing with fire.*

"And how is Pops doing?" Clara asks before I can make a move to leave.

I rub my beard and lean forward with my elbows on my knees instead. "Ah, no changes to report, unfortunately." I stare at the fireplace, at the decorated Christmas tree still sitting on the hearth, unsure of what else to say. The fear of losing Pops on top of . . . well, everything else, sends me to a dark and broody mind space.

"Hmmm," Clara hums, not saying anything further. I'd expected her to jump in with more ideas on how to get Pops active again. But she seems to sense that's not what I need right now. I glance over at the empathetic expression on her face and fight the urge to bury my face in her neck. To get a closer inhale of that spicy sweet scent always emanating off her skin.

"Well, I should let you get some sleep now. Syd is going to expect a functional human being to show up at her house tomorrow," I say with some reluctance. Clara gives a small smile, and we both stand up. "Thanks for sharing a cookie with me," I add. "They're a lot fancier than anything we have around here."

Clara shrugs. "True. But everything you have around here seems pretty fantastic, too."

She peers up at me, and I notice a smear of powdered sugar on her cheek. Without thinking, I reach up and brush it off with my thumb. Surprise flashes in her eyes, but not scared surprised . . . more like, pleasantly surprised. "Uh, just a smudge of powdered sugar there," I mumble.

"Oh, thanks," Clara responds, a faint blush spreading across her cheeks. "And thanks for coming to the rescue. Again. I promise to work on my Girl Scout skills."

"No need; I got you covered any time," I say. I'm treading water in the ocean of Clara's blue eyes, seconds away from going under. I whisper goodnight and turn toward the door before it's too late.

CHAPTER TWENTY-FOUR

Clara

"I can't wait to see it in person!" Mads squeals next to me from the passenger seat.

"You're going to love it," I tell her. "The backyard is a secret woodland oasis."

I've been begging Madison to come with me to see the cabin and meet Sydney. After making biweekly trips to Noel the past three months, Syd is beginning to feel like one of my closest friends. I want her and Madison to meet since I talk about them to each other all the time. My parents came with me the first weekend I visited in April, so I assured Mads that I had practice sleeping on the couch and she could sleep in my bed.

The true reason that Mads is here, however, is the irresistible opportunity to meet Mayor McScrooge for herself.

It's a tiny town, meaning I've seen Clark on multiple of my trips here. Although, he must have sworn off Davis and Syd from planning any other arranged meetings. I thought maybe after the smoke detector rescue, he might act more casually around me, but not so much.

In March, he came into Noland's while I was listening to Emily share about how many extra gray hairs three teenagers had inflicted over the course of spring break. He couldn't ignore Emily talking to him, so he just stood there, visibly uncomfortable until he was able to excuse himself from the conversation.

Last month, I was taking a walk along the river, and I saw him out with Chase. When Chase saw me, he came running out of the river and attacked me with his soaking wet fur and kisses. Clark scolded him, but I loved it. As I scratched Chase's belly, Clark asked me how writing was going. I gave a vaguely positive answer, remarked on the nice weather, then asked how things were going around town. He evaded answering, pulling Chase away for a quick exit instead.

So it goes with Mr. Magic Eye puzzle. Thoughtful and semi-approachable one minute, evasive and cold the next.

Part of me thinks that I should write him off completely—quarantine him to the acquaintance zone and go about writing at the cabin the way I originally intended. But every time I convince myself of such, I remember all that he's been through, all the pressure weighing him down. And gosh darn it—I just want to help the man.

The magnetic attraction drawing me toward him also doesn't make the acquaintance zone option any easier.

We pull into the driveway, and Madison is appropriately impressed by my quaint cabin. I give her the grand tour—which takes all of two minutes—ending with the sunroom. Madison stops abruptly in the doorway.

"Clara, I love you, but has anyone ever told you that you have a problem?" she asks.

"What? They're just plants. You know I like plants," I say, pointing to the *You're Unbeleafable* shirt I'm wearing.

"Yeah, but this is . . . obsession level," she replies, face laced with mock seriousness.

I scan the room. Sure, it's on the verge of overflowing with foliage, but I couldn't resist finally buying all the plants I've had my eye on for years. Not now that I have adequate sunlight to keep them alive. Thus far, the plants have all survived with being watered approximately every other week, so adding a new plant or two on each trip just kind of happened.

Ignoring Madison's teasing, I lead her out to the back patio. I purchased a padded love seat to go along with the rocking chair on the deck, and I also put up poles for strings of patio lights. I managed it all by myself without calling Clark for help, thank you very much. We don't talk about how crooked they may be.

"Wow, this is gorgeous," Mads says, awestruck. "I can see why you come down here frequently."

"Yeah, it's pretty perfect." I sigh. "I mean, it would be *more* perfect if it was No-el and not Nole, but at least *this* space is perfect."

"Speaking of Nole, when do I get to meet the Grinch incarnate?"

"Tomorrow afternoon," I reply with an eye roll. "Syd and Davis are hosting a big cookout at their house. I assume he'll be there."

Mads rubs her hands together, an evil glint in her eye.

"Behave yourself, Mads," I chasten. Not that I actually expect her to.

CHAPTER TWENTY-FIVE
Clark

My chest constricts as I pull into Davis' driveway. Pops is in the passenger seat with Chase behind us; a déjà vu moment from Christmas.

But this time, we're not coming for Christmas. We're coming for Clara.

Of course, Syd claims this is a fun barbecue to gather some people together before the summer rush. In actuality, the purpose of this gathering is for Clara's best friend, Madison, to meet her friends in Noel.

I think I'd rather endure Christmas again than attend this cookout. Even though I'm friendly with everyone who will be in attendance, I don't prefer gatherings of more than one or two people. Especially not a gathering in honor of the woman I keep unsuccessfully trying to erase from my daily thoughts.

Clara's made good on her intent to visit Noel every month, usually twice a month. There's no scientific explanation that could be used in a court of law, but I swear, every time she's come to town, I've sensed it before even seeing her. Like her crossing the boundary of my hometown plucks a string tied to my heart, vibrating to announce her presence.

I might be going crazy.

After helping her with the smoke detector that night, I lay in bed, wide awake for hours. I attempted to analyze why I felt inescapably drawn to her when I naturally hold people a safe distance away. I've had no problem shutting down the efforts of the handful of Noel single women who have shown interest in me over the years. My close circle of friends is the same small group I've had since childhood.

Did my inner walls malfunction from the beginning with Clara because there was a physical wall between us for our first conversation? Is it the fact that she isn't a Noel local, so her first encounter was with *just* Clark, not with Clark *Noel*? Or is it simply something about *her*?

I can't put my finger on the exact reason I feel so connected to Clara. I also can't sever the connection, try as I might. And it's driving me insane.

Which is why I've tried to avoid her as much as possible. Unfortunately, that's hard to do in a small town, so we've bumped into each other a couple of times. Last month, she caught me down at the river with Chase, who couldn't hold his chill together in the slightest. He was all over Clara, exactly the way my instincts want to be. Watching her love on Chase made enough of a crack in my walls that I asked how her writing was going.

But then she peered up at me with those cornflower eyes, her cheeks flushed from walking outdoors, grinning from Chase's affection. She asked me how the town was doing. And that string tying me to her was tugging, beckoning me to open up to her. To pour out all my worries and anxieties and fears about how I'm losing the one thing I have left. How it's slowly dying under my watch.

So I took Chase and left.

I wish I could take Chase and leave now.

But this is the first time that Syd and Davis have attempted to plan something with Clara and me in the same vicinity. Ever since I let them have it about that Deer River Bar ambush, they've been less blatant, at least. Today seemed important to Syd, though, so I reluctantly agreed. On the bright side, this is getting Pops out and around other people for a while. And there will be more bodies here as a buffer between Clara and me, unlike dancing at the bar.

We make our way around back slowly since Pops is still refusing to use a cane. I hear the chorus of voices and laughter filling the air, along with the smell of the grill. Pausing to drop my offering of watermelon slices on the food table, I walk alongside Pops to make sure he makes it safely to a lawn chair. Junior scampers over to greet him, lured by the butterscotch candies Pops always hides in his pockets.

With Pops settled, I say a quick hello to Paul and Emily seated next to him, then move to the grill to see if Davis needs any assistance. I halt mid-step, taken aback by the sight of Clara standing next to Syd.

She's wearing a baby-blue sundress that makes her eyes even bluer than usual. A few strawberry-blond tendrils escape from the ponytail she's pulled her hair into. Clara is laughing at something her brunette friend said. The sound carries on the breeze straight to the deepest corners of my mind, where the fodder for my dreams lies.

My vision of Clara is interrupted by a hard clap on my back.

"You're right—I see it now. You definitely *don't* have a thing for Clara," Davis says in a deadpan tone that's canceled out by the mirth in his eyes.

"Shut up."

"Hey babe, look who's here!" Davis calls out to Sydney.

"Clark! So glad you could make it!" Syd says with an extra-wide grin, gesturing me over. She's also wearing a dress, and Clara's friend has on one of those shirt/short onesie romper things that are in fashion for reasons I don't understand. Even Davis has on a polo shirt. I didn't realize everyone was dressing up for this barbecue. I'm suddenly self-conscious in my plain black tee shirt and jeans, but at least I didn't wear a ball cap today.

"Hey Syd. Hi Clara," I greet as I walk toward them. *Be a civil human being, man!* I lecture myself, trying to shake off the way Clara flusters me. I hold my hand out to her friend and introduce myself. "Hi there, I'm Clark Noel."

"Madison," her friend replies. She shakes my hand and doesn't even try to hide the way she's eyeing me from head to toe. "So. We meet at last, Mayor *Nole*."

She also doesn't try to hide her exaggerated emphasis on my last name pronunciation.

Her greeting was a loaded statement if ever there was one. I clear my throat. "Um, Clark's just fine. Welcome to town, Madison. Glad you could come for a visit with Clara."

"Oh, she talks about this place and the people in so much detail, I had to come see for myself!" Madison says. Her tone somehow manages to sound lighthearted and threatening at the same time.

I notice Clara subtly poke her elbow in Madison's side. The movement draws my gaze from Clara's elbow up the curve of her shoulder, along the dip of her neck, past her perfectly pink lips, and up to her eyes. I'm paralyzed in starstruck silence.

Syd chooses this moment to be uncharacteristically considerate of my social awkwardness and asks me to help carry some things out from the kitchen. Addie is characteristically attached to Syd's leg, so I scoop her up as we walk toward the house and blow raspberries on her tummy. That adorable toddler giggle melts even my heart.

Inside the house, Syd turns to me. "Clark, are you okay?"

"What do you mean?" I ask, pretending not to know. I focus on Addie scratching her fingers in my beard instead.

"I mean, are you going to be okay being here around Clara? I'm sorry I pushed things too far at the bar back in February, and I'm sorry if inviting you both over tonight is uncomfortable for you. But I honestly don't understand *why* you get this uncomfortable around her."

"I'm not uncomfortable," I bluff.

"Liar," Syd calls me out, hand popped on her hip. "You lock up like the Tin Man the second Clara steps into view. I know she's pretty, but I've never known you to act weird around pretty women before."

I bite my tongue from correcting her that Clara isn't just pretty. She's gorgeous, stunning, bewitching.

"I'm fine, Syd. I guess I feel awkward about our conversations about the Christmas stuff when she first got here," I lie again. "I'll try to loosen up, though."

I know Syd's not buying my explanation, but she knows me well enough to drop it. She hands me a stack of plates to carry with my hand that's not holding Addie, and we rejoin the crowd outside.

Davis has finished cooking the meat, so everyone makes their way through the buffet and takes seats around the tables. In addition to Paul, Emily, and Pops, Syd also invited James and Becky, who are a few years older than us but have a son Junior's age. Becky owns the coffee shop, Becky's Brews, next to the grocery store. As a result, she and Emily are good friends. Syd frequents the coffee shop as often as possible when it's open during tourist season.

I overhear Clara's conversation with Becky as we move through the line. "You didn't grow up here in Noel?" Clara asks.

"Goodness, no!" Becky responds with a laugh. "I grew up in Austin, Texas. But I went to the University of Arkansas for college and met James there. Since his family owns the cabin rentals along the river, I knew saying yes to marrying him would mean saying yes to moving here. Not gonna lie—it was an adjustment at first, going from big city to small town life. But I wouldn't trade it for anything. I love it here now. Although, I do sneak back to Austin occasionally to get coffee ideas," she adds with a wink.

I go through the line last and take the final seat open at the table—directly across from Clara and Madison. The troublesome twinkle in Madison's eye lets me know she's happy with this arrangement. Her opening comment also lets me know she's locked and loaded, ready to fire.

"So, Clark, I hear you hate Christmas," Madison says, before taking a big bite of her burger.

"Mads!" Clara whisper-scolds, elbowing her friend in the ribs for a second time. I notice Syd and Davis fighting smiles, and a stifled laugh escapes from Emily.

I exhale before answering. "I don't hate Christmas. Granted, it's not my favorite time of year, but I have no personal animosity toward the holiday."

"Just a professional vendetta as mayor against public displays of Christmas spirit?" Madison quips, one eyebrow raised.

I glance briefly at Clara, whose cheeks are fiery-red as she tries to give Madison an evil eye. Madison isn't looking at Clara, though, because she's waiting for me to respond to her prodding.

"Long-standing town tradition goes against major holiday displays, but individual residences and businesses are more than welcome to decorate however they choose," I answer diplomatically. My eyes can't help but flit toward my truck and means of escape from this social interaction.

"Madison, tell me about what you do at Clara's company. She mentioned you work together." Syd jumps in, rescuing me for a second time. *I must really have her worried—I need to get a grip, so she gets off my back.*

Madison shares about her work as a proofreader, but I'm only half-listening until she starts talking about Clara as her boss.

"Clara's the perfect boss for anyone who actually comes to work and does their job, but a terrible boss for slacker employees," Madison says with an eye roll.

"Hey! Rude," Clara responds with a joking tone. But I sense some genuine hurt, or maybe annoyance, beneath the surface. This must be a conversation they've had before.

"What do you mean?" Becky inquires, saving me from having to be the one to ask.

"She's too nice to be firm," Madison says. "There's this one writer on the team who's always making up excuses for not getting his work done. But rather than fire him, Clara just writes his articles for him. She's a total pushover."

"There's nothing wrong with being nice!" Clara defends herself. "And you have no proof that Michael's excuses aren't legitimate. I can choose to help him if I want."

A flare of jealousy sparks hearing Clara mention another man—a man who gets to see her almost every day. *Does Clara give this guy special treatment because she's attracted to him?* I tamp the jealous spark down, reminding myself that I don't want to see Clara every day. I try to coax my thoughts: *Maybe if she did have a man back home, she wouldn't be here meddling and causing trouble for me. Yes, that's what I truly want.*

"Michael has exactly zero legitimate excuses. His never-ending litany of medical emergencies and fights with his girlfriend can't be valid. He's capitalizing on your lack of backbone to be lazy," Madison scoffs.

A wave of anger rushes through me at the thought of Clara's sweet disposition being exploited by this guy (who has a girlfriend who is *not* Clara). "You shouldn't let him take advantage of you, Clara."

Everyone turns to me with shock, surprised that I spoke up. No one is more surprised than I am, though.

Except maybe Clara. She appears mostly dead in response to my interjection. Miracle Max might need to whip up a concoction to bring her back to consciousness.

"I just mean, every employee should pull their weight. It's okay to make exceptions when you deem appropriate, but you shouldn't let someone continually mistreat you," I conclude, wishing I hadn't spoken in the first place.

"I can't believe I'm going to say this, but I agree with Clark," Madison says with an approving nod to me. "He hit the nail on the head, Clara. You always get so caught up in helping other people that you don't have time to do what you want to do. Michael is simply the prime example."

Clara's clearly uncomfortable being the topic of current conversation, and Davis kindly jumps in to redirect. Unfortunately, he redirects my way.

"Clark, any update on that company interested in purchasing the plant?" he asks. I know he regrets the question the second it's out of his mouth when there's a collective gasp around the table. I stare him down with my well-honed death glare.

"Wait, what? There's a company buying the plant?" Syd asks breathlessly. She slaps Davis hard. "You didn't mention this to me until now."

"That's because I told him not to," I growl. All eyes are on me. "I've been in contact with several companies, hoping to find someone who could utilize the building. Bring some jobs back to Noel. There's a company that's considering buying the plant to convert into a pet food production facility. But it's not a sure thing yet."

"But is it promising?" Paul asks, sitting up straighter.

"They are seriously considering it, but I'm not counting the chickens until the eggs hatch," I say, hoping to caution everyone from getting their hopes up.

They've all thrown caution to the wind though, hooting, hollering, and excitedly talking about the chance of having stable jobs year-round for the town again. Becky's gushing to James about how great it would be to keep the coffee shop open all year. Emily's already listing off the people they could hire if the grocery store started seeing more business again. Even Pops has some pep in his voice. All their eager conversations fill me with equal doses of optimism and dread.

Everyone is talking over each other, but Clara just eyes me with a small smile. "That's really exciting, Clark. I hope it works out for you. I mean, for the whole town."

Clara's well wishes only pile on the pressure. Since she arrived, she's only seen this town slowly dying—my failure as a mayor. I want to prove to everyone that I'm competent enough to keep this town running. But I especially want to prove it to Clara, even if she's only ever a visitor to Noel.

But that kind of irrational response to her is exactly what's getting me in trouble, tangling up my practical thinking. Logically, Clara and I don't work together as anything more than part-time fellow residents of the same town. Her driving passion to be involved with helping other people doesn't fit with my solitary preferences. Not to mention her dogged commitment to Christmas. We don't match.

I need to keep my focus on the people of Noel, not worrying about what Clara thinks.

If only it were that easy.

CHAPTER TWENTY-SIX

Clara

I've spent the past month trying not to think about Clark. Trying and failing.

I didn't make a second trip to Noel in May. Work was busy, and I was helping my parents with some projects around their house. In actuality, I could have made time if I'd wanted to.

Instead, I'd avoided the town because I didn't trust myself seeing Clark. I was already seeing enough of him in my daydreams. And in the movie script I'm writing.

As antithetical as the heroine, Renee, is to me, my main male character, Jack, bears a striking resemblance to a certain mayor. Right down to the absurdly attractive beard and grouchy personality. Despite writing him in to my character, I've been nervous to see Clark again ever since we had dinner at Syd's house.

I'd expected Madison to help me out on my quest to dismiss Clark from my list of eligible men. However, Mads came home declaring him to be worthy of my affection. Apparently, his admonition to not let Michael take advantage of me was the key to her heart. That, plus his grumpy love for his town, won her over. Her assessment of Clark as an "extremely hot, broody woodsman" rounded out her closing argument in his favor.

She updated his contact in my phone to "Hottie McScrooge."

Hearing Clark talk about the potential of a company buying the plant and the ensuing joy put into perspective the burden he's carrying. I can't imagine shouldering the weight of an entire town. Although, I still wish he'd let me help him share the load by planning a Christmas tourist experience.

I can't avoid Noel or Clark any longer because I promised Sydney I'd come for a long weekend to experience the height of tourist season. It's the first weekend in June, the launch of peak river season. Although I'm nervous about seeing Clark again, I am looking forward to understanding what the town of Noel is like in its prime.

I pull into the driveway of my cabin late Friday night, having driven here straight from work. I stayed later than planned in order to finish an article for Michael, a fact I will not be sharing with Madison. Or Clark. After unlocking the door and putting my stuff down in the living room, I text Sydney.

My eyes are too tired to do any writing tonight. I do a quick plant check to make sure everyone is doing okay after I sent Syd over to water them last weekend. After a short bubble bath, I change into pajamas and collapse into bed.

Saturday morning, I leave early to stop by Becky's Brews to pick up coffee for Sydney and me. I'm so thrilled to begin my day with a fancy coffee, I can hardly stand it. Parking in the Noland's lot, the increase in traffic around town is evident. I enter the small coffee shop and take in the modern but homey vibes. *I'll have to pay compliments to Syd for her design*. I greet Becky behind the counter.

"Clara! It's great to see you again!" she says. "What can I get for you?"

I peruse her handwritten menu. "Ooo, a blackberry hazelnut latte? That sounds intriguing!"

Becky smiles. "I enjoy making unexpected drink combinations. When I was a teenager in Austin, I loved going to trendy coffee shops with interesting drinks. Most people around here don't appreciate them, so I only buy enough supplies to make small batches for a week or two. But this is one of my favorite experiments yet! You should try it iced."

"I'll take your word for it. Give me a large, and then whatever drink Syd typically likes to order," I tell her. We make small talk as she crafts our drinks, and a line starts to form at the register. I'm glad to see the customers, all dressed like they're heading out for a day on the river.

I take a quick sip of my latte. "Oh, Becky, this is *amazing*!" Holding up my cup in the air, I announce to the waiting customers, "You won't regret the blackberry hazelnut latte!" Becky calls goodbye as I exit, making way for more people to enter.

Sydney greets me with a zealous embrace when I get to her house. "Girl, it's been too long! I've gotten used to my biweekly Clara fix!"

Laughing, I hand her a coffee cup. "Here, this is whatever Becky picked for you."

"Oh, she makes the best caramel macchiato," Syd says, taking the cup with eager hands. "Ahhhh, I love tourist season," she says airily.

An hour later, we're changed into swimsuits, lathered with sunscreen, and fully caffeinated. "Davis' employees are handling the rentals today, and my parents are watching the kids, so you get the full tourist experience," Syd tells me with a grin. The corners of her smile fall slightly before she adds, "I hope it's okay with you, but we invited Clark to come with us?" Her inflection turns the statement into more of a question.

"I, yeah, of course, that's okay. Why wouldn't that be okay?" I mumble.

Syd pins me with a pointed look. "Uh-huh. We'll keep pretending there's nothing awkward going on and that you and Clark have zero attraction to each other."

My mouth drops open, and I stare at her, unable to respond. She rolls her eyes.

"Look, I haven't known you long enough to be thoroughly acquaint-ed with what goes on in your head, and I've never understood what goes on in Clark's. But I think we can agree it wouldn't kill you two to just admit you like each other," Syd says casually.

"You ladies about ready?" Davis loudly questions, entering the front door before I can respond to Syd's observation. "Clark is meeting us down by the river. Let's get a move on!"

We drive in Davis' truck to the end of the route we'll float today. He has supplies for dinner stashed in a cooler with dry ice to leave there. Clark is already waiting in the parking area when we arrive, so we pile into his truck. I'm trying not to be awkward as I greet Clark, but Syd's observations aren't helping me on that front.

After parking in the lot at the start of the route, we unload the tubes from the back. Davis' company rents out all kinds of kayaks and canoes. But Syd insisted we should take a relaxing float trip in the inner tubes today, since the lack of rain has made the river current slow. These deluxe commercial tubes are nothing like the kids' pool rings I was picturing. They're enormous and look comfortable, even for an extended time.

"This is a whole new world that I never knew existed," I say, awed by the cooler float Davis is attaching to his tube. Apparently, we'll have snacks and drinks close at hand for the duration of our five-mile float.

"You need to get out of the city more often," Clark teases, catching me off guard. Aside from the first night we met, this might be the most cheerful I've ever seen him. I assume the influx of people to the town must have a lot to do with that.

"Hey, sunscreen first, gentlemen!" Sydney scolds. Davis and Clark stop pushing the tubes toward the water and accept her sunscreen bottle.

I don't have time to fortify myself mentally before Clark is pulling his shirt over his head. My imagination no longer has any work to do to picture the rest of his tattoo. Or any of the hard muscles that hide under his clothing. I should avert my gaze, but I can't. I'm mesmerized as Davis and Clark take turns spraying each other with sunscreen, cracking jokes and oblivious to my perusal.

My eyes don't know what to focus on. The details of the tattoo running the full length of Clark's left arm up to his shoulder? Or the lines of hard muscle running beneath the ink, across his chest, and down his abs?

An elbow digs into my ribs as Syd's voice singsongs, "I know my husband isn't the one you're over here ogling, so I won't have to slap you."

Her comment is enough to jolt me out of my embarrassingly obvious drooling over Clark. I turn away from the guys and face her. "I don't know what you're talking about," I say, but the breathy tone to my voice gives me away. Syd smirks. "Whatever," I say, rolling my eyes and walking toward the river.

Syd and I sit down in our tubes, and the guys push us out into deeper water before getting into theirs. I try to play it cool when Clark's muscular arms and chest are mere inches away from me. But I'm pretty sure he could have heard the pounding of my heart even if he was a mile away. I splash some river water across my face.

I wasn't sure exactly how much I'd enjoy sitting in an inner tube for hours, but it turns into one of the most fun experiences I've had in a long time. Davis keeps the snacks and drinks flowing from the cooler, and the guys splash enough to keep us cooled off. I'm constantly laughing at the memories and stories that Davis and Sydney take turns sharing, with occasional additions from Clark. I've seen him smile more today than I ever thought he was capable of.

After a couple of hours, Sydney and I decide to take a quick dip in the river to cool off. I leave my jean shorts on, doubting that I could gracefully remove them while sitting in the tube. But I do take off the tank top I've been wearing. I have a fairly modest two-piece swimming suit on underneath, and I stay in shape with barre classes at home. So I shouldn't be reluctant to forgo the tank top. But after seeing Clark's extremely fit upper body, I've been too self-conscious. With the sun now scorching overhead, I decide to reapply sunscreen and leave it off.

I glance up and catch Clark staring at me. He has a baseball cap and sunglasses on, so I can't see his eyes. But I can't *not* see the firm set in his jaw, or the clench of his fist hanging over the side of his tube. I hope he can't see the blush spreading across my cheeks and neck.

By the time we reach the end of our float, I'm exhausted from the sun and starving for a real meal. I perch my sunglasses on top of my head and awkwardly paddle my hands on the sides to try to guide my tube to the riverbank. I'm not overly eager to jump into the murky water—it's much browner here close to the river bank than where we jumped in earlier. Syd and Davis are already on the shore, pulling their tubes out of the water. My paddling is failing miserably when my tube lurches forward.

"Afraid of the river snakes?" Clark asks in front of me, submerged in the water up to his thighs.

"What?!" I jump, pulling my feet into the tube. "There are snakes?! Why didn't you tell me that before I jumped in earlier?!"

Clark's deep laugh fills the air. "I'm kidding, Clara. I mean, of course, there are snakes in the river; it's their natural habitat. But I won't let 'em getcha, I promise."

His baseball cap is now backward, and his sunglasses are off. I have a clear view of the crinkle lines around his eyes as a wide grin lingers from laughing. He pulls my tube closer to the shore, then holds his hands out to help me stand up. My eyes snap magnetically to Clark's tattoo, mentally cataloging the specifics of the design—bare tree, storm clouds, lightning, raindrops trailing the tree trunk and dripping from the roots.

I gulp and place my hands in his. He gives an effortless tug to lift me to my feet in the knee-deep water. My foot slips in the slimy mud, but Clark catches my elbow to steady me. I'm now face-to-chest with Clark's chiseled pectorals, and I can't stop the hitch in my breath. His grip on my elbow momentarily tightens before releasing me.

"You steady now?" he asks, voice husky.

"Mm-hmm!" I squeak, finally moving my eyes to his face. A torrent of emotions seems to be flashing through his eyes. Possibly a lot of the same emotions flashing through me. I don't miss Davis and Syd smirking from the shore as they watch us.

Syd is going to be insufferable now, I think as I drop Clark's hand and make my way out of the water. *Absolutely, positively insufferable.*

CHAPTER TWENTY-SEVEN

Clark

Today has been the best day I've had in, well, a long while.

Yesterday afternoon, I got a call from the pet food company that they're officially moving forward with the purchase of the old Byers plant. I haven't told anyone yet since the details aren't settled, but it's relieving to know there's a solid plan for the building. A plan that can secure jobs for Noel residents.

Consequently, I came into this float trip in a good mood. Such a good mood that even being alone with Clara, Syd, and Davis couldn't put a damper on it. Or maybe that fact amplified the good mood. I'm too confused to know, and too afraid to try to sort it out.

Hanging out as the four of us felt so natural. Like it was exactly how I should be spending my free time *all* the time. But I'm not the type of guy for the type of relationship that a girl like Clara is looking for. So, I've spent all day halting those thoughts in their tracks every time they rear their heads. It's an exhausting game of whack-a-mole.

Pretty sure I officially lost the game the moment I pulled Clara out of her inner tube. She stood there, inches away from me, in her swimsuit top and jean shorts. Her curly ponytail was disheveled from a day on the water, her freckles popping from the sun. I thought I was going to have to call out to Davis to rescue me from kissing her.

I shake my head to clear the mental picture for the hundredth time since we sat down to eat dinner. We'd made a simple meal of watermelon, chips, and hot dogs cooked over a small campfire on the beach. The sun is dipping below the horizon when we pull out the bag of marshmallows.

The sound of Syd's phone cuts through the air. "Oh, it's my mom; let me answer."

We only hear Syd's side of the conversation, but it quickly escalates into alarm. "When?! How? Where?" Davis is on his feet now, crowding close to her to try to hear. "Okay, we'll meet you there."

She turns to us with panicked eyes. "Junior was jumping in our bed and hit his head on the frame. Mom said he's going to be fine, that he's not even crying, but he needs stitches. We need to go meet them at the urgent care."

"Oh no!" Clara gasps.

"Shoot," Davis says, quickly pivoting around to pack up the cooler.

"Leave it; I'll clean everything up," I tell him. There's no urgent care in Noel, so they'll have to drive thirty minutes to the next town over. "Hit the road and get to your kid."

"Thanks, man," Davis responds before they start running to his truck. Syd skids to a stop and swivels back toward us.

"Wait, Clara!" she says.

"I got her, Syd. I'll find someone to come give us a ride back to my truck, then I'll take her home. Just go!" I yell. Seconds later, they're peeling out of the parking lot.

I turn to face Clara. "So . . . you want to go ahead and leave?"

It's getting darker by the second, which means I can't see Clara's face clearly. But I can see enough to know she's staring straight at me, assessing. She bites her lip, and now I'm thinking about kissing her again. But this time, there's no Davis to rescue me if I need it.

Back away! The alarm bells sound.

Before I can make a move, she says, "We could stay and roast marshmallows. I mean, if that's okay with you."

"Yeah, okay," I respond, sitting back down in my lawn chair. Clara sits next to me, and I hand her a roasting stick with a marshmallow on it. We sit silently roasting marshmallows for a few seconds. It only takes those few seconds before I'm thinking about her lips again.

"Perfectly toasted or burned?" Clara asks.

"Huh?"

"Your marshmallows. Do you like them toasty brown or burned black?"

"Oh. Definitely toasted brown," I answer, turning to her. "Are there even people who truly prefer them burned?"

"You tell me after you try yours," Clara giggles. In gazing at her, I'd taken my eyes off my marshmallow, which is now a flaming torch. I quickly blow out the flames.

It's charred to a crisp. "I'm not eating that," I say, moving to pull it off and throw it in the fire.

"Don't waste it! I'll eat it, you big baby," Clara says. She holds my hand briefly to steady the roasting stick while she pulls the marshmallow off. Now my hand is flaming. Clara gives a quick blow to cool the marshmallow off, then stuffs the entire thing in her mouth. Her nose crinkles.

"If there are people who think marshmallows taste good burned, I'm not one of them," she says, then coughs. "That was disgusting."

Chuckling, I slide a new marshmallow onto the roasting stick. "Just pay more attention to the flame spurts than I did, Buttercup." Clara smiles at my *The Princess Bride* reference as she holds her marshmallow close to the embers. We fall silent, watching the fire.

The gentle sounds of the river and occasional sparks from the flames fill the quiet. I'd be perfectly content to sit here next to Clara all night without saying a word, but I know she's more the conversational type.

"So," I clear my throat as I remove my toasted marshmallow from the flames to let it cool. "You've mentioned your parents and your late aunt. No siblings?"

Clara shakes her head. "Just me." She pauses for a moment. "My parents experienced secondary infertility after they had me. They tried for years to have another baby, but it never happened."

Unsure of the right way to respond, I settle on, "I guess that was probably tough." I pop my marshmallow in my mouth as an excuse to not say anything else. I want to follow Clara's lead.

She nods. "Yeah, it was extremely tough for them. I remember a lot of times hearing them quietly talking about it and my mom crying when I was young." She pauses, pensive. "Aunt Gloria and my parents doted on me, but their sadness at not having any other children was always there in the backdrop of my childhood. I was determined as a kid to not cause any trouble and be as helpful as possible. I guess, in a way, I was always worried that I wasn't enough."

Clara stiffens as she seems to realize what she shared. "I'm sorry, I shouldn't have said that. That sounded so whiny. I didn't mean it that way."

"Clara, you're more than enough," I respond, eyes locked on Clara's. Hers widen, and I scramble to recover. "I mean, I'm sure that your parents felt that way. That you were more than enough for them. You're incredible—how could they not?"

So much for that recovery.

Needing to remove my eyes from Clara's, I lean in to prop my roasting stick in the fire to char off the remainders of marshmallow. *This is why I don't attempt small talk.*

We fall quiet again as Clara chews her marshmallow, giving me the opportunity to replay all the awkward things I've said. I know I shouldn't stare, that my fixed attention would be too obvious, but I can't stop my gaze from settling on Clara every few seconds. The soft glow of the firelight brings out the red tones in her hair, the flickering light making her eyes take on a life of their own.

"Will you tell me about your tattoo?" she asks, breaking the silence and catching me staring.

I drop my eyes to the fire, my right hand subconsciously moving to rub my tattooed left arm. When I don't answer right away, Clara tries to backtrack.

"I'm sorry. Maybe that was a personal question. I think I'm tired after being out in the sun all day, and my brain isn't operating within accepted social norms." She stands abruptly. "Maybe we should pack up."

"No, sit down," I say, unintentionally gruff. "I mean, I'll tell you about it. I'm sorry, I didn't mean to order you to sit. I guess my brain is also tired."

My brain *must* be tired. Because the significance of my tattoo isn't something I talk about with people. Ever. Davis and Pops are the only two who know its meaning.

It could also be that string wrapped around my heart that I keep trying to ignore, but one way or the other, I start talking. Clara sits back down, angling toward me. "I'm sure you've already heard about what happened to my parents and brother," I begin, glancing at her.

Even in the firelight, I can see her blush. "Yeah, I have."

I shrug. "Small towns talk. It's okay. Although I didn't get the tattoo until a few years after the accident, the inspiration started a long time before that. When I was growing up." Clara settles deeper into her chair, rapt attention on me. It makes me nervous, but rather than clamming up about my personal life like I typically do, I force myself forward.

"I didn't exactly get along with my dad growing up. He was a successful financial planner in addition to being mayor. My older brother, Sam, was so much like him. Sam and I never were very close because he was six years older than me. He was always mature for his age, even as a kid. And always doing everything with my dad. By the time I came along, my dad already had everything he wanted in a son. They were both book smart and business savvy. Two peas in a pod. And I was on the outside from the start."

I pause, swallowing down the old insecurities that still manage to flare up even in my father's absence. "Let's just say I was the opposite of Sam and my dad in every way. School was never my thing. Don't get me wrong—if something intrigued me, I would read every book about it I could find. The school librarian had her work cut out for her, helping me find books about whatever topic had caught my attention that month. But I was always more interested in doing things with my hands, taking things apart and figuring out how they worked. But that wasn't an acceptable pursuit in my dad's eyes. And . . . he let me know that constantly."

Clara's quiet voice cuts in. "What about your mom? Were you any closer to her?"

I shrug, staring at the fire. "I mean, closer to her than to my dad, sure. But she was always a more passive personality. She went along with whatever my dad said or did. Mom also handled a lot of the administrative tasks for my dad's business, so she was pretty busy. I knew she loved me, but she never stood up to Dad on my behalf."

I don't dare glancing at Clara to see her reaction. I just continue talking.

"Anyway, it was never an option to not go to college after high school. But I didn't know what to do. My dad agreed to let me start at a community college and take some gen eds. He came to terms with the fact that I wouldn't follow in his business footsteps like Sam did. But he hoped I might pursue engineering or some other 'respectable profession,'" I emphasize with air quotes. An ironic laugh escapes before I can stop it.

Clara hasn't said anything else. She's quietly listening with a neutral expression, putting me at ease.

"After the accident, I was a mess. I didn't know how to handle all the emotions—grief, anger at the driver who hit them, sadness. But also . . . relief. I felt relieved to be out from under my father's expectations. But that relief only added guilt into the mix. I mean, who feels *relieved* that their dad has died?"

I swallow hard, embarrassed that I admitted this to Clara. Especially knowing how close she is to her parents. I can't risk meeting her eyes, afraid of the judgment I might find there.

"Clark, I know those are complicated emotions. But they make sense. You aren't wrong for feeling conflicted," Clara says in a calm voice. I dart my eyes back to hers and see empathy instead of judgment. "What did you do after the accident?" she asks.

"I knew I wasn't going to finish college, but I had no idea what to do with myself," I answer. "I moved back into my parents' house, and their life insurance money plus inheritance more than paid for my basic necessities as I floundered through the grief for a year. Totally purposeless."

My chest tightens as I dredge back up the memories I mostly ignore now. "Pops is the one who finally snapped me out of it. He convinced me to shadow him in his carpentry work, taught me how to use tools to shape wood into something new. How to repair broken furniture. He was semi-retired already, but he started going back out to his workshop every day to teach me everything he knew about woodworking.

"I made a pair of barstools on my own, and although they weren't perfect by Pops' standards, they were sturdy. And I felt good at something for the first time in a long time. That's when I got this." I point to the leafless tree traveling the length of my forearm. The exposed roots start just above my wrist, and branches wrap around my bicep. Clara leans forward for a closer look, and my heart temporarily stops beating at her nearness.

My internal warning sirens are blaring at this intimate moment, but I silence them by continuing to speak. "I wasn't convinced I wanted to be a full-time carpenter like Pops, but I knew for sure after his training that I enjoyed fixing things. Knew that I could be good at it. I decided to learn residential electric work. I took classes at a trade school and worked as an apprentice to get a residential journeyman electrician license. I added this." I push the sleeve of my shirt up to expose the storm clouds above the bare tree branches, pointing to the flash of lightning striking the tree trunk.

"I enjoyed learning electric work, but I realized I didn't want to be a full-time electrician either. After my apprenticeship, I learned basic plumbing repairs like replacing faucets and fixing leaky pipes—all the minor jobs that don't require a license," I say.

"Let me guess," Clara interrupts as she reaches to trace her fingers over my tattoo. "You added the raindrops trailing down to the tree roots."

The feather-light touch of her fingers on my arm renders me utterly paralyzed. And mute.

She eventually looks back up into my eyes in the silence. "A piece of the picture for every skill you mastered."

My vocal cords are still disabled, so I simply nod in response. She sits back in her chair, giving me space to inhale. "That's really beautiful, Clark. I mean, beautiful in a manly way. And obviously everything with your dad and the accident isn't beautiful. Just the tattoo and Pops helping you was beautiful. Again, manly beautiful." She slaps a hand to her forehead. "I'm going to stop talking now."

At least I'm not the only one whose brain malfunctions when we're around each other.

"If it's beautiful in a non-manly way, I'm going to need to go back and have a word with my tattoo artist." I smirk, unable to resist the urge to tease her. Clara pushes my shoulder, but one corner of her perfect lips turns up in a smile. My mind tumbles down the rabbit hole of wondering what Clara's lips would feel like against mine. *Are they as pillowy-soft as they look? Would the sweet taste of marshmallow linger there?*

Warning! Warning!

"I should probably try to find us a ride back to my truck before it gets too late," I announce, effectively popping the bubble of this intimate fireside chat.

"Oh, yeah, that's a good idea, I suppose," Clara responds, although her voice sounds disappointed. I stop myself from changing my mind and drawing this evening on longer. This night needs to end precisely because of how badly I want it *not* to end.

A quick phone call later, Paul is on the way. Thankfully, almost every household in Noel owns at least one truck. Clara packs up the food containers as I put out the fire. When Paul arrives a few minutes later, we make quick work of loading everything into the bed of his truck.

I try to let Clara sit up front with Paul, but she insists on taking the back to give me more legroom. I have to hide my disappointment about not being able to secretly watch her profile from the backseat.

We transfer everything to my truck, and I assure Paul I'll let him know when I hear an update from Davis about Junior. On the drive to Clara's cabin, she's quiet, staring out the window. "The stars are so breathtaking here," she says softly.

I can't respond. My breath has been stolen by a different sort of star. It's taking every ounce of energy I have to fend off the desire to reach over and take her hand, to lace her slender fingers through mine. To ask her to sit with me out on her porch all night long.

Parking in her driveway, I turn off my truck and open my door. Clara tries to stop me. "Oh, you don't have to get out. I'll be fine. I left the porch light on."

I'm afraid of what I might accidentally confess about wanting to extend my time near her. I attempt to lighten the mood instead. "Right after two-step class, our next lesson was that a Southern gentleman always walks a lady to her door."

Clara laughs her beautiful, musical laugh, making me smile in the dark. I follow her up the stepping stones to her porch, waiting as she unlocks her door.

She turns to face me. "Thanks for getting me home safely. And for the float trip and the fire and . . . everything."

"Of course."

Clara's blue eyes scan my face, and she bites her lip. Just when that urge to kiss her is about to break down every internal wall I have, she speaks again.

"It was amazing seeing the town brimming with life today, experiencing the energy at its peak. I guess I just wonder . . ." Her voice trails off momentarily as her eyes dip. My heart sinks. "I wonder why you wouldn't want this for another month during the holiday season. The excitement, the liveliness, the boost to the local economy. You could have that again for Christmas, to get people through the winter. I know it would work. I want to help you make it work."

Her words are a bucket of ice water splashed over me. Which is exactly what I needed to cut through the haze our beachside chat put me under. I take a step backward.

"We've been over this, Clara," I say with a sigh. "I don't want a Christmas festival. I don't want your help."

A spark of hurt flickers in her eyes but is quickly replaced by defiance. "Well, maybe you don't, but what about the rest of the town? How do you know that they don't want an opportunity to keep their businesses open during the holiday season? To have a couple more months of income to make it possible for them to stay? How do you know they don't want the boost of life tourists bring to town? Maybe other people do want my help."

I cross my arms. "Stop trying to help all the time. Aren't you supposed to be here to write your movie script? Maybe Madison was right. Maybe you always get so caught up in helping other people that you don't spend any time on your own dreams. Why don't you focus on what *you* want and stop trying to help people who don't need it?"

In the porch light, I see her eyes well up as she flinches away from me.

"That's not fair," she says, voice wobbly. She points at my left arm. "You have a permanent reminder of everything you're good at. Maybe helping is what *I'm* good at, Clark."

"Maybe it is. But I don't need help," I firmly reply. I say the words that I desperately need to convince both of us to believe. "So, maybe you need to look elsewhere for . . . whatever it is you're hoping for, Clara. You're not going to find it with me."

I take another step back. "Goodnight," I gruffly call and stalk back to my truck. As I open the door, I realize I'm holding my breath that Clara will still be there standing on the porch when I turn around, watching me.

But she's gone. I start the ignition and break every speed limit driving home.

CHAPTER TWENTY-EIGHT

Clara

I close the door and lean against it, chest heaving. I'm unsure if hurt or anger is the source of my tears. Probably both. *But am I angry at Clark, or myself?*

Probably both.

I send a text to check in with Syd as I run bath water with an extra-large pour of pumpkin spice bubble bath. She quickly responds.

SYD

> Junior is fine, thank God. He asked the doctor random questions the whole time they were stitching up his forehead. Ten stitches take long enough to find out a doctor's favorite dinosaur, cartoon, song, Bluey episode, color, food, and motor vehicle, as it turns out.

ME

> Oh my gosh, that is the most hilariously adorable thing I've ever heard!

SYD

> Yep. Doctor said he'd never seen anything like it. Leave it to Davis' son.

ME

> Glad he's ok. Get some rest!

Minutes later, I'm soaking in the bath and questioning my existence.

Am I avoiding going after what I want by helping other people all the time? Do people not really want my help? How do I stop caring, stop helping? I enjoy helping. But maybe I should help less? Would people not want me around as much if I'm not helpful? Are there any good synonyms for the word "help" so I can stop thinking about that word this much?

I groan and massage my temples.

But also, why does Clark have to be SO GRUMPY every time I bring up the idea of a Christmas festival? Why can't he take a step back and at least consider it? What does he have against Christmas? Or does he have something against me?

I think back on everything Clark shared by the fire. It's the most I've heard him talk, ever. Certainly the most I've ever heard him talk about himself. I was slightly shocked that he shared such personal feelings. I was so afraid of interrupting the magic of him being open with me that I stayed still as a statue. At least, until I couldn't resist the almost palpable pull to trace my fingers along the lines of his tattoo.

After hearing him share tonight, I can understand why he's so closed off, at least to a certain degree. He's been hurt. I can't imagine growing up without experiencing the love and approval of your parents. And then to lose your whole family so suddenly . . . who wouldn't be messed up by that?

I close my eyes, and I can see Clark's face lit by the firelight as he talked tonight. Do I want to help the town of Noel? Yes. But do I want to help Clark Noel even more? Definitely yes.

But if he doesn't want help, what am I supposed to do?

Why don't you focus on what you want and stop trying to help people who don't need it? Clark's challenge floats back through my mind, and I decide I may as well take his advice.

I drain the water, dress quickly, and sit down to write.

CHAPTER TWENTY-NINE

Clark

It's been two-and-a-half weeks since our float trip, and I haven't heard a word from Clara.

Not that we typically stay in touch when she's back home in KC. But the second weekend after she left, I kept waiting for that invisible string to vibrate with her presence, thinking she might fall back into her biweekly visit rhythm.

No sign of her.

The decreased amount of sleep I'm getting is making me sluggish, but I don't know what to do about it. Every time I lie down in my bed, my thoughts take it as their cue to replay that day with Clara.

I think about floating on the river together, watching her laugh with Syd and catch snacks tossed by Davis. I remember the flush that spread across her cheeks when she caught me staring at her reapplying sunscreen. I'm tormented by the ghosts of her touch. Her hands in mine when I pulled her out of her inner tube. The lightness of her fingers against my skin tracing the lines of my tattoo. I think about how *not* uncomfortable it felt to tell her about my complicated family history.

It's that lack of discomfort that makes me terrified of her effect on me.

I also replay the sight of her flinching away from me after I forcefully turned down her repeated offers to help. I know I was *too* forceful, but at this point, I need both of us to get the picture that we aren't a good idea. Her trying to help me isn't going to end well for either of us.

She lives to feel needed, and I live to not need anyone.

So I've been spending a lot less time sleeping and a lot more time in Sam's old room, which I converted into a home gym. Trying to occupy my mind and tire out my body to encourage sleep. The strategy hasn't worked yet.

I'm at Pops' house replacing a couple of boards in his front porch. The lack of sleep must be making me grumpier than usual because Pops hollers at me from his rocking chair. "What bee flew up your bonnet?"

"No bees. Other than this heat wave," I grunt. I pull the bottom of my t-shirt up to wipe the sweat off my forehead, just for extra emphasis. Chase dashes over to lick my forehead, then returns to his place at Pops' feet.

Pops gives me a serious stank eye. "I'm not buying what you're putting down, or whatever it is the kids say these days."

I bypass correcting Pops' mash-up of phrases. "I don't think 'the kids' are using that saying anymore."

"Don't matter. Something's clearly bothering you, and you may as well spit it out. I got nothing else to do but listen," Pops says. His words add another layer to my worry about the lack of meaningful things to keep him occupied.

"Fine," I give in. "Got a few things on my mind."

"Things such as, oh, I don't know, a certain pretty redhead?" Pops quips, eyes boring into mine.

"It's more strawberry-blond than—" I stop myself from finishing my comment, but that doesn't halt the merry twinkle in Pops' eyes. I roll mine.

"Yes. It's partially Clara," I say. Pops gestures a hand for me to continue. "When she was here a few weeks ago for the float trip, she tried bringing up the Christmas festival idea again. Went on and on about the energy in the town during tourist season, trying to guilt me into giving it a try for the holiday season."

"And?" Pops questions.

"And I shut her down again. Told her to stop trying to help, that we didn't want a Christmas festival and didn't want her help. I figured with this new company coming in to purchase the old Byers plant, we'll have secure jobs in Noel again. What would be the point in trying to add some gimmicky festival?" I blow out a breath. "But then last week, I found out that they won't even begin converting the building until the start of next year. It might be another eighteen months until there are regular jobs."

The timeline is a detail I haven't shared with anyone else. People were excited about the prospect of the plant opening back up. I haven't had the heart to delay their dreams just yet.

Pops is quiet for a minute before responding. "Clark, why are you so dead set against having a Christmas festival?"

I eye him incredulously. "Pops, you knew my dad, my granddad. A touristy Christmas festival is the antithesis of what Noel men have always stood for. I can't be the one to ruin our family name."

Pops stays quiet for another beat. "Son, you have no idea how much those Noel men standards cost."

Now I stare at Pops quizzically. "What are you talking about?"

"I know it's not upstanding to speak ill of the dead, but your granddad could be a real piece of work. And I say that as one of his closest friends in life," Pops adds. I take a seat in the rocking chair next to him, anticipating the need to be sitting down for whatever he's going to say next.

"Bev and your grandma were friends. Good friends. Your grandma would do her cross stitch while Bev would paint, and they'd shoot the breeze all afternoon. So I got to hear the intimate details of how your granddad's stubbornness soured their marriage.

"Your grandma grew up loving Christmas, before she married your granddad. One year, when your dad was a boy, she planned a small Christmas party for the town. Nothing too over the top, just some Christmas caroling that would end with hot drinks in the town square and a tree lighting. Bev helped her map the whole thing out."

I'm silent, but I can guess where this story is headed. All signs point to "that didn't end well."

"When your grandma shared her plan with your granddad, he blew up at her. Ranted about the upstanding Noel name, the respectability of the town, his disappointment that she would dare plan a 'circus event' behind his back." Pops pauses for a long minute, staring out at the horizon. "Your grandma never was quite the same after that. Lost her spirit, I guess you could say. Made Bev terrible sad."

I soak in Pops' revelation. I'd never been especially close with my grandma because she came across rather stoic. It pains me to know that there had once been a more lighthearted version of her I never experienced. Chase leaves his post by Pops to come rest his chin on my knee. I absentmindedly scratch behind his ears.

"You're regurgitating all the same lines your grandad and daddy ever said about this town and the Noel family name. But far as I can tell, you never much wanted to be like either of them," Pops concludes with a side eye toward me. He lets me sit with his observation for a minute before adding, "Clara reminds me a little of the old version of your grandma. Creative, kind, soft around the edges but a little spit-fiery underneath. Don't let these notions your ancestors put in your head ruin your chance at a relationship with such a woman."

"Pops, this is not about a relationship with Clara. That's not something I'm in the market for. This is about our town," I counter.

"Fine then, don't let your Noel-men stubborn streak get in the way of you doing what's truly best for the town. Maybe things have been the way they are for long enough, and it's time to let in some ideas about the way things could be."

CHAPTER THIRTY

Clara

Are you coming to Noel this weekend? I'd like to talk to you about something.

My eyes widen, and the gears stop turning in my brain as I stare at the text on my phone.

I really need to change his contact name.

Reading Clark's text sets loose a net of moths in my stomach. I'd say butterflies, but he's too confusing to associate with beautiful butterflies fluttering around in there. Definitely moths. Stirring up gray dust to float around my insides.

Clark hasn't communicated with me since the night of our float trip. The night I was starting to think he felt the gravitational pull toward me as much as I did toward him. The night when he drew me in with his uncharacteristic vulnerability but then shoved me back away.

I've been dedicating time here and there to writing my script ever since that night. My main character, Jack, continues to sound more and more like a Clark clone, keeping him fresh in my mind. But I haven't gotten over the emotional whiplash of that day. Which means I haven't gone back to Noel.

Once again, my thumb acts before my brain thinks, and I hit the call button.

Clark's gruff voice greets me after two rings. "What's with you refusing to text and having to call all the time? Are you secretly two decades older than the rest of our generation?"

"Just had to be sure I wasn't seeing things. Because what I thought I saw was you requesting for me to come to Noel to talk about something," I respond, trying to keep my voice breezy. I stand up and close the door to my office.

"Congratulations. You can read," Clark deadpans. One corner of my mouth twitches.

"What do you want to talk about?" I ask.

"Not sure if you caught on to this, but you called me. I didn't call you. I simply texted like a normal person and asked if you'd be in town this weekend so we could talk. Talk *then*. Not talk *now*."

I twirl the ring on my finger, considering my response.

"Fine. Yes, I can come to Noel this weekend," I say after a short pause. "But first, I need to know which version of Clark I'll be talking with."

"What the heck does that mean?" he growls.

"I mean, am I talking to the Clark who talked to me by the riverside fire, the one who rescued me from bathroom jail and took meticulous care of my plant? Or the one who trashed the list of ideas I worked on all night and hates me every time I say the word Christmas?"

There's a moment of silence, and my pulse pounds in my ears. *I can't believe I said that out loud.*

"Clara, I've never hated you. I could never hate you." His voice is husky, only making my heart pound harder. "You're the most un-hateable person in the history of the world."

"I think Mother Teresa would disagree with you," I quip back, trying to lighten the mood. Because I'm wobbling on thin emotional ice.

"All right, in the history of America," Clark amends.

While I'm warmed by his sentiment, he hasn't answered my question. "Well?"

I hear a sigh. "Clara, I'm . . . I'm sorry. It's true I prefer solitude over being around people, but I swear I'm not usually outright mean. I don't know how to explain why I've been rude to you in the past. But I am sorry that I've treated you poorly because that's the last thing you deserve. I promise to be the better version of myself with you this weekend."

Although I don't have decades of history with Clark, I know him enough to recognize how hard that was for him to say. A pool of warmth puddles in my chest, slowly spreading through my limbs and up to my cheeks.

"I accept your apology, Clark. And I'll see you this weekend."

No sooner do I hang up than there's a knock at the door.

"Come in!" I call. I stifle a sigh when Michael's head pops in.

"Hey Clara, how's the day going?" he asks, flashing me a too-wide grin.

"Fine, but busy," I reply, not in the mood for small talk. "What do you need?"

Michael takes a seat in the small chair on the other side of my desk, settling his face into a frown. "Here's the thing. I have two more articles scheduled to turn in tomorrow, but my girlfriend called, and she's cat sitting for her cousin. The cat has been acting funny today. She's so freaked out. I might need to go with her to the vet to get it checked out."

I grit my teeth. "Your girlfriend's cousin's cat is acting . . . funny. And?"

He flashes another smile at me. "I was hoping you might be able to pitch in to help me out with the articles, so I can help my girlfriend out."

Normally, I would acquiesce—say yes and stay late doing his work for him. A case of "toxic helpfulness," as Mads likes to call it. Maybe it's because I just got off the phone with Clark, but his doorstep accusation flashes through my mind. That I'm too busy helping other people to chase what I truly want. And what I *want* is to spend time working on my script tonight. I've had an idea for a dialogue exchange buzzing around in my head all day.

Michael appears disconcerted by the fact that I didn't agree right away. But he's about to be *very* disconcerted. Because I'm not going to.

"No, Michael."

"I'm sorry?" he asks.

"No, I won't take the articles for you. You're going to need to figure out a way to get them done. Stay up late tonight, come in early tomorrow, whatever it takes. I expect polished articles to be finished by the deadline," I say, strength growing in my voice with each word.

Michael looks flustered. "But, I just need a little assistance this once—"

"No, Michael, you consistently don't complete your work on time and ask for 'a little assistance,'" I emphasize with air quotes. *Who am I right now?! I like it! I wish Mads was here to watch this! With popcorn!*

He stares at me, as though unnerving eye contact will make me change my mind. I double down.

"I'm making a note in your personnel file that you've repeatedly missed deadlines and turned in less-than-quality work. This is your chance to turn things around, or I'll be speaking to Mr. Douglas about your future here." I stand up, effectively dismissing Michael.

His face conveys hand-in-the-cookie-jar energy as he slinks out of my office. As soon as he leaves, I exhale and fall back into my office chair, fighting the urge to squeal aloud. I look down at my hands, expecting to see power visibly surging from them.

I did it! I set a boundary! I can't wait to tell Mads.

Then again, maybe I shouldn't tell Mads. I'm not sure yet if I want to give her more reason to join "Team Clark."

I take a half-day off work on Friday so I can drive down to Noel in time to make a supply run to Noland's before dinner. Emily greets me enthusiastically but briefly, as there's a long line of shoppers ready to check out. It's a night-and-day difference during tourist season versus the dead of winter.

Stopping in at Becky's Brews on my way to my car, I order a decaf special—a simple sweet cream iced coffee—to take home. I'm determined to take full advantage of quality coffee being available, even if it means being awake later tonight. Maybe it will fuel some writing hours.

I've barely had time to unload my groceries and take a few sips of coffee when I hear a loud knock. Startled, I tiptoe my way to the front door, standing to the side where I can see out the window without being seen.

Clark stands outside, baseball cap turned backward. His dark-gray t-shirt hugs the muscles of his biceps as he balances a pizza box in one hand. The other hand reaches up to rub across his beard, then knocks again.

"Clara?" he calls through the door. "It's Clark. I, uh, saw your car back in town and decided to come over."

I lightly run my hands over my loose curls, hoping they're not too wild. I'm still wearing the athletic shorts and *You Grow Girl* Monstera plant graphic tee I wore for the drive, but I don't have time to change.

What are you thinking, Clara?! You don't need to dress up for him! Just answer the door.

I turn the knob and swing the door open, hit by a wave of woodsy sandalwood mixed with pizza. Unclear which smell I'm hungrier for.

"What are you doing here?" I ask, trying to divert my brain away from fixating on his scent. Chase is sitting at Clark's feet but dances up when he sees me. Clark stills him with a command to sit before responding to my question.

"I told you I wanted to talk this weekend. And I come bearing gifts," Clark answers, tipping up the pizza box. "I figured you would be hungry after the drive."

I eye him without inviting him in yet. My hesitation is half confusion about him showing up here before I even told him I'd arrived. The other half is that I'm knocked off-kilter by how much I missed the sight of his hazel eyes, bearded jaw, and tall, muscular frame. Not to mention that darn tattooed arm I once traced my fingers over. A moment I've mentally replayed more times than I'll ever admit to on record.

"How did you know I was in town?"

Clark flinches but quickly rolls his shoulders, as though he's a teenager who got caught texting during class and tried to play it off. He raises his free hand to rub his beard again, looking around at the trees before resting his hand against the door frame. "I . . ." He sighs and locks eyes with mine. "I just knew."

Now I'm the one feeling caught. I awkwardly stand staring at him, suppressing all the hormones screaming at my muscular system to move forward and lean into Clark's chest.

I take a giant step backward. "Come on in."

Closing the door behind Clark, I gesture toward the back of the house. "Why don't we go sit on the back porch? I'll get some plates and water." Clark nods and heads toward the sunroom, Chase on his heels.

I take advantage of my few seconds alone in the kitchen to take a deep breath. I don't know what Clark is here to talk about, but my brain has gone into full-on anticipation mode. Complete with a racing pulse and overactive underarm sweat. I stand in front of the open fridge for an extra few seconds before taking out the water pitcher.

A minute later, I approach the sliding back door balancing plates, two stacked glasses, the water pitcher, and my iced coffee like the one-trip champion I am. I pause when I see Clark standing on the porch, talking to Chase and gesturing with his hands like he's giving a speech. Chase peers up at him, tongue hanging out of his mouth as he appears to nod along to whatever it is that Clark is saying. I'm mesmerized by the scene. Mesmerized by the man who still remains such a mystery.

Until he turns to the door and catches me staring.

CHAPTER THIRTY-ONE

Clark

I've been practicing my speech on Chase, but I look up to see Clara standing on the other side of the glass door, staring at me. Her hands are ridiculously full, and she startles when I make eye contact with her. Thankfully, she doesn't drop anything as a result.

I see her raise her leg like she's going to open the sliding door with her foot, but I jump forward to open it first. "It's okay to ask for help, Clara," I bemuse.

"Hi, kettle. I'm pot," she sarcastically quips back. "I mean, pot as in a kitchen pot. That's black. Not pot like, *pot* pot," she adds quickly.

"And here I thought things were about to get *really* interesting," I say with a twinkle in my eye. I take the plates and glasses from her hands, then mentally scold myself. *Stay focused. Don't get distracted by her wit or eyes or smile or adorable punny shirts.*

"P.S.: your fiddle leaf fig in the sunroom looks sickly," I observe, distracting my train of thought.

"Does it?" Clara asks, retreating inside for a moment before coming back out. "Shoot, it does. I asked Syd to come over and water them when I was gone so long."

"You asked Syd to take care of your plants?!" I exclaim. "Well, there's a sure-fire way to kill them off."

"Hey!" Clara laughs. "She was doing me a favor!"

"Do your plants a favor and let me take care of them next time you need help. Syd has the blackest thumb I've ever seen. Pretty sure she could kill an artificial plant. She probably set a reminder to water them every few days without even bothering to check the soil," I explain.

"She didn't!" Clara gasps. "That would explain the yellow leaves on more than one plant." She sighs. "Wait, how do you know this much about plants?"

I shrug a shoulder. "When I took care of your Tineke, I did a little research." Clara eyes me. "Okay, I did a lot of research. I went down the black hole of Instagram and blog posts by the plant lady who makes that fertilizer."

There's a tangle of emotions in Clara's eyes as she regards me. Those deep blues are sucking me in, tugging me closer. I change the subject.

"I didn't know what kind of pizza you prefer, so I ordered their best seller. It's a three-meat pizza," I say, opening the lid of the box.

"As long as there are no black olives, I'll eat pretty much any pizza," Clara replies.

"Ugh, who likes that dirt fruit garbage anyway?" I respond with disgust.

"Right?! Only psychopaths think olives taste good," Clara says as she pulls a slice of pizza onto her plate.

"Just don't let Syd hear you talk that way," I tell her, taking a slice for myself.

"Nooo!" Clara groans. "Don't tell me Syd is on the dark side."

"I won't say anything then," I respond, unable to hold back a smile any longer.

Chase is sitting right next to Clara's chair, ears perked, lip tucked behind his bottom tooth. His best puppy eyes are plastered on her. He knows better than to beg me for people food. I'm determined to keep Chase alive longer than any dog has ever lived, so I'm strict about his diet and exercise.

Clara coos at him before handing him a meatball from her pizza. All of my friends know better than to feed Chase scraps from their plate. But I can't bring myself to stop Clara.

Chase is going to be even more obsessed with her than we already were. I mean, he. *Than he already was.*

"Sooo," Clara draws out, eyebrow arched. "You wanted to talk?"

I chew and swallow my bite of pizza, setting my plate down beside me. "Um, yeah," I begin, clearing my throat. "I wanted to talk to you—or, really, I guess I wanted to ask you . . . I just mean, I needed to say . . ."

The more I stumble over my words, the wider her eyes grow. I don't know what thoughts are running through that beautiful mind of hers. If they're as conflicted as mine, I need to spit this out and clear up any potential confusion.

"I need to talk to you about the Christmas festival idea."

Her eyes flash with the tiniest moment of disappointment before lighting up like a Christmas tree.

"Precisely what about the Christmas festival do you want to talk about?" she asks coyly, head tilted.

"I think I've decided that it could be a good idea for the town. For morale, for the economy, for resident retention. I'm ready to explore the possibility," I state as unemotionally as possible.

"What was that?" she asks, setting aside her plate. Chase eyes her half-eaten pizza, but stays obediently in place. "I'm not sure I heard you correctly."

I sigh. "The Christmas festival might be a good idea. To bring in some tourists. I'm thinking we should do it."

"And I play into this conversation how, exactly?" Clara asks.

This woman. She's really going to make me spell it out.

"I'm asking for your help to plan a Christmas festival, Clara. Please?" I acquiesce.

She's now the spitting image of the Cheshire Cat. But her smile is so intoxicating, I can't even be annoyed.

She sits forward and literally claps her hands like an excited child. "Finally! You won't regret this, Clark. We can make it beautiful and classy and magical—it doesn't have to be gimmicky at all, I promise. I mean, maybe a teensy bit gimmicky. But not over the top. Let me get some paper, and we can brainstorm," she says, standing up.

"Wait," I say as I grab hold of her wrist, urging her to sit back down. My hand is now on fire after touching her smooth skin. I picture a fire extinguisher shooting through my veins before I continue.

"Why don't we use these ideas as a starting point?" I ask, reaching into my back pocket to pull out a folded piece of notebook paper. A crumpled, folded piece of notebook paper.

Clara's eyes double in size, and she gasps. It's the most attractive intake of breath I've ever heard. She stares at the paper in my hand, then looks up into my eyes.

"My ideas," she whispers. "You . . . you saved them?"

I nod.

"But you crumpled them up. You threw them in the trashcan," she says, still breathless.

"And then I took them out of the trashcan," I reply, unfolding the page. "I didn't read them until recently. But I kept them."

Moisture pools in Clara's eyes, and she blinks rapidly to clear them. Crying has always made me uncomfortable, but I resist the urge to retreat. I clear my throat again and motion to the list.

"Some of these ideas I'm going to veto—no changing the town name to No-el, no fake snow machines, no mistletoe kissing booth," I say.

"But—" Clara starts to interject.

"No. Kissing. Booth," I state firmly. Clara huffs but nods. "There are a lot of reasonable ideas here. I think we should call a town meeting and present this list. Give everyone a chance to vote on it."

"I have an even better thought," Clara says, eyes twinkling. "If the town is on board with the festival idea, we should have a Christmas in July Heartmark movie marathon and let everyone brainstorm ideas together. Give people more ownership of the plan."

I nod. "That's not a bad idea."

"Of course, it's not a bad idea. When have you known me to have bad ideas?" Clara quips. I tilt my head with a deadpan expression in my eyes. "Hey, you just admitted to my festival idea being *good*. So none of the sarcasm leaking out of your eyeballs shall be directed my way from now on," she says, looking infinitely pleased with herself.

"Fine."

"How soon can you pull together a town meeting to vote on the festival?" Clara asks, sitting back and taking another bite of pizza.

I sit back in my chair as well. "That's the great thing about small towns. Doesn't take much notice to pull everyone together. I'll put out the call to gather early Monday morning."

"Can I stay for the meeting?" Clara asks quietly, twirling the ring on her finger and not making eye contact with me.

I lean forward to force Clara to look into my eyes. "This was your idea, Clara. Of course, you can come."

The corners of her mouth turn up slowly, pulling on the string knotted around my heart.

"The town has to be able to blame the right person if this goes sideways," I joke, trying to relieve the tension in my chest.

"Har har," Clara scoffs. "I'll be sure to share credit with Noel's finest mayor when this turns out to be the best thing that ever happened to this town."

The jury is still out on the Christmas festival, but I'm trying to ignore the persistent feeling that *Clara* might just be the best thing to ever happen to this town.

Chapter Thirty-Two

We've got an official date for the Christmas in July brainstorm session. Wednesday after the week of the Fourth. Town shouldn't be too busy midweek after a big holiday week.

Sounds good! I'll put in a request for PTO that day and plan to work remotely the days around it.

Have you picked the movies for the marathon yet?

Of course! I narrowed down all my favorites that have Christmas festival scenes in them and picked the best five.

Absolutely not. I will not subject my town to five Christmas movies in a row.

But Clark! All five have good ideas! It will be fun!

No. You get three. Keep narrowing.

ME

What about four?

HOTTIE McSCROOGE

Nope. Three.

ME

<sad eyes emoji> <broken heart emoji>

HOTTIE McSCROOGE

My heart is immune to emoji manipulation. Three is my final answer.

ME

<Bah Humbug GIF>

HOTTIE McSCROOGE

Why did a giant shipment of Christmas lights and garland just arrive at my office?

ME

Oh, yay! They made it! It's so you can decorate the town hall for the movie marathon!

HOTTIE McSCROOGE

Nope. Not doing that.

ME

But you have to set the mood, Clark! Get everyone in the Christmas spirit *<Santa emoji>*

HOTTIE McSCROOGE

You have the movies for that. This is a brainstorm session. Not the actual festival. I'm returning these.

ME

Don't you dare!

HOTTIE McSCROOGE

Oh, I dare.

ME

You WILL keep those decorations and I will drive down early to hang them up myself.

HOTTIE McSCROOGE

<GIF of Michael Scott yelling no>

ME

Clark. Don't make me call you. So help me, I will hit that telephone icon so fast.

HOTTIE McSCROOGE

Fine

ME

What time are we going to start the first movie in the marathon?

HOTTIE McSCROOGE

We need to be done with movies and the idea brainstorm by 6:00. I decided we'd do a big cookout for everyone as a reward for sitting through 5+ hours of Christmas. So work backward from 6 p.m.

ME

Oh, that's a great idea! *<clapping emoji>*

HOTTIE McSCROOGE

You think I can't have good ideas too?

ME

I mean, you HAVE been known to not recognize good ideas when they're staring you in the face, so . . .

HOTTIE McSCROOGE

I'm not dignifying that with a response

ME

Except you totally just responded, so ha! *<grinning emoji>*

HOTTIE McSCROOGE

<eye roll emoji>

ME

CLARK NOEL JUST USED AN EMOJI *<wide eyes emoji>* Mark this down as the day I successfully converted you to the bright side!

HOTTIE McSCROOGE

And I'm turning my phone off now.

ME

Is everything good to go for next week?

HOTTIE McSCROOGE

Yes

ME

Any other help you need from me?

HOTTIE McSCROOGE

No

ME

<thumbs up emoji> See you next week, Clark!

HOTTIE McSCROOGE

Looking forward to seeing you.

I mean, looking forward to the whole deal.

I mean, NOT looking forward to the Christmas spirit torture. But looking forward to the morale boost for the town.

ME

I know what you mean. *<smiling emoji> <Christmas tree emoji>*

CHAPTER THIRTY-THREE

Clara

"**D**o you need me to pick up anything from the store on my way?"

"No, honey. We have plenty of food. Just come hang out with everyone," my mom responds.

"I'm sorry; I was trying to get ahead on some work since I'm going to Noel next week. I totally forgot to make the strawberry pies," I say, blowing out a breath. "But I could stop and pick up some other desserts."

"Care-Bear, stop worrying," my dad's voice calls out. Speaker phone strikes again. "The neighbors are making homemade ice cream. We'll have plenty of sugar. Just get over here and eat before we do fireworks."

"Dad, it's illegal to shoot off fireworks in Overland Park," I chide.

"I mean, technically . . ." His voice trails off.

"Daaad? Need I remind you that you've already taken one trip to the emergency room in the past year?"

"I didn't buy any fireworks, but I can't be responsible for what other people in the neighborhood have planned." He sounds smug.

I sigh. "I still feel bad that I'm not bringing anything. I should have set an alarm last night."

"Clara Jane." My mom's voice has switched to scolding mode. "We're glad that you get to go to the cabin next week. No one is going to go hungry because you forgot the pies. Please, just come straight over."

"Okay, okay," I acquiesce. "I'll be there in twenty minutes."

I arrive at my parents' house empty-handed, still feeling guilty about it. A proper block party setup spreads from their front yard to the two neighbors on either side. The unmistakable smell of burgers grilling fills the air, along with the lingering scent of the multicolored smoke bombs the kids have been lighting. I greet my parents and their neighbors, fielding questions about work, the cabin adventure, and, inevitably, my love life. Such is the fate of a single adult.

Mom heads inside to bring out a fruit salad now that the food is ready, and I follow her. "Need any help, Mom?"

"I got it, honey. I don't need any help. You go back outside and enjoy yourself," she responds.

Her comment pokes the bear of confusing emotions I've been burying ever since Clark told me to stop helping people all the time. To go after what I want. "You know I enjoy myself more when I'm helping," I try to joke. "It's not a good time if I'm not pitching in somehow."

Mom cocks her head as she regards me. "You're allowed to just *enjoy* yourself sometimes, Clara. Why do you think you have to be helpful in order to have a good time?"

I manically spin the ring on my finger, hoping to divert the panicked energy her question prompted in my mind. Unfortunately, my mom knows my tell, so one glance at my hand has her setting down the bowl of fruit and crossing the room to me.

"What's going on, honey?"

I chew on my lip. "It's just something Clark said to me when I was in Noel for the float trip. I can't get it out of my head." Mom eyes me, silently urging me to continue. "He basically accused me of pushing to help where I'm not needed instead of doing what I really want to do."

Mom purses her lips and hums. "Do *you* think you focus too much on others instead of doing what you want to do?"

"I don't know." I sigh. "I've never known how to be any other way. I mean, ever since I was a kid, I needed to be helpful to you and dad so that, you know . . ."

I trail off, but my mom looks confused rather than sympathetic. "What do I know?" she asks.

"Never mind," I attempt to dismiss. "Let's go back outside and have some food!"

My attempt at being casual epically fails.

"No, ma'am," my mom says sternly. "You have some explaining to do. What do you mean about needing to be helpful to your dad and me?"

I'm trapped. This is the last conversation I want to have, but I can't find an escape hatch. The only way out is forward.

I can't quite meet my mom's eyes as I explain. "You know, you and dad were always so sad about not being able to have another baby. I wanted to make sure that I wasn't burdening you, that I could help make you happy."

Stunned silence fills the room. *Why has no one invented a real-life rewind button?! I'd pay good money for that right now.*

"Honey, did we say something to make you feel that way?" my mom asks, eyes misty.

"No, Mom; of course, you didn't. It's something I put together in my own mind, I think. I hated seeing you and dad discouraged or crying or disappointed. Little-kid Clara just assumed the best way I could help you feel better was to be helpful instead of being needy." The confession dam has broken, and everything is pouring out unhindered. "And, I guess, there's part of me that still thinks I need to be focusing on other people's needs all the time so that . . . so that they'll need me. And love me. But that's not your fault—this is all in my own head."

Mom steps closer and takes my face in her hands. "Clara, I love you *so* much. And that has nothing to do with any of your actions. It's because I'm your mother. Because the day I knew you existed, I *chose* to love you with every ounce of my heart for the rest of my life. You could have been the most rebellious, angst-inducing tornado of a child, and I still would have loved you with my whole being. I *will* always love you, no matter what you do or don't do."

She pauses to wipe a tear from under her eye. "I'm sorry that we inadvertently made you feel like you had to act a certain way to be loved."

"Mom, it's not your fau—" I try to interrupt, but Mom cuts me off again.

"I know you think it's not our fault, and it certainly wasn't intentional. But maybe we should have hidden our pain from you better all those years when you were young. You've always been the greatest joy of our lives, Clara. Simply because you exist—not because you're helpful or considerate or supportive. I wish I could go back and amplify *those* feelings in your memory." She leans in to wrap her arms around me, and I hold on to her tightly.

"Thanks, Mom. I do know that you love me. You and Dad gave me the best childhood. I promise those are the memories I think about most. Clark's comments just got me thinking about myself in a different way. I'm a little off-kilter, I suppose," I conclude as I pull back from our hug.

Mom's head is once again cocked to the side, a sparkle in her eyes. "Maybe you need someone like Clark to help you approach life in a different way. Someone who pushes you to focus on yourself more."

I roll my eyes. "I already have that someone. Her name is Madison. I just mostly ignore when she pushes me." Mom raises an eyebrow. "Mom! You've never even met Clark! You don't understand how . . . how . . . infuriatingly contradictory he is."

A smug smile settles on my mom's face. "I'm just saying *he* is the one who finally got you to examine your helping habit. But then also *asked* you for help with the festival. Maybe he's the perfect kind of contradiction for you."

This conversation is decidedly *not* helping my stomach settle down the Clark moths. Thankfully, my mom knows me enough to see my inner scramble for an escape. She takes the bowl of fruit and walks toward the door. "Come on out when you're ready, sweetheart," she calls back over her shoulder. I accept her invitation to stay put for a few minutes, collecting my thoughts.

Let's be honest—zero thoughts are collected. They're free-range chickens scattered across the sprawling farmstead at this point. Still, I appreciate sitting in the quiet before rejoining the red, white, and blue chaos outside.

My mom refuses to allow me to lift a finger all evening as we share dinner with their neighbors and watch the unsanctioned fireworks. As though she's going above and beyond to prove a point—that I don't have to help all the time. If I didn't know better, I'd think that she was already in cahoots with Madison and Clark.

The Wednesday after the Fourth of July, I'm keyed up with inadvisable amounts of excitement. Movie marathon day is finally here. Ever since the town unanimously voted to host a "Christmas Fest," I've been anxiously anticipating this moment.

We'll binge-watch three movies, have a group brainstorm session, then celebrate with a massive crawfish boil dinner. I'm not sure what to think about that last bit, but everyone else is excited, so I'm trying to play along.

Anxiety gnaws at my stomach as I think about seeing Clark today. I saw him when I came back to Noel the weekend before the Fourth of July. We had a strategy dinner with Syd and Davis to plan the Christmas in July brainstorm day, and Clark acted almost normal toward me.

But ever since my conversation with my mom, I'm torn on whether I think contradictory Clark is a good or bad fit for me.

Now that Clark has come around to the Christmas Fest idea, the primary reason behind his rude behavior aimed at me is no longer an issue. However, he still vacillates between acting mildly flirty and mildly grumpy toward me. I've decided I have no choice but to guard my heart and conclude that he doesn't have the same attraction to me that I feel to him.

Because I *feel* it. Mega-feeling it. I can admit it: my heart is drawn to that gruff, tattooed, towering force of a man like a kid to the candy aisle.

I'm just not going to do anything about it. Having my *ideas* rejected by Clark when he was adamantly against the Christmas Fest idea stung so badly. I don't think I could handle it if he rejects *me*.

Therefore, I'm switching to my helper mindset and staying far away from the Fire Swamp of my feelings for Clark Noel. Who knows what lightning sand or rodents of unusual size might be waiting to take me down?

I head into the Town Hall to make sure everything is ready to go for the movie marathon. Seeing the garland and lights draped on the sides of the room brings a smile to my face. We'll take short stretch breaks between each movie, with snacks and drinks ready to keep everyone satisfied. Becky is testing out several coffee concoctions she hopes to serve during Christmas Fest, and the Ladies Who Bake Club has a mountain of festive treats to sample. Everyone will be able to vote on the favorites to keep.

The room slowly fills with conversation as people enter and sit down. Ten minutes later, Clark stands up at the front of the room to shush everyone. *For goodness' sake, why does he have to look so attractive?*

His appearance is more professional mayor today, dressed in dark jeans and a black button-up shirt. A far cry from his typical tee shirt and baseball hat wardrobe. However, he's rolled the sleeves up to his forearms and still has on his regular boots, making the look slightly more casual. Also, *more* handsome, somehow.

I use my notebook to fan myself.

"Welcome, everyone," Clark announces. "Thanks for taking time off today to join us in planning our first Christmas Fest. Maybe the only one, depending on how things go."

"Boo!" Syd and Davis heckle from the back of the room.

Clark holds up a hand. "I'm just saying we'll see how this turns out and evaluate from there. But I'm grateful to see everyone rallying together for our town." His sincerity and protectiveness over his town make my heart pound harder.

Clark invites me up to speak next. "Please welcome to the stage . . ." He pauses, glancing around. "Well, welcome to the front of the room, Clara Sullivan, the mastermind behind this whole deal."

I walk nervously to the front as people clap, wishing Clark would stay standing next to me as moral support. But he already sat down in the front row. His facial expression is on the encouraging side of neutral, though. I'll take what support I can get.

"Thanks again, everyone. Not only for coming to brainstorm ideas together, but for welcoming me to your town," I begin, surprising myself by getting choked up. "It's been a true honor to become a part-time resident of Noel," I add with a smile. Syd cat-calls, making everyone laugh and snapping me out of sappy-mode into business-mode.

"My lovely assistants, Sydney, Emily, and Becky, are going to pass around some note cards and pens," I announce as they move through the room. "As we watch the movies today, jot down any festival ideas that stand out to you—could be events, decorations, goods or services offered, anything and everything! At the end of the afternoon, we'll share ideas and figure out what could work here in Noel. And be sure you taste-test Becky's drinks and the ladies' holiday treats during the breaks, so we can give them feedback. Now, let the Christmas cheer commence!"

Davis hits play on the first movie while Sydney turns off half the lights. I leave the main area to help Becky prep her drinks. I walk into the kitchen to see Becky pouring syrups into mini measuring cups. If the North Pole had a chemistry lab, this is what it would look like.

"Whoa, how many different drinks are you making?" I ask. "Not that I'm complaining!"

Becky is sheepish as she meets my eyes. "This is seriously my dream come true—the chance to try out all these unique flavor combinations! I'll have to narrow it down, of course, but today's the perfect day to throw everything at the wall and see what sticks!"

"Well, why don't we throw everything in my mouth, instead," I laugh. "I'm the only taste tester you need!"

I inspect Becky's note cards with each drink's ingredients listed. Naturally, she has a traditional peppermint mocha planned, but she has several other festive combinations. There are recipes for spiced gingerbread lattes, maple pecan macchiatos, eggnog frappés, apple cider chai lattes, cranberry white chocolate mochas, and extra-rich hot cocoa.

"That's it, you're not cutting any of these," I joke. "What can I do to help? We have about seventy minutes until the first movie ends." Becky assigns me the task of setting out the sampler cups on one counter behind the paper tents listing the various drinks. There's not a lot we can do this far ahead of time. We mostly stand around chatting about how the summer season is going at the coffee shop and sharing excitement for the festival.

Forty minutes later, Clark comes through the door. He's undone the top button of his shirt, and his hair looks like he's been running his hands through it nonstop.

"Feeling a little stuffy in there, Clark?" Becky muses, smirking at him.

"Ugh, I'm about to go home and get a t-shirt and hat," Clark groans, leaning against the counter next to me. "Dressing up for this was a dumb idea."

"Whatever, you look very dignified, Mr. Mayor," I tease, reaching up to tug on the collar of his shirt. Even through Clark's full beard, I swear I see the hint of a blush on his cheeks. The thought brings a flush to my own. "What are you doing in here, though? You should be out there watching the movie."

"I can't take it anymore," he responds, running a hand through his hair. "Besides, *you're* not out there."

"That's because I've seen all of these movies multiple times. And I already made a list of my suggestions, remember?" I say, ignoring the *other* possible meaning behind his assertion that he wasn't watching the movie because I wasn't out there.

"Boy, do I," Clark huffs. "You're getting your Christmas Fest. Don't make me regret this decision."

"Actually, I have the perfect idea for a name," I share excitedly.

"We already have a name. Christmas Fest," Clark asserts.

"Yes, but since this first year is special, we should have a special name—The First Noel," I say, bouncing on my toes. Becky *awws*.

"You're doing the literal opposite of 'don't make me regret this decision,'" Clark says flatly, narrowing his eyes.

"But it's perfect!" I counter.

"It's ridiculous. Ridiculously cheesy."

"Clark, we're Christmas lovers. Cheesy is the name of our game."

He groans again and buries his head in his hands, elbows propped on the counter. I smile smugly, knowing I've won. Glancing victoriously over at Becky, I see an amused expression on her face as her eyes bounce back and forth between Clark and me.

"Just give me a task to do," Clark demands. "I'm not going back out there."

"But this is my favorite of the three movies! All of *The Nutcracker* references—it's the perfect Christmas movie," I gush.

"Wait a second," Clark muses. "Clara . . . you're named after *The Nutcracker*? You literally have a Christmas name?"

My cheeks burn, but I raise my chin. "So?"

"This explains so much."

"I come from a long line of Christmas enthusiasts, okay?" I say as Clark throws his head back in a laugh. "Becky, give the man a task, will you?"

Becky sets us both to work steaming milk extra hot as she pulls espresso shots. We mix large pitchers of the various drinks, carefully following her recipes, then pour them into stainless steel carafes to keep them hot.

"What scene is the movie on?" I ask Clark as I twist the lid on the final carafe.

"I told you, I'm not going out there again," he responds, defiantly crossing his arms.

I roll my eyes. "Fine, I'll go check, Scrooge."

"I am not Scrooge. I'm just not Buddy the Elf," Clark harrumphs.

"Whatever you tell yourself." I pause to pat his arm as I walk past him and immediately regret it. *Well, now I know what my imagination will fixate on tonight. Clark's insultingly firm biceps coupled with his sandalwood scent.*

Shaking off the zing of attraction, I peek my head into the main room to gauge how much time is left in the first movie. Returning to the kitchen, I tell Becky we have about ten minutes. She tests her whipped cream dispenser and triple checks the various sprinkle toppings assembled.

With about five minutes to go, Clark and I start carefully pouring drinks into the sample cups, and Becky follows behind, adding the embellishments. Moments later, a wave of Noel residents floods the room, ready for a jolt of caffeine. I'm delighted to overhear snippets of conversations—excited voices bouncing ideas for the festival from the first movie.

This is really going to work!

Several hours later, I'm standing at the front of the room again, dry erase marker in hand. People are calling out ideas faster than I can write them down.

"Why don't we have a 'Santa's Workshop' store where people can sell their handmade goods? Pearl's pottery would sell like hotcakes!"

"I loved all the strands of twinkle lights draped between the poles."

"I enjoy arranging flowers—I could fill some barrel stands for the poles with some nice evergreen arrangements!"

"We should have some Christmas carolers!"

"And plenty of photo ops with different themes!"

"I think we should have a small Living Nativity scene—make sure to remember the reason for the season."

"What about a place to write letters to Santa with a cute mailbox?"

"Ooo, a whole craft station for kids would be wonderful!"

My hand is cramping, but my smile is wide as I finish writing down everyone's ideas. We quickly star the best ones that are feasible to pull off in Noel, and everyone seems intoxicated by the anticipation in the air.

I stand there in front of the townspeople of Noel, scanning their faces as they stand up and converse on the way to the riverside for dinner. I'm positively beaming.

Glancing down at Clark still seated in the front row, I catch him staring up at me with a small smile. He notices my eye contact and drops the sides of his mouth along with his eyes. But not before I saw the warmth in those hazel greens. A warmth that spreads right through me in an already overheated room.

I came into today convincing myself that nothing was ever going to happen between Clark and me. Convincing myself to guard my heart and focus solely on helping the town. But that look in Clark's eyes is doing a fairly effective job of unconvincing me.

Chapter Thirty-Four

Clark

We're at the crawfish boil, and Junior is showing Clara how to eat a crawfish. She regards Junior with amused affection, and the crawfish with skeptical disgust. Chase is stuck to them like glue, knowing they're his best chance at a bite of food from the table.

Today's "Christmas in July" event went better than I expected. Everyone acted genuinely excited about the festival. Even I have to admit there were a lot of good ideas thrown out in the brainstorm session.

Still, it was a tough basket of emotions to sort through. Gratitude to see the people of Noel full of hope. Anxiety about what my dad and granddad would have to say if they were here to see this. Relief that they aren't here to say anything. Guilt over the relief.

I haven't experienced this much inner turmoil since the years following the accident. Except maybe with the introduction of Clara into my life.

I observe her as she watches Junior bring the crawfish head to his lips, sucking out the butter and juices. Her attempt at a smile falters, and it's evident she's trying her hardest not to gag.

I bring a hand to my mouth to cover my smile. Then I decide to put her out of her misery.

Ambling over to them, I ruffle Junior's hair and tell Clara, "Looking a little green around the gills there. You're taking this Christmas thing too seriously."

She casts a glare my direction, and I can't hold back a laugh any longer. I hold up the hot dog I've been hiding behind my back. "Here. Looks like you could use an alternative meal."

Relief floods her eyes as she accepts my offering. "Oh, bless you. I'm sorry. I know this is such a cliché city girl move, but I just don't have . . . that . . . in me." She gestures toward Junior eating another crawfish, who's oblivious to Clara's discomfort.

I chuckle again as Clara takes a bite of the hot dog. "The brainstorm went pretty well, I suppose," I say. I try not to be affected by the spark in Clara's eyes or the perfect smile that draws my attention to her mouth. Try and fail.

"It did, didn't it?" she replies. "People were full of fantastic ideas."

"You know almost every idea thrown out was already on your original list," I observe. Her cheeks flush at my admission of having memorized her list, but I don't try to backtrack the statement. My resolve to keep her on the outside of my internal walls has been waffling today.

"Still, it's better for it to be *their* ideas coming to life. Everyone has to own this if it's going to work," she says, eyes locked on mine.

"Hey, I'm owning it," I respond. She raises an eyebrow, and I hold up my hands. "Okay—reluctantly—but I'm still owning it."

Satisfied, she takes another bite before tearing off a small piece and feeding it to Chase. As if he needed any more reason to follow her around. Clara finishes her last bite and brushes her hands together. "We should probably talk through some of the practical logistics," she says, turning to face me.

"Why do I feel like I should be grabbing a notepad and pen for this?" I reply.

"You should absolutely grab a notepad and pen for this," she quips. "And possibly a cranberry-orange scone if there are any left!"

I shake my head but smile. "Why don't you go raid the dessert table, and I'll get stationery supplies."

Clara nods and walks toward the food table, Chase on her heels. I whistle and call him, "Chase! C'mere, boy!" He glances back at me, then up at Clara, then back at me. He whines. "Traitor!" I yell as he follows after her. The smug smile she gives me over her shoulder ignites a fuse of dynamite in my chest. I quickly stride toward my truck before it detonates and I wind up the same love-struck puppy that Chase has become.

Five minutes later, we're sitting at a secluded picnic table with a legal pad between us. I brush Clara's scone crumbs off the page before writing a list of logistics to discuss—installation, upfront investment, advertising, and marketing. Chase makes camp between our feet, lying down in the cool grass.

Clara leans toward the page, squinting. "Need your glasses there, ma'am?" I tease in my driest deadpan tone.

She rolls her beautiful blue eyes at me. "Ha ha, *Mayor* Noel. No, I don't need my glasses. I just can't read that chicken scratch."

I examine the paper. "What? It's perfectly legible."

Clara scoffs. "Puh-lease. No one—except maybe you—could read that. Are you sure you didn't secretly aspire to be a doctor?"

As soon as the words leave her mouth, her sarcastic smirk falls as her lips and eyes go wide. "Oh my gosh! I didn't mean that, Clark! I'm sorry. That was poor taste in jokes."

The fact that she would not only be aware of the possible impact of that joke, but also care enough to apologize, evaporates any potential sting from the comment.

"Clara, it's fine. I know you didn't mean anything by it. Although Junior's stitches run did get me thinking that we could use an urgent care here in Noel. Maybe I'll learn that next. A scalpel might make a nice addition to my tattoo."

My mention of the tattoo sends Clara's gaze to my arm, and my forearm flexes at the memory of her soft fingers tracing my skin. Her eyes track the movement of my muscles, and suddenly the tension between us is so thick, a butter knife would do the trick. No scalpel necessary.

After what could be five seconds or five minutes, I clear my throat. "Okay. Kick-starting this festival is going to take some capital, but I have some ideas on that front. I'm more concerned about advertising and the logistics of pulling off a big event."

"Well, I have some ideas on that front," Clara chimes in. "As you might recall, I work in the print marketing industry."

"I do recall a certain skeptical friend of yours mentioning something along those lines. A friend who harbors ill feelings toward me," I reply.

Clara waves a hand. "Mads is over it. You won her over to your dark side."

I'm genuinely surprised by that remark. "Really? What was it? My charm? My smooth-talking social skills?" I joke.

She laughs, but appears slightly embarrassed. "Ah, don't worry about it."

I will absolutely be worrying about it. I'm immensely interested to know what it is that Clara alluded to but isn't saying.

I attempt to press her on it, but she continues rapidly speaking. "What I mean to say is, I have plenty of connections in the marketing industry, and even some journalist friends from college. I can get word about The First Noel spread far and wide."

"We are absolutely not calling it that."

"Oh, we absolutely are."

I stand, leaning my hands on the table between us. Chase stands up and barks. "I'm still the mayor of this town, and I say we are *not* calling it that."

Clara matches my stance. "Well, this festival is *my* baby, and I don't think you're really going to tell me no."

She's leaning so close, I can count the freckles across her nose, the flecks of navy blue in her stubborn eyes. A breeze blows a curl across her face, and my eyes follow the movement. Before the rational part of my brain can kick in, my hand raises to tuck the stray curl behind her ear. Her hair is pure silk. The brief contact of my fingers on her neck has me imagining what that satin skin would feel like against my lips.

Warning! Warning!

I abruptly pull back and sit down. Picking up the pen, I write a check mark and Clara's name next to the "marketing and advertising" point on the list. "Fine, call it what you want," I mutter under my breath.

Clara slowly sits down, silent. *Good going, Clark. You've successfully made this the most awkward business meeting in history.*

I keep my eyes on the list and off her face as I say, "What about the setup and installation of everything? This is a lot to arrange. Any thoughts?"

I'm making a list of all the available spaces in Noel to use, both empty buildings and outdoor areas that would make good gathering spots. Clara's still quiet, but I can't risk making eye contact yet. Chase nuzzles his nose against her hand.

She clears her throat. "My parents could be a good resource on that front. They've helped plan a massive Living Nativity event at our church for a decade. My dad would have a lot of pointers on setup and traffic flow. Give me your phone."

I can't avoid looking up at her now. "My phone? Why?"

Clara rolls her eyes. "I'm going to put my dad's phone number in for you. I'll give him a head's up that you'll be contacting him." I unlock and hand over my phone. She's typing with a smirk when she adds, "Fair warning—he's a terrible texter, so you'll have to call."

Taking the phone back from her, I see the contact she added. A laugh escapes before I can stop it.

"Your dad's name is Joseph?"

She makes a dismissive scoffing noise.

"Hold on, Nutcracker Clara—your aunt's name was Gloria, and your dad is Joseph. Don't tell me your mom's name is Mary."

Now she makes an indignant gasp. "No! You're ridiculous." The evasive expression on her face negates all the nonchalance in her statement.

"Claraaa . . ." I draw out. "What's your mother's name?"

She huffs and crosses her arms. "My mom's first name is Holly."

My head drops back with a deep belly laugh. "Ohhh, I couldn't have made that up if I tried!"

Clara glowers at me but can't conceal the hint of a smile playing at her lips. "I told you, I come from a long line of Christmas enthusiasts . . . on *both* sides of my family."

My laugh settles into a smile. "Well, at least you come by it honestly."

"Now, if you're done teasing me about familial traditions beyond my control, I need your help with something," Clara says.

"Not until you tell me the names of your grandparents," I counter, unable to help myself.

Clara mimes zipping her lips. "You'll never crack the safe."

"Give me five minutes on Google, and I'll prove you wrong."

She reaches across the table and softly punches my bicep. "Stop it! What's gotten into stoic Clark today, huh?"

I'm definitely not answering that.

Thankfully, she continues before I have to respond. "But speaking of grandparents, my request relates to *your* grandfather-figure." That quiets me down.

"Pops? What about him?" I ask.

"I want to convince him to make some wood carvings to sell in the gift shop," she replies. "You mentioned he used to whittle animals."

I lean back, clasping my arms behind my head. "I don't know if we could talk him into it. He's stubbornly refused every attempt Davis and I have made to get him back into his workshop."

"I have a plan," Clara says, eyes gleaming. "I just need you to take me to see him."

Pops attended part of the Christmas in July festivities, but I think the energy of the crowd drained his. Davis drove him home early for an afternoon nap when he was worn out.

I drive Clara to Pops' house, Chase practically sitting in her lap the whole way. She laughs and gushes in the sweet voice she reserves for him. I'm quiet, mentally sorting through a pro/con list of acknowledging feelings for Clara.

Con: Trusting people enough to let them in close is not my strong suit.

Pro: Clara has proven herself pretty trustworthy.

Con: I don't like disrupting my social circle comfort level.

Pro: Clara already fits like a missing puzzle piece into my small social circle. A funny, spunky, gorgeous puzzle piece.

Con: I'll never leave Noel, and Clara's real life is in Kansas City. Noel is a getaway destination to her.

I don't have a pro to offset that one.

When we arrive at Pops' house, I knock loudly on the front door. "Pops? It's Clark. You awake in there?"

A muffled but cranky voice calls back. "Go away!"

I pound the door again, earning a, "What do you want? Can't an old man have some peace after a long day?"

"Not today, you can't."

Clara steps up next to me. "Hi, Pops. It's Clara Sullivan. I made Clark bring me over here so I could ask for your help with something."

A few seconds later, the door opens. "Why didn't you tell me you'd brought Clara along, Clark? I would've opened up sooner."

Clara beams back at him, her smile the hot fudge melting his frosty disposition. "Could we sit out here on your porch?" Clara asks sweetly. "Did Clark tell you he brought me one of your rocking chairs? It's my favorite place to sit."

Pops gives a proud smile before responding. "Sure can—let me grab the pitcher of sweet tea."

"I'll get it, Pops, you come on out and have a seat," I say. Then I add lowly in Clara's ear, "Mentally fortify yourself to drink the sweetest liquid ever created." She giggles softly, face so close to mine that her breath tickles my neck. I turn away into the house before I do something stupid. Like brush my nose along her jawline, or kiss the skin behind her ear. Like pull her body flush against mine, or any of the other fifty tempting ideas clamoring in my mind.

I listen to Pops and Clara talk about the day's events as I grab glasses and the pitcher of sweet tea. Joining them on the porch, I pour drinks for everyone before taking a seat. Pops rubs Chase's head, and I can't miss the pronounced curl of Pops' fingers. *I don't know if he'll even be capable of doing any whittling.* The thought makes my heart hurt.

"What can I help you with, Miss Clara?" Pops asks. Clara's demeanor manages to pull the Southern gentleman out of the curmudgeon.

Clara takes a big swallow of sweet tea, completely hiding any reaction she may have to the overpowering amount of sugar. Then again,

I've seen the drinks she orders from Becky's. Maybe this is par for the course for Clara's taste buds.

"It's about the Christmas Fest," she begins. "Have you heard that we're going to call it The First Noel this year?"

Pops grins at me. "I'm not even going to bother asking how you felt about that."

"I got vetoed," I say flatly.

He turns his grin to Clara. "Well, I love it. Don't listen to this one."

"Oh, I'm way past listening to this one," Clara chirps. "And he's way past arguing with me."

I'm not sure if Clara is intentionally buttering Pops up, or if this is just her natural people skills at work. Either way, he's putty in her hands. I think he'd say yes to anything she asks.

I know the feeling.

"One of the main features of the festival will be a gift shop called Santa's Workshop. Pearl has already agreed to sell her pottery, and two talented high schoolers are going to make some artwork. The Quilt Bunch is sewing several varieties of fabric gifts, and we have someone making jewelry. But I can't help thinking we need something slightly more masculine to round things out."

Pops is listening closely as Clara continues, "A while back, Clark mentioned in passing that you used to whittle wood figurines before you got busy with furniture orders. I can't stop thinking about it. Would you be willing to make some pieces to sell in the gift shop?"

His mouth twists into a half frown as he looks down at his hands. "I'd really like to help ya, Miss Clara, but I'm not sure that I'd make anything people would want to buy."

"*I'm* sure that you would, Pops. If your carvings are a fraction as good as your rocking chairs, people will be fighting to buy them before they're gone," Clara asserts. "We have lots of time before the festival kicks off after Thanksgiving." She leans forward to place a hand on Pops' arm. "Would you at least consider giving it a try, make a few things and see how it goes? Please?"

Who could say no to that? How did I ever say no to her?

Pops' face goes soft. "Well, all right. I suppose I could give it a try. My doctor gave me some new medicine to help the inflammation in my joints. I'll take it for a few days and see if it loosens up the ol' fingers. I'll give it my best shot, Miss Clara."

She thanks him, and then looks over at me with a dancing, victorious spark in her eye. The smile on her face is so full of warmth, a chill courses through me. Today has magnified what I already knew about Clara—she comes most alive when she's helping other people.

The realization hits like a gut punch. It's the only "con" on the pro/con list I need to convince myself I have to shut down this pull toward her.

Even though I've allowed her in to assist the town, *I* don't need help.

My chest aches, wishing I could be a different man than who I am. The type of man who naturally lets others in, accepts help. The type of man who had a healthy family environment instead of a toxic father who conditioned him to never rely on anyone else.

Just for her, I wish I could be that man.

But I am who I am, and she is who she is. We'll never work together. For her sake, I have to reconstruct those walls she's slowly broken through.

CHAPTER THIRTY-FIVE

Clara

Joy threatens to burst my heart as Clark drives me home. I've rolled the window down, letting the evening breeze blow through my hair. Chase is sitting on my lap, his head hanging out the window as I watch the scenery roll by.

This day couldn't have gone any better. Everyone in town is buzzing with positive energy—a buzz I helped create. *And* we found a way to get Pops involved. A way that will hopefully give him something to look forward to each day.

And Clark. I'd have to be either completely blind or completely stupid to deny the chemistry between us after today. All of his teasing comments—it was the most at ease, dare I say, *flirtatious*, I'd ever seen him. When we were having our standoff at the picnic table and he reached up to tuck my hair behind my ear, I thought I might faint from the contact.

The glint in his eyes hinted that he was experiencing all the same attraction that I was. But then he stepped back so abruptly, I thought maybe I imagined it. *Did I imagine it, or is Clark just too afraid to admit what's there?*

We pull into my driveway, and I climb out of the truck, hoping that Clark will walk me to my door again. Whatever might be going on in his mind, I guess his Southern gentleman genes won't quit because he follows me to my front porch. My heartbeat morphs into the hoofs of a racehorse, sprinting and pounding with abandon.

I punch in the code to unlock my front door but then turn to face Clark. He's several steps back from me, in what could only be an intentional attempt to put space between us. My heart drops, but I force a smile.

"Thank you for today, Clark. Thanks for saying yes to this, for letting me help," I say, taking a tiny step closer to him.

He shrugs a shoulder. "Seemed like the best move for the town. We'll see how it goes. But if today's excitement was any indication, it was the right decision."

"I know it was a hard idea for you to get on board with," I press, wanting him to understand how I feel about his decision. About *him*. "I just want you to know how grateful I am. How happy it makes me to be able to be here with you and help."

A shadow flickers across his face, killing the edges of my smile. He takes another step backward. "I'd do anything for the people of this town. Even if it means the opposite of what past generations of Noel men thought was needed." He clears his throat, and I hear Chase whine from the truck window. "I'll let you get some sleep. Let me know if you need anything from me for the advertising."

He strides away from me, then pulls out of the driveway while I remain frozen on the porch.

Every time I think I've figured out the Clark puzzle, that I've found the true design hidden behind the Magic Eye camouflage, I find myself back at square one. I was so sure he was opening up more, letting down some of his walls. Now I'm not sure of anything.

Stunned, I just stand there staring at the empty driveway for a few minutes before I open the door. I pull my phone out of my pocket, tempted to call Syd and process through all this Clark confusion with her. But her friendship with Clark has too much back-story, and his relationship with Davis is too important. I can't bring myself to unload this on her.

I call Madison instead as I make my way to the back porch, plopping down in my rocking chair in the darkness. Just when I think it's going to voicemail, she answers.

"Clara! How'd the Christmas planning party go?"

"Hey, Mads. It was good. Everyone was excited. And we have a solid plan to execute, so I count that a success," I say.

"Then why do you sound like Christmas got canceled?" she asks.

I sigh.

"Ah," Mads says. "I take it Hottie McScrooge is behind the low-key depressing tone. Did he try to cancel Christmas?"

"No, nothing like that," I respond. "He's totally rolling with the festival idea, and even seems pretty convinced that it will be worthwhile."

"Sooo? What is it then?"

"I don't know. I think that's the most frustrating part—that I can't figure him out," I groan. Madison waits silently for me to continue. "I just . . . I feel all this attraction, this chemistry between us, and I keep thinking that he might be feeling it too. But then he'll push me back out to arm's length again. And I'm not talking T-Rex arm's length—what animal has the longest arm span?"

"Please hold. I'm searching," Mads replies. A second later, she says, "Humpback whale."

"Okay, so he pushes me out to humpback whale arm's length. I thought the whole Christmas festival was a sign that he was opening up to me, but maybe I was wrong."

"Do you think he's afraid to get close to people after what happened with his family?" Madison asks.

I hum. "Maybe? I mean, that would make sense. But I think it's something else, something more than that. Something specifically about *me*. Then again, maybe that's just me over-analyzing why he won't like me."

"You do hate it when people don't like you. What are you going to do?"

"I don't know. Nothing, I guess? Just focus on making this Christmas festival the biggest success it could possibly be," I muse, twirling the ring on my finger.

"That's fine, Clara," Mads says. I can hear in her tone that there's a "but" coming. "But as you're working on the festival, don't forget the original reason you wound up at that cabin in Noel."

"The movie script," I sigh. "You're right."

"Of course, I'm right," Mads scoffs. "When have I ever not been right?"

"Uh, maybe when you said you were entirely confident that Ivy was the type of person to make a good roommate?"

"Touché."

The next three months are a whirlwind of Christmas activity. As a girl, I'd always wished that the holiday season could last year-round. Between preparations for The First Noel and slowly chipping away at my movie script, I'm living out all my childhood Christmas dreams.

I reach out to several contacts I have in the journalism sector. Articles advertising the Christmas festival will appear in newspapers based in Kansas, Missouri, Arkansas, and Oklahoma. I also comb through our client lists to find any located in the general vicinity and work short blurbs into the November newsletter issues. It may be an abuse of power, but it's a chance I'm willing to take in order to get the word out about The First Noel.

My parents accompany me on two of my trips to Noel, offering their logistics expertise to the planning committee, which consists of Clark, Emily, James, and Sydney. Clark's mayoral office is brimming with boxes of Christmas decor, a mental picture I take delight in projecting any time I need a smile.

Mom knows there's ambiguity in my friendship with Clark, but she's kind enough not to bring it up. Which is good because I wouldn't even know what to explain. The ambiguity only thickens when I watch how polite and borderline *friendly* Clark is with my parents . . . but I'm personally still out at humpback whale's arm length.

The first week of October, Sydney comes to visit me in KC. She's been hired by James to decorate the tiny cabins used by float trip vacationers in the summer. Each cabin will have a different Christmas decor theme, hopefully drawing even more people to drive to Noel and stay a few days for the festival. Madison knows all the best thrift stores that put out Christmas decor early, and she's going to help Syd find good deals—even though Sydney said she has a healthy budget.

"Where did the money for the festival supplies come from?" Madison asks Syd as we wait in line for our coffees.

"Ya know, I'm not sure," Syd replies, brow furrowed. "Clark said he found some funding to get the festival kicked off. I didn't think to ask questions—I figured there were some mayor strings he pulled to get a grant from the state or something."

Six hours later, all three of our cars are filled to the brim with Christmas decorations. We found what we could thrifting and then hit up some of the big home decor stores. Ranging from traditional red and green, to more modern whimsical colors and patterns, Syd has plenty of material to work with. I'll have to plan a trip to Noel with Dad's truck to get the rest of the supplies to Syd. There's no way it will all fit in her car, and she needs to start decorating soon so James can take photos and get the cabins listed on the rental website.

That night, I take Syd to one of my favorite Kansas City barbecue restaurants for dinner, making sure she orders the Z-man sandwich with extra crispy fries. She's moaning over her bite of food, and I try to inquire about Clark nonchalantly.

"So, how has Clark been holding up with the invasion of Christmas?"

She shrugs and swallows. "He acts reluctant about it all, but I think he's secretly enjoying it. He even agreed to rename the town 'No-el' for the duration of the festival, per your suggestion. I'm no psychologist, but I suspect that planning the Christmas event is helping him work through some of his childhood trauma from his dad's disapproval."

I nod and bite a French fry rather than responding.

"I honestly still don't understand why he won't admit that he likes you, though," Syd adds before taking another giant bite of her sandwich.

"Syd!" I exclaim, cheeks on fire.

"What?! I'm just speaking the truth! I know Clark's not naturally one to open up to relationships, but his avoidance of his feelings for you seems over the top—even for his vulnerability issues," Syd says. "It's obvious to everyone that y'all like each other."

I bury my face in my hands. "Who's everyone?"

"Paul, Emily, James, Becky, Pops, us, obviously," Syd replies, ticking off the names with her fingers. She adds with a grin, "Literally anyone who has ever watched the two of you interact for even a millisecond."

Now I drop my head fully into my arms on the table, groaning.

"I'm not trying to embarrass you," Syd says, patting my arm. I look up and raise an eyebrow at her. She laughs. "Okay, *sometimes* I try to embarrass you, but I promise I'm not this time. I'm simply letting you know that I sincerely don't know what his deal is. I'm on your side here."

"There are no sides, Syd," I say. "I'm trying to stay focused on my full-time job while also helping make this festival amazing. I'm trying *not* to worry about what probably won't happen with Clark."

"I hope your movie script is also on your to-do list," Syd says. "How's that coming? When can I read it?"

I take a bite of my sandwich to buy time before answering. "It's coming. I swear I'm making progress. But I'm not sure when I'll be ready for anyone to read it. In fact, I may not ever let anyone read this first script. I might use it as practice but then try a new storyline."

I'm too afraid that my feelings for Clark not-so-subtly woven into the script will be displayed for everyone to decipher.

"What?! Unfair!" Syd whines. "I'm giving you a deadline—I expect to see that script by the end of the year, or I'll speak with Becky and remove your coffee privileges."

I gasp. "You'd never!"

Syd quirks an eyebrow. "Girl, you know I would. Get me that script!"

CHAPTER THIRTY-SIX

Clark

I can see it on my tombstone now: *Here lies Clark Noel. Killed by Noel.*

The past few months have stretched me outside of my comfort zone so much, I think I've surely reached my lifetime allotment of growth zone minutes. I want nothing more than to retreat to my old, quiet routines—complete my handyman jobs, attend to mayoral duties, return home to laid-back evenings with Chase. Make occasional contact with a small handful of friends.

Instead, my life has been a revolving door of people. Townspeople, suppliers, journalists, Christmas enthusiasts. My office and spare bedroom are slowly filling with Christmas decor, a constant reminder of the chaos on the horizon.

I think I've developed an ulcer.

On the flip side, I have to admit that preparations are running more smoothly than I expected. Clara's dad had lots of practical suggestions to streamline the event. He helped me think through logistics that never would have crossed my mind—parking, restrooms, traffic flow. The town is buzzing with anticipation, everyone looking for ways to pitch in. Beau even reached out to ask if he and his family could come back and help with the festival setup.

I've spent many a late night sitting alone or with Davis, mapping out ideals and contingency plans. I've scoured the websites and social media of every similar event I could find.

And, although I'll never admit it to anyone, I've even watched a few more of those cheesy Christmas romance movies. I'm simply making sure I thoroughly understand what people will be expecting coming in. Chase gets excited every time I settle on the couch with a bowl of popcorn.

The first time I sat down to watch one of the movies, I almost turned it off. A torrent of emotions bubbled to the surface with such force that I couldn't fend it off. I thought back to my childhood, to all the snide comments my dad would make if someone tried to suggest a town Christmas celebration. I thought about the lackluster holiday memories I carry from my family, which led to a rabbit trail of lackluster family memories, period.

Saying yes to this Christmas festival has conjured competing emotions about my father's memory. On the one hand, it's almost liberating to do the one thing he was always so against. He'd made it so clear that I never lived up to his expectations, so why not spectacularly let those expectations down now that he's gone?

On the flip side, I've realized that the part of me hoping I'd one day earn my dad's approval never truly died. Even after Dad's death, there's still that boy inside me wishing that his father would be proud of him. Wishing that he'd regard me the way he always looked at Sam—a competent, successful man he was proud to call a son.

Like the cherry on top of my sundae of conflicted emotions, Clara's biweekly visits have been their own combination of sweet relief and acute torture. Leave it to Clara to pull off such a contrast. Considering the fact that this festival really is *her* baby, she's insisted on sitting down together every time she's here to go over updates and plans. The conversations talking logistics on her back porch or over dinner at the Deer River Bar leave me craving *more* mundane, everyday time with her. Denying the craving has become plain painful.

November rolls around, and I'm as prepared as I possibly could be. The weeks leading up to Thanksgiving are spent building and installing as much of the booths and decor as won't interfere with everyday life. The public areas of town are strung with Christmas lights and greenery, and about 90 percent of the residential houses are lit up before Thanksgiving. Paul and Emily have had a healthy boost to their store's income, placing bulk orders while still giving the townspeople a good deal on lights and decorations.

The First Noel officially opens the Sunday after Thanksgiving, making Saturday our final walk-through to ensure everything is ready. Clara is spending Thanksgiving with her parents and driving down Saturday morning to be here.

Paul and Emily have invited Pops and me to join them for Thanksgiving dinner. I drive to pick up Pops, making mental notes along the way of a few places that need light strands tightened.

When I knock on Pops' door, there's no answer. I call out for him, but the lack of response has me worried. I enter the house, finding it empty. Puzzled, I check upstairs, even though I don't know the last time Pops attempted climbing the stairs. Finally, I head out back to his workshop.

Pops is deep in concentration, a cardinal taking shape in his hands. I glance around the workshop, shocked to see dozens of animal carvings lining the shelves.

I fight back the moisture in my eyes. Once I have my emotion under control, I knock on the door, trying to get Pops' attention without startling him while he's holding a whittling knife.

"You ready to go, Pops?" I ask when he looks up from his work.

"Oh, is it time for dinner already? Guess I lost track of time," he responds, setting down the cardinal.

I take a few steps in and examine the carvings. There are bears, dogs, cats, and horses. But mostly, lots of birds. I glance over at Pops watching my appraisal of his work.

I'm fighting off emotion again, clearing my throat. "You know, Bev would be really proud of you. She would have loved to see these—I'm sure she's looking down and smiling."

Emotion clouds Pops' face now, his eyes turning foggy. He nods, and then grips my shoulder and adds, "And your grandma would have loved to see all of this. She'd be proud of you. *I'm* proud of you, son."

As two stoic men not used to feeling much emotion—much less displaying it—we stand there awkwardly for a beat before turning to walk to my truck.

Despite the extra load on her plate, Emily has still managed to pull off a Thanksgiving feast. Paul deep-fried the turkey, and every comforting side dish is present on the table spread. We pause while Paul blesses the meal, then begin passing plates.

"How are you feeling about Sunday, honey?" Emily asks me.

I swallow a bite of sweet potato casserole. "Honestly? Ready for this whole thing to be over."

Emily laughs.

"The lack of knowing exactly what to expect is driving me crazy. I wish I knew how many people will show up. I hope this turns out being worth everyone's time," I explain.

"Yeah, I can understand that," Emily responds. "There are a few thousand people who marked interested on the Facebook event page, but it's hard to know the real numbers of visitors that will translate to."

"James told me that every cabin is booked solid for the entire three weeks of the festival. There are even a few booked all the way through Christmas," Paul says before taking a bite of turkey.

"Really?" I ask.

"I'm not surprised. Syd did such a good job decorating—those cabins all look so cute and cozy. Who could resist?!" Emily remarks. "Is Clara still coming down for the first week?"

Mention of Clara catches me off guard, even though I know it shouldn't, logically speaking. After all, she is the mastermind of this whole thing. For better or worse.

"Um, I assume so? I haven't talked to her since her last trip here," I reply, met with a telling *hmmm* sound from Emily. "What?"

"I just assumed you were keeping closer tabs on her, that's all," Emily says. Her attention is diverted to scold her son for hiding his phone under the table, saving me from having to respond.

"We'll be at the store, but let us know if you need any help with the final setup tomorrow or Saturday," Paul interjects. He changes the subject to fill me in on Noland's extended operating hours for the festival. I'm grateful for the diversion away from Clara.

That night, I'm lying in bed, wide awake for hours. Chase has a dog bed on the floor, but at 1:00 a.m., he stands and whines next to me. He nuzzles my hand with his nose.

"You think I need some attention, huh?" I ask, scratching him behind the ears. He reaches a paw up, whining again. "All right, come on up. Just this once." He jumps into bed and lays down next to me, head resting on my stomach.

I absentmindedly stroke his fur, mind refusing to calm down.

I'm anxious about how this festival is going to go. *How many people will come? Will they love it and tell others to visit? Or have we missed the mark? Is this enough of a boost to keep the town going until the pet food facility finally opens up?*

What if it fails? What if I'm a failure?

Clara's face also competes for space in my anxious thoughts loop. I close my eyes and picture her dancing blue eyes. The way the wind catches her strawberry curls. The freckles like constellations across her cheeks, begging to be memorized. The way her full, rose-pink lips twitch when she's trying not to smile at something I said.

My mind wants to replay a montage of every moment I've been near her. From the first day I stumbled into her bathroom, to sitting shoulder-to-shoulder ordering bulk Christmas decorations online last month.

No! I shout to that persistent part of my brain that won't let her go. *It won't work. We can't do it.*

Frustrated with my lack of control over my thoughts, I abandon my attempt at sleep. Chase follows me as I pad into the living room, pausing to throw a bag of popcorn in the microwave. His ears perk up at the sound, and he preemptively jumps onto the couch to wait for me.

I dump the popcorn into a bowl and join Chase on the couch, turning on the TV. I find the Heartmark Channel, ready to watch another cookie-cutter version of the same sappy love story. In the name of festival research. *Not* because it makes me feel connected to Clara.

Deciding to make an exception to my "no people food" rule, I hold out a piece of popcorn to Chase. His tail wags, but he considers me with those confused doggie eyebrows. "Go ahead. It's okay." He eagerly takes the piece of popcorn from me, then another. "But only this once. Don't get used to it," I add sternly.

I watch as a man and woman *obviously* in love repeatedly deny their feelings for each other. The man finally professes his love and kisses the girl at the end of the movie.

I rub my hand across my chest, heart physically aching as the invisible string tightens.

CHAPTER THIRTY-SEVEN

Clara

My body is practically vibrating with anticipation as I drive into the Noel city limits. The First Noel is finally here, and I'm equal parts thrilled to experience it all and terrified that I talked Clark into something that will epically fail.

As I drive through town, I see the transformation of Main Street from sleepy city street to event destination space. There are temporary booths, photo ops, portable restrooms, traffic signs—all the evidence of a well-planned event. And Christmas decor galore, of course.

"This looks like a real festival!" I exclaim out loud to myself.

I swing by my cabin to drop off my duffel bag before meeting Sydney and Becky in the center of town to go over a final readiness checklist. We walk through the various booths, making a list of any last-minute items missing.

We meet Davis, James, and Clark at the bar for dinner, prematurely toasting to a successful three weeks for the town. After eating, the two couples have to return home to their kids, and I gear up to head back to my cabin.

"Would you want to walk around and see everything all lit up?" Clark surprises me by asking as we walk out into the crisp night air.

"You're turning the lights on tonight?" I ask.

"Yep. Want to walk through and make sure everything is working before tomorrow," he replies, sounding perfectly practical.

"Of course, I do!" I reply, bouncing on my toes. I swear a smile flashes across Clark's face, but he rubs a hand across his beard before I can confirm.

We walk to the center of the action. The temperate climate in Arkansas may not make for picturesque white Christmas scenes, but it's ideal weather for an outdoor Christmas event. I'm perfectly warm walking around with only a light coat. As we near the main festival square, Clark pulls out his phone.

"I have everything plugged into smart devices that I can control from an app," he says, then angles toward me with a smirk on his face. "Maybe you've heard of this genius invention that allows you to control power switches remotely?"

I roll my eyes and shove him hard. Which only serves to throw me off balance, not Clark. I huff. We stop walking, and he asks, "Ready?" I nod, and he taps the button on his phone.

I gasp as we're instantly surrounded by the soft glow of thousands of twinkling lights strung from poles, tacked onto buildings, wrapped around trees. I turn a full circle, taking it all in. Strung over Main Street is a huge "Merry Christmas" light display.

The Becky's Brews stand is decorated with whimsical pink and purple tinsel trees, with her hand-painted menu sign prominently displayed. The Ladies Who Bake stand has a three-foot gingerbread man figure holding a chalkboard list of baked goods for purchase. Traditional greenery and crimson bows are draped under the counter. There's something for everyone's taste in Christmas decor.

Although there are no items filling the tables tonight, Santa's Workshop looks as though Clark enlisted the help of Buddy the Elf to decorate. I can picture crowds streaming through the covered but open area, then making their way to purchase drinks and treats. They'll be able to take their food down the path bordered by string lights to the picnic area set up along the river. It's like I'm standing on set of a Heartmark movie.

I'm smiling, but I can't stop tears from slipping down my cheeks.

"Did it live up to your vision?" Clark asks, breaking the silence.

"It's perfect. Everything is beautiful. It's just . . . *perfect*, Clark," I whisper, still overwhelmed.

His hands are in his pockets, but his face is pleased. Then again, I don't entirely trust myself to interpret Clark accurately anymore. "Tomorrow will be the moment of truth," he muses.

"Not *just* tomorrow," I say. "We have three whole weeks of Christmas festivities to look forward to," I add with a wry smile.

Now I'm positive he smiles back at me as he responds, "Don't remind me."

The opening days of The First Noel start off with simmering magic. We decided to kick the festival off on a Sunday, banking on a few slower weekdays to help us get our footing before larger weekend crowds.

Still, even more people have come than we anticipated. Becky's Brews is a raging success—no surprise there. But that means we have to make a rush order of more syrup supplies to arrive before the weekend.

Santa's Workshop is teeming with Christmas enchantment. The sight of Pops' table full of animal carvings brings tears to my eyes. It's not taking much to bring tears to my eyes this week. The magic of the season paired with the feeling of helping this town come to life has my tear ducts ever-ready to produce moisture.

A friend of Madison's arranged for a TV crew to come on Thursday to film a short spot for an Arkansas news station. Clark and I guide the crew around the town to get B-roll footage of the Christmas-themed cabins, the town decorations, the Letters to Santa craft station, and the evening festivities. When it's time to do the on-camera interview, Clark tries to pawn off the job to me.

"This whole thing was your idea, Clara! I don't want to be on the news. You talk," he asserts, arms crossed and eyebrows furrowed.

"But this is *your* town, Clark. The city of Noel—this is your family, your history. It has to be you," I counter equally as adamantly.

He groans. "Fine, but when all the potential visitors are scared away by my face on TV, you'll be to blame."

I snort. "Your face isn't scaring anyone away." My cheeks heat as I realize I said that out loud. "Just . . . try to smile a little," I add, trying to breeze over the foot in my mouth.

We find a spot with the festivities perfectly framed in the background, and the reporter asks Clark a series of questions about the festival and the town of Noel. Clark does a stand-up job of looking neutral, bordering on amiable, as he answers. He never mentions me by name, but at one point, he meets my eyes as he talks about "The First Noel" tag line. A hint of a smile crinkles the sides of his eyes.

I hold my breath as I watch him. My thoughts are caught up in all the positive connections I've shared with Clark over the past year. Sure, we had our difficult moments too—times when he crumpled my heart. But now, watching him stand in front of a news camera talking about the very festival he was stubbornly opposed to, I'm overwhelmed with affection for this complicated man. Affection I can't bury anymore.

Late into the night, I furiously type at my writing desk. My mind is playing out scene after scene, line after line of my movie script, faster than my fingers can keep up. Tears blur my view of the computer screen as I write Jack and Renee's first kiss into existence, when they finally stop avoiding their feelings for each other.

At 3:00 a.m., I type those epic words: The End.

I sigh and lean back, arching with my hands overhead. It's far from the end—I'll go through a rigorous edit of the script before I decide if I'm even going to submit it. But finishing the first draft is still a huge accomplishment.

Staring at the screen, my ears tune in to the music playing from the speaker— "The Waltz of the Snowflakes." I can almost *feel* the physical hug from Aunt Gloria. Almost see the wide smile on her face, the light in her eyes. Almost hear her soothing voice telling me she's proud of me.

I look around my cabin with tears in my eyes. "We did it, Aunt Gloria. You made it possible for me to chase this dream."

And just like that, I know that I'm going to submit this script to Heartmark. I might be terrified to put it out there, to potentially tip my hand to show my interest in Clark. The script might get rejected and never turned into a movie. But I owe it to Aunt Gloria to follow this dream as far as I can take it.

Chapter Thirty-Eight

Clark

"Clark, we need more boxes brought over from the storage unit," Pearl calls to me.

"You mean my *office*, Pearl?"

"Call a spade a spade; it's temporarily a storage unit and you know it," she scoffs back. "Can you run and get some or find someone who can?"

"I got it. Let me finish changing out the trashcan liners at the picnic area," I call back.

I've been running around like a chicken with its head cut off for the past two days, jumping in to fill every job from barista to photographer to garbageman. Nothing could have prepared me for the number of people that have circulated through town this week—and it's only the first week of the festivities. We've easily had as many, if not more, tourists as we do during the height of float season.

The news spot we filmed on Thursday aired yesterday on the Friday morning news, and I swear, every person within driving distance of Noel made their way to town today. Paul and Emily have been placing rushed order after rushed order of more supplies for Becky and the baking ladies, as well as gift wrapping for the gift shop.

Every high schooler in town is now making bank working odd jobs. They're taking pictures at the photo ops, supervising children as they write and decorate letters to Santa, cleaning up trash, and wrapping gifts sold by the local artisans. The kids who are selling their artwork can't even man the booth themselves—they've been working around the clock creating more to keep the booth stocked.

Beau and Abby are here this weekend helping out. They'd planned on bringing their kids, but my SOS text prompted them to come unattached in order to pitch in where needed. Becky's been delighted to have Abby's help in addition to Clara's with her coffee drinks, and they make much better assistants than I did.

I'm hoping the combination of the Christmas festival, plus the impending factory jobs, might entice Beau to move his family back to Noel. He's hinted at how much they've missed the town, and I spouted off a long list of reasons why they should move back. The energy of the festival seems to be working in my favor on that front.

Although my DNA predisposed me to be opposed to this whole spectacle, I understand it now.

Clara was right.

It somewhat hurts to admit it, but her lack of lording the fact over me has made it easier to acknowledge. She's been 100 percent beaming and delighted all week, without a hint of "I told you so" energy.

It's only making it agonizingly harder to keep her at arm's length. That stupid tether around my heart is beginning to feel like a noose—the more I struggle against it, the tighter it pulls.

But I won't risk hurting Clara's heart by letting things progress beyond friendship between us. Being with me wouldn't be fair to her. Even if I like her—even if I might love her—she deserves a man who needs her. And that's not me. It won't ever be me.

Late Saturday night, I open my front door only to be bowled over by a whining, energetic Chase. After a quick trip outside, he comes back in and stays plastered to my side as I heat up some dinner.

"I know, boy. I'm sorry you've been alone all week. I'm trying to think of a way for you to come to the festival without getting in the way," I tell him, stroking behind his ears.

As if she'd secretly wiretapped my house, a text from Clara comes through.

Been thinking about how to let Chase come with you to the festival. He must be miserable at home alone! Do you think he'd be content to sit in Santa's Workshop with Pops while he whittles live for people to observe? I talked Pops into the idea.

It's worth a shot. Let's try it tomorrow and see how he does.

Of course, she talked Pops into the idea. I'm becoming convinced Clara could talk a cattle rancher into going vegan. Still, the thought fills my chest with warmth. Pops has been living with a second wind the past few months, faithfully taking his medication and even doing some of the exercises suggested by the physical therapist.

That alone is enough to make me want to kiss Clara—aside from all the thousands of things about *her* that make me want to kiss her.

After eating a quick dinner, I fall into bed at 11:00 p.m. Sleep overtakes me, and I dream of Clara's face softly lit by the glow of Christmas lights.

We have a special line-up of activities planned for each weekend night of the festival. It was Syd's idea, meant to encourage people to book entire weekends at the cabins. There's a miniature parade down Main Street on Friday nights, and Saturdays boast a Rockettes-inspired performance by the high school dance team plus carolers singing Christmas favorites.

On each Sunday at dusk, we'll make a big show of packaging up all the week's letters to Santa in burlap bags and loading them into a canoe. Syd convinced Davis to dress up as an elf—a sight I literally paid her to see—and he'll paddle the canoe down river. As darkness settles, we'll time fireworks to go off from a nearby dock, giving the illusion that the letters were rocketed off to the North Pole.

Tonight will be our first run at the letters send-off, and I'm crossing my fingers that everything goes off without a hitch. Or a fire.

When I arrive at the festival grounds with Chase at 9:00 a.m., Syd, Clara, and Abby are already there with Becky, prepping drink mixes. I make my way over to check on Becky's supply stock. *Not* to see Clara. Chase, on the other hand, sprints right to her.

"Morning, ladies. Becky, you need any supplies ordered today?" I ask, not missing the sweet smile Clara gives me.

"I already made a big order of syrups yesterday, and Emily's bringing more milk and cream by later. But we'll probably need another order of cups and sleeves. I'll let you know at the end of the day what needs to be restocked," Becky responds.

Clara squirts whipped cream into a small cup and holds it down for Chase to lap up. Becky and Syd stare at me with raised eyebrows, knowing the "Do Not Feed the Dog" rule I impose on everyone. Everyone except Clara, apparently. I look away, not giving them the satisfaction of a reaction. That doesn't stop their very satisfied smiles, however.

I whistle for Chase to follow me as I walk the grounds, making sure everything is in order for the day. Townspeople slowly arrive to man the various stations, and everyone I talk to mentions how encouraged they are by the energy of the festival. I walk Chase back to the gift shop to sit with Pops before things get too chaotic. Pops promises to call me if Chase gets out of hand. But I have a feeling Chase will be on his best behavior if it means not being cooped up at home.

The weather is chilly without being truly cold, especially once the crowds start to fill in after lunch. The Letters to Santa tent is constantly chaotic with a never-ending supply of children coming through. I'm sent on multiple restock runs to my office and to Noland's for more craft supplies.

I'm so busy keeping everything running smoothly, it feels like no time at all before the sunlight is sinking away. An announcement over the loudspeaker encourages families to gather at the river front for the ceremonial Letters to Santa send-off.

I head in that direction with Chase, happily surprised when Clara bumps my shoulder and falls into step beside me. Chase gives her a small bark in greeting.

"Seems like things are going well so far," she remarks.

"Yeah, it does. Here's hoping the fireworks go off when they're supposed to. And that the kids think it's exciting and not gimmicky," I reply.

"Oh Clark, the more gimmicky, the better. The kids will totally eat it up," Clara says with confidence. "This whole week has been amazing. Even better than I dreamed."

"If it's better than the dreams of Christmas fanatic Clara, daughter of Joseph and Holly, then we must have done something right," I respond with a smirk.

Clara laughs—that musical, magical laugh that lights up her whole face. "You're practically Clark Griswold now." She taps my forearm. "Might need to add some Christmas lights to the tree trunk here."

I resist the urge to grab her hand and hold it there in the crook of my arm, wanting the heat of her touch searing through my sleeve.

As we walk toward the river, Clara says, "There's one thing I keep wondering about. This festival turned out flawless—all the decorations, the supplies, the tents. But this had to be expensive. Where did you find the money for all of this?"

Heat rushes from my neck up to my face, even though Clara's not touching me at all. "Oh, it just worked out. Found some pools of funding to get things going," I attempt to evade.

"Right, but how? Did you tap into state funds, or a private grant?"

"More like a private grant," I respond, hoping she'll drop it. I glance over at her, and she's staring at me intently. *Not dropping it then.*

I sigh. "When my parents and Sam passed away, I received life insurance settlements from all three of them, plus the inheritance they left behind. The money has been sitting in a trust fund, so I decided to put some of it to good use."

Clara's mouth drops open, and she comes to a standstill. I pause beside her, regretting telling the truth.

"Clark, that's . . . unbelievably generous. I'm . . ." she trails off, wide eyes locked on mine.

Her appreciative attention makes me sweat. My palms get clammy. "That inconceivable, huh?" I joke. I'm trying to dispel the tightness in my throat caused by the way she's regarding me. But her lips do that adorable "I'm trying not to laugh at your bad jokes" twitch, and the tightness comes back full force.

Chase nudges my hand with a whine, giving me an excuse to look away from Clara. "Uh, Chase did good with Pops today. Thanks for thinking of that," I awkwardly transition.

"Of course," she responds quietly. We continue walking to the river in silence. Clara might think this is a comfortable silence, but I'm experiencing rock-in-my-shoe discomfort. More accurately, I have a rock in both shoes. One, because I'm kicking myself for admitting to her that I paid the festival start-up costs. The other because I'm losing the raging internal battle against my desire to be close to her.

We reach the river's edge, and Syd takes the microphone. She does a masterful job of hyping the kids up for the send-off. Syd could have had success as a children's librarian or voice-over actress in another life.

"Everyone wave goodbye to Santa's elf as he paddles to the magic portal to the North Pole!" Syd says. All the kids are cheering and waving and jumping and generally losing their minds. It's clear that they ate their fair share of the bakery treats. Good thing Becky kept the parents dosed on caffeine to keep up.

Syd has an ear piece so she can coordinate her countdown with the fireworks, but I still worry that the timing could go amiss. She starts counting down from ten, and I hold my breath until there's an explosion of fireworks right on the count of one.

If the kids were losing their minds before, they're having full on, out-of-body experiences now. I make a mental note to avoid this particular event for the next two weeks, if at all possible. I glance over and notice moisture pooled in Clara's eyes, her hands clasped over her heart. The soft light makes her content smile look almost angelic.

There goes that string again, vibrating, tightening, pulling me toward her. It would be the easiest thing in the world to wrap an arm around her shoulders, tuck her to my side. Lean down and kiss her temple.

Lean further down and find out if her lips are as soft as my imagination has decided they are.

I'm surprised when Chase paws at my leg, whimpering next to me. Given Clara's teary eyes, I would have expected him to be plastered to her leg, lending her emotional support. But he's peering up at me with his concerned little eyebrows.

You're right, boy. You should be concerned about me. Because I need Clara to be okay, even if it will mean I'm not.

"I'm going to drive down and help Davis out with the canoe. I'll see ya next weekend," I mumble to Clara. I turn away from the bewildered expression on her face and make my way through the crowd, Chase close on my heels.

I don't look back.

CHAPTER THIRTY-NINE

Clara

"He could be scared to get close to someone again after what happened to his family," my mom muses from the passenger seat of my car. We're driving down for the second weekend of The First Noel, and my dad is following in their car. They have to be back for church on Sunday, so they won't get to see the musical performance tomorrow night or the Letters to Santa send-off. At least they'll get to see the festival and the parade tonight.

"You sound like Mads. She said the same thing," I respond. I've been trying to honestly share about my complicated feelings for Clark. I'm usually an open book with my mom, but my inability to figure Clark out has made me less confident to talk about how I feel. Being able to focus on the road and not make eye contact has made it easier to open up. Not that she was surprised to hear me admit that I'm attracted to him.

"Well, maybe we're right, then," Mom says. "If I'd lost my whole family in one blow, I might be afraid to let someone close again."

"True. Although, he wasn't especially close to his family in the first place." I chew my lip. "I don't know. Syd told me that Clark's always been a private person who doesn't really let people in. Which also makes sense, given his childhood. But he's let me get close enough as a friend to spend all this time together planning the festival. I mean, he caved and let me plan this festival in the first place!"

I pause, a snowstorm of thoughts swirling. "I know Syd said he *likes* being alone. But . . . he still seems lonely. Maybe he doesn't even see it as loneliness. He has this small world of people he feels responsible for in Noel, but an even *smaller* world of truly close relationships. It's like he wants life to stay all the same. Never wants anything more."

Mom is quiet for a beat before responding. "Not everyone has to have a big life. Maybe he's okay with keeping his world small. Maybe he truly doesn't care about having more."

"What if more could be . . . us? And what if it could be beautiful?" Emotion catches my words, and I take a steadying breath. "I guess I just want to help Clark see possibility. He took a risk and let me help the town. And he can see the joy that the Christmas festival has brought to everyone. Why not let me help bring him a different kind of joy?"

At this point, I think my mom knows I'm speaking more to myself than to her. We drive the rest of the way, silently listening to Michael Bublé.

We drop off our bags and my parents' car at my cabin before driving to the festival parking lot. Positive buzz about The First Noel must be making the rounds because there are almost twice as many people here as last weekend. The town is overrun with crowds and children and Christmas cheer.

I love it.

My parents match my enthusiasm and then some. They buy multiple gifts from every booth in Santa's Workshop and take pictures at every photo opp. They enjoy baked goods and Becky's coffee drinks, rounding out the day by cheering on the parade participants.

I've been not-so-subtly searching for Clark ever since we arrived, but he hasn't shown up anywhere. Either he's nowhere to be found, or he's actively avoiding contact.

I take my parents to say hi to Syd and Davis at the Letters to Santa tent, where Junior and Addie are busy coloring their letters. Soon, my dad is sitting down beside them, writing his own letter while my mom chats with Sydney.

A throat clears behind me, and I swivel to see Clark. He's wearing a black fleece jacket, half-zipped to show the hunter-green shirt underneath. His signature baseball cap is turned backward, allowing his shirt to accent the striking green in his hazel eyes. He runs a hand over his beard, drawing my attention to his mouth. Not that it takes a lot to draw my attention to his lips. They're becoming more irresistible every time I see him.

"Clara—welcome back," he says. *Is he happy to see me? He looks happy-ish to see me?* My heart smacks against my chest like a paddle ball.

"I wanted to thank your parents for all their input. We couldn't have pulled this off without them."

"Oh." My heart slowly loses momentum—the missed ball dangling from the paddle string.

Clark steps around me to greet my mom, and my dad stands up to join the conversation. *It's fine. This is good. Of course, he's grateful for Mom and Dad's help. I* want *him to be grateful. This is fine.*

After a short conversation with everyone except me, Clark excuses himself. I keep trying to convince myself that everything is fine, but it's not a very effective pep talk.

Back at my cabin, my parents turn in early, so I sit in the sunroom, marking up edits on a copy of my movie script I printed off. Reading all of Clark's qualities in Jack's character only leaves me frustrated by Clark's recent behavior. Again. I give up.

I make a quick pass checking on each of my plants, testing the soil to see if any need water.

How can I test the soil with Clark? How can I find out what he truly thinks about us?

The next morning, my parents load their car, and we make our way to the festival grounds early. We pop in to see Becky, who hooks us up with large, sugary cups of caffeine. We chase the liquid sugar with cinnamon rolls and scones from the bake shop.

After a few hours, my parents say their goodbyes to make the drive back to Kansas City before dusk. I keep hoping Clark will suddenly show up again, but I hope in vain. Hugging my mom by the car, she whispers in my ear, "Don't stress about him, baby girl. Keep your heart open and see where it takes you."

My dad wraps me up in a hug next. "I love you, Care-bear. I know you're worried, but I have a good feeling about Clark. Keep your chin up."

I guess that confirms that my mom tattled on me to Dad.

"Thanks, Dad. I love you too," I reply.

Walking back to the festival, I jump in to help Becky with coffee drinks, giving Syd a break. There's a steady line of customers the entire afternoon, so I grab dinner from one of the food trucks for Becky and myself. Syd mans the drinks while we quickly stuff our faces with warm panini sandwiches. We spend the first several minutes in silence, both inhaling the sustenance.

"So," Becky starts. This is definitely one of those uncomfortable "so" remarks where I'm expected to fill in the blanks.

"You and Clark are . . . ?" she asks, taking a giant bite of her sandwich.

"Me and Clark are . . . what?" I respond, taking an equally large bite.

Becky rolls her eyes. "Come on. Everyone has lost the pool already. It's taken longer than any of us bet it would for you two to get together."

I inhale too quickly and choke on my half-chewed bite. "Pool? Bets? What the actual heck, Becky?!"

She simply shrugs. "Whatever. It's obvious to everyone that you two are attracted to each other. Not to mention a great match."

I stare at her.

"What? Take it as a compliment! We all want you around more. And we all want Clark to be happy. We can put two and two together," Becky reasons.

I sigh. "Well, maybe you all can put two and two together, but I'm not sure Clark wants to. I'm not sure what page he's on, or what book he's even in." Becky skewers me with a look. "All I'm saying is I don't know what we are. Or what we'll ever be. I just don't know."

Crumpling my sandwich wrapper, I hope that's a sufficient signal to end this line of questioning. Becky catches my drift and leads the way to take over making drinks while Syd mans the register.

The Saturday evening show by the dance team and carolers starts in ten minutes, so the coffee line is slowing down as people crowd around the pavilion. I need a moment to clear my head after my brief chat with Becky. I meander away from the crowds.

Are Becky and Sydney right? Are Clark and I a good match for each other? I still can't figure out if he sees things the same way or not. His messy Magic Eye picture projects a solid "no" at first glance. But the glimpses I've seen of the image underneath seem like maybe he does want something more with me.

Is he scared of getting close to someone, like Mom and Mads said? Or is it more than that? Is he afraid of things not working out because we'd be long distance, at least at first? Is he just uncertain of how I feel?

What do I do?

I try to sort through all the rapid-fire questions barraging through my mind. The music from the dance show starts playing in the background, cheers from the spectators mixed in. I should make my way back to the pavilion to watch, but I'm too confused to be surrounded by crowds.

Instead, I turn down a small alley lit by overhead white Christmas lights that I haven't noticed before. I do a double take when I see sprigs of mistletoe hanging from the strands of lights. There's a sign at the entrance of the alley that reads *Mistletoe Lane*.

Ha! So Clark caved. Syd must have convinced him to include this. Or did it behind his back. But even if she set it up without his knowledge, he didn't tear it down. The thought makes me smile—maybe he's not as unwilling to change his mind as he tries to project.

Maybe he just needs a chance to make up his mind about us? Maybe I need to give him a straightforward opportunity to say yes or no.

I swivel to leave the alley but bump right into a solid, human-shaped wall. My hands instinctively come up to steady myself, landing smack dab on Clark's firm chest. The flashback to the first time we met in my bathroom is inevitable.

The positive memories of Clark that first weekend come flooding back. His witty comments through the door, his respectful approach to helping me, the options he brought the next day to give me a choice in fixing the door. The way he took my Tineke, no questions asked—and then researched the heck out of plant care to make sure she thrived.

This is the same man who repeatedly—and harshly—shot down my suggestions as Mayor Noel. Who ruthlessly crumpled my list of ideas. But this man *also* pulled the crumpled list out of the trash and held on to it for months.

This man took down my Christmas lights to keep me safe and brought a rocking chair so I'd have somewhere to sit on my porch. He opened up to me about the pain in his life, and he challenged me to overcome the pain in mine to chase *my* dreams.

To top it all off, we're standing in the middle of the very festival I'd dreamed of and pushed for. Because he loves this town, yes—but, I think, maybe because he also feels something for me?

I have to know. One way or the other, I have to know.

"Sorry, Clark, I didn't mean to run into you," I apologize as I take a small step backward. It's a mild evening, so Clark doesn't have on his fleece jacket tonight. Just a long-sleeve, navy Henley shirt, clinging to the muscles of his biceps as he fidgets with his hands. He finally puts them in his pockets before acknowledging my apology.

"It's fine. I was just escaping the crowd for a minute. I took Chase and Pops home and knew I should come back. But my social capacity is shot," Clark says, then abruptly cuts himself off. Maybe he didn't mean to admit that, but anyone who knows him the slightest bit would know it's true.

"Yeah, you might need to hide in a cave for a couple of weeks after this is all over," I joke. "I know this has been your worst nightmare, but I'm really grateful you made it happen."

He shrugs, not saying anything else. But the spark in his eyes as he holds my gaze has my insides melting and my courage fortifying.

"Clark, I need to say something to you," I begin. "It's not a secret that I've struggled to understand you over the past year. We've had rocky moments—"

Clark interrupts. "You know I'm sorry about that, Clara. I've tried to keep better control over my reactions."

I place a hand on his forearm, where the sleeve of his Henley is hiding the reminders inked onto his skin. "I know you have, and I've already forgiven you for that. *And* I acknowledge my role in being too pushy. What I was going to say is that we've had rocky moments, *but* we've also had some really . . . magical moments."

Pausing, my eyes bounce back and forth between his, watching for signs of what he's thinking. He must be a phenomenal poker player. I'm getting zero clues as to what's happening in that brain of his.

I continue anyway. "Even as a friend, you've pushed me to grow in ways that no one else has before. I'd like to think that I've maybe played the tiniest role in helping you grow a little bit too. I guess I'm saying that I think that we could be . . . Well, maybe we could be better as Clark-and-Clara than we are as Clark"—I gesture toward him and pause to punctuate my statement. Then I gesture to myself separately—"and Clara."

He doesn't respond verbally, but his eyes are still locked on mine. The gold flecks of his irises draw me in. "I just want you to know that I *want* that. I want to find out if we're better together."

Before I can talk myself out of it, I lean onto my tiptoes and wrap an arm around Clark's neck, gently pressing my lips to his. His beard is softer than I imagined it would be, tickling my chin in a way I could easily become addicted to. My lips have found their missing puzzle piece locked with his.

My heart sings for the two seconds it takes me to realize he's not kissing me back.

He's not kissing me back.

An electrician jumping away from touching a live wire has nothing on the speed and force with which I spring back from Clark.

He looks as stunned as I feel. Which is not fair considering *I'm* the one who just kissed someone who didn't want to be kissed. Clark's obvious discomfort only makes me more embarrassed.

"I'm so sorry; excuse me," I mumble as I dart past him out of the alley.

"Wait, Clara, let's—"

"Please forget everything that just happened!" I call back over my shoulder, voice unnaturally high. Logically, I know I should attempt to play this cool and walk away as if unbothered. But my heart is both pounding out of my chest *and* my chest is so tight I think my heart can't beat. Which should be an impossible combination of biological responses. I break out in a dead sprint toward my car.

Oh my gosh; I am such an idiot. I laid it all out there like we were on the same page, but, boy, was I wrong. We're not on the same page. We're not in the same book. Clark isn't even in a book.

I'm such a fool.

I want nothing more than to crawl into a hole and curl up in the fetal position. No—my one wish would be to take back everything about the past ten minutes, to extract it from Clark's mind like a lobotomy. *Where are the Men in Black with those flashy memory-eraser sticks when you need them?*

Every ounce of logic in my brain knows that I'm in no state to drive for hours. In the dark. But the shame of rejection is overpowering all sense of logic.

Not even bothering to stop at my cabin, I speed away from Noel—and Clark—as fast as I can.

I cry the entire drive home.

Chapter Forty

Clark

"You've reached Clara! Leave me a message, and I'll get back to you as soon as I can!"

I hang up before the beep, groaning.

It's been almost a week since I pulled the most Clark move of all time. And by "Clark move," I mean royally messing up a relationship by reacting to a situation in the most idiotic manner possible.

Clara kissed me. She told me she thought we could be great together, despite all the ways I've been a complete jerk to her in the past. She saw through all that and thought we could be something.

Then kissed me.

And what did I do? Locked up like the Tin Man, exactly the way Syd accused me of at the cookout for Madison.

I *wanted* to kiss Clara back. I wanted to pull her body flush against mine and *kiss* her until she forgot she loves Christmas. Kiss her until nothing else existed outside of the Clark-and-Clara picture she painted.

But I didn't. Because I know that the Clark-and-Clara would fall apart. Know I'd stifle Clara's eager spirit with my self-sufficiency. She wouldn't stick around once she truly understood that I don't need anyone. And she'd get hurt in the process. I can't do that to her.

So I stood there, still as a statue, while the opportunity to kiss the woman I love slipped through my fingers.

Yes, I love her. Despite all the willpower I've put into trying to push her away, to sever that cord between her heart and mine, to kill the feeling by denying its existence. But it exists. I love her.

I've texted her twice this week to try to get her to talk. Not so I can profess my love—that can't happen—but to try to help her not be embarrassed about the kiss, to apologize for my poor reaction. Blame it on a lack of sleep. Or overstimulation from the crowds, or anything other than the excruciating pain of loving this woman but needing to stay away from her for her sake.

She wouldn't text me back, so as I walked to the festival grounds tonight for the final parade, I pushed that dreaded icon on my phone and tried to call her.

No answer. It's what I deserve. I only wish I could give her what she deserves.

The crowds at The First Noel have been bigger than ever this week, the final week of the festival. I've tried my best to rein in my grouchiness, but haven't been entirely successful. At least everyone close to me knows how much I hate these social situations. So I've had their benefits of the doubt that my foul mood has to do with the multitudes of people.

My benefits have apparently run out, though. Syd sees me coming and marches toward me with murder in her eyes. Probably because Clara hasn't shown up today.

"What did you do?" Syd demands.

I narrow my eyes at her but don't respond.

"First, Clara left early last weekend, citing some emergency at home that she never gave details for. She avoided texting me all week. Now, she finally texts me that she won't be here this weekend because of some 'work thing' that came up," she huffs. She mimes air quotes to show how much she believes Clara's excuse.

"This festival is her baby—there's no way she'd let some 'work thing' keep her from the final days." Extra exaggerated air quotes this time. Syd's turned feisty, and I need to get out of her line of fire. Unfortunately, I'm exactly the right person to blame.

Syd pops her hands on her hips and stares down my silence. "Don't make me get Davis."

I groan, rubbing a hand down my face and across my beard. "Fine. Last weekend, Clara may have said something to me about having feelings for me that went beyond friendship. And I may have reacted in . . . not the way she was hoping I'd react."

Syd full-on punches my biceps with a mean right hook. "Ow!" I say, rubbing my left arm.

"Don't be a baby in addition to being a complete fool," she glowers at me. "Clark, you *obviously* reciprocate Clara's feelings. Why in the world wouldn't you tell her? You're not making any sense!"

I sigh, rubbing my arm. It still stings. Syd could apparently also have a future as an MMA fighter if the children's librarian or voice actress gig didn't work out.

"Even if I was attracted to Clara, that doesn't mean a relationship would work out between us, Syd. I'm just . . . not starting something that I know we couldn't finish."

"But why?" Syd jumps back in. "Is it the distance? Because there are plenty of people who have made long-distance relationships work until they figure out what they're going to do long term."

"No, Syd, it's not the distance. I need you to just drop it, okay? I don't want to talk about Clara anymore," I say.

"If you won't talk to me about this, find someone you can talk to, Clark. And then talk to Clara and fix this! Because you made a mess of things with my new best friend, and I'm not going to let you get away with that." Syd's eyes are shimmering with moisture in addition to the rage. Her emotion cuts through my defensiveness.

"I promise I'm trying to patch things up, at least make it to where Clara can still come to town and just avoid seeing me."

"You're trying how hard?" Syd questions.

"I've texted her a few times this week, and when she wouldn't respond, I tried calling her a few minutes ago."

Syd sniffs. "You tried an actual phone call? Like, talking with your voice through the phone?"

I roll my eyes. "Yes, Syd, I tried a real-live phone call. She didn't answer, but I'll keep trying. I've never intended to hurt her."

She studies my face. "Maybe. But sometimes the impact matters more than the intention, Clark."

Ouch.

Syd stalks away, but whirls around to face me again. I brace for another sucker punch.

"And go check on Clara's plants! She asked me to do it, but the last thing we need is me killing off her favorite plant and giving her one more reason to abandon Noel!"

The First Noel is officially over, and I've never been more grateful for the end of something. We'd decided not to extend the festival into the week before Christmas so that everyone could enjoy a quiet holiday with their families.

I work Monday and Tuesday to take apart some of the larger festival booths that are no longer needed, but we'll leave the decorations up until after Christmas. On Tuesday afternoon, Davis tries to bring up Clara with me as we work alongside each other.

"I don't want to talk about it," I cut him off.

Davis gives me a look that's not quite a glare. More in the neighborhood of concerned disappointment. It makes me uncomfortable.

"Look, man. I know Syd laid into you the other night. And I agree with every word she said, for the record. I won't pile it on, but you need to know that I'm worried about you," Davis says. I swallow hard and avoid eye contact as he continues. "You're my best friend—nothing's ever going to change that. I know every circumstance of your past that's rolled into how you tick. Been there with you through every hard thing. And I love you like a brother."

Davis pauses, and I swallow even harder. He claps a hand on my shoulder. "I'm worried about *you*, Clark. I just want you to talk to me if you need to."

After a long pause, I manage to reply. "I appreciate it, man. But I'm not ready to talk right now. Can we put this off a little longer?" Davis nods, and we continue working in silence.

Maybe if I put off talking long enough, everyone will forget and leave me alone.

Unlikely.

Clara has either blocked my number or developed willpower of steel to continue ignoring my texts and second phone call attempt. As much as I want to make peace between us, I'm almost relieved that she's avoiding me. Because I still don't know exactly what I'd say to her to make things right.

Dear Clara—I love you, but I don't need you, so I'm staying away from you for your sake.

As far as building bridges goes, somehow I don't think that would go very far.

I drive to Pops' house on Wednesday to check in now that the town has calmed down. Chase has matched my morose mood this week, but he has his head hanging happily out the window now, sensing where we're going.

He bounds up to Pops' front door, barking to announce our presence. Pops opens the door before I even have to knock, steadier on his feet than he has been for a long while. I may have ruined things with Clara, but at least she fixed things with Pops.

We wordlessly take seats on the porch rocking chairs, Chase resting his head in Pops' lap. The afternoon sun should warm us enough to enjoy the crisp air, but I brought a thermos of coffee for us to share as a backup.

Pops takes a long sip of black coffee, then turns his furrowed brow on me. "I spoke with Sydney yesterday."

Knowing exactly what Syd would have spoken with him about, I close my eyes and pinch the bridge of my nose. "And?"

"Clark, I mean this in the most loving way. You're a complete and utter idiot," Pops declares.

I refuse to dignify his insult with a response.

"You are so obviously in love with that girl. Truly, madly, stars-in-your-eyes in love. And despite your best efforts to be a disagreeable moron, Clara seems to love you back. Why would you push that away?" Pops presses.

I flip my hat forward to provide a shield for my eyes before answering. "You've seen Clara. She's a city girl. This town will only ever be a getaway for her, a quiet place to write and nothing more. And I'll never leave Noel. We don't make sense long term."

"Bull crap."

"'Scuse me?"

Chase barks next to me.

"I said bull crap. That's not the reason you're pushing her away and you know it. I see through that excuse plain as day, and I'm darn near blind, son. Tell me the truth. Tell *yourself* the truth," Pops says.

I sigh, throwing my hands up in the air. "Because I don't *need* her, Pops! Clara's DNA is hard-wired to care for other people. Helping people brings her to life in the most captivating way possible. She'd eventually resent our relationship when she can't scratch that itch with me."

"You don't need her, or you don't *want* to need her?" he questions.

"Is there a difference?"

"Maybe, maybe not. But either way, why's it such a bad thing to need someone?" Pops asks.

I pause to consider my answer. "Pops, you know better than anyone that I grew up learning not to depend on anyone but myself. I'd rather take care of my own business, take care of myself, even if that means being alone."

Pops assesses me. "Lord knows you haven't had someone truly take care of you in a long time. Maybe ever. I s'pose you just don't understand how good it can be. What if you let someone take care of you, and you find out how much more color and joy and beauty it brings to life?"

I roll my eyes. "I'm a competent, grown man. I'm the town handyman *and* the mayor. I'm literally the person everyone in Noel calls when they need something. I don't need someone to take care of me."

"Fair enough." Pops pauses. "But what about someone to care *with* you? You've carried the burdens of this town on your shoulders ever since your folks passed. You've carried the burden of your family name long before that. Would it really be that bad to have someone care with you for this town? Because evidence indicates that Clara has a lot of care to give Noel." He emphasizes the new "No-el" pronunciation with a wry grin.

He quietly finishes his speech. "Needing the love of a kind, generous woman like Clara doesn't make you less competent, son. It just makes you more loved. And there ain't nothing wrong with that, no sir."

Pops takes another sip of coffee and stares off into the distance. His eyes get the kind of misty that reveals he's thinking of Bev. I glance away to give him privacy with his thoughts. Chase looks torn between nudging his nose under Pops' hand or tucking his head under my arm. I wave him toward Pops and stare down at my hands.

Needing someone is a sensation I've stifled since childhood. I've learned to be self-sufficient. The comfort of competency is the drug I crave. It's brought me a sense of satisfaction knowing that I'm taking care of myself and the people around me. I've always been content being a one-man show.

It's okay to be content with what is, but it's also okay to want what could be. Davis' unsolicited advice from the first day I denied my attraction to Clara comes crashing through my mind.

What could be?

I clear my throat but avoid making eye contact with Pops as I speak. "What if I admit that I want Clara—that I *need* Clara—and it doesn't work out? And we both wind up devastated?"

Out of my peripheral vision, I see Pops shrug and hold up his hands. "Such are the gambles of life. But I say it's worth the risk. Because a life loving a good woman is the biggest jackpot the world has to offer."

I leave Pops' house and drive aimlessly around the outskirts of town. I rolled the window down for Chase, but he's kept his chin propped on my thigh the whole time.

Reaching to run my hand down his back, I think about the day we found each other. When I was in the middle of my electrician apprenticeship, I'd found Chase abandoned along the side of the road.

He was a tiny, quivering puppy, crouching there in the grass. Nursing him back to health and gaining his trust had added a layer of purpose to my life. Now, I can't imagine life without him. I think about how wrecked I'll be the day that Chase's life with me comes to an end.

The thought chokes my throat, but I know that I wouldn't trade away the time I have with Chase in order to avoid that pain.

Chase whimpers, reading my thoughts, as always. I scratch behind his ears. "I suppose it hasn't been so terrible needing you in my life, has it, boy?"

It's getting dark, and I find myself driving up the ridge toward Clara's cabin. The beacon of her Christmas lights is less of a standout this year, now that we have thousands of lights strung up all over town. I pull into her driveway and cut the engine.

I'll check on the plants, per Syd's order. Even though I know that Clara won't be here, my chest is heavy as I follow the stone pathway to her front porch. Maybe the heaviness is *because* she won't be here.

Punching in the code on the lock, my mind falls back to the first time I did this. The first night I met Clara—literally stumbling into her. The vision of her wide eyes, her damp curls, her black robe is easy to recall, considering how many times I've replayed it over the past year. Rubbing a hand across my beard with a sigh, I open the door.

I flip on the light and look around the room. It's obvious she left in a hurry—there's a pair of shoes in the middle of the floor where she must have toed them off. A dirty bowl and coffee mug sit in the sink, a box of Cocoa Puffs left open on the counter.

Running water in the sink, I wash the few dishes and put them on the drying rack. Then I fill her watering can with fertilizer and water, carrying it to the sunroom to assess which plants need care. The Tineke plant sitting at the end of her writing desk catches my attention, and I think back to her shock when I returned it to her in good condition.

Something else on her writing desk catches my eye—a stack of papers, marked with red pen. I peer more closely and realize what I'm staring at: Clara's movie script.

She did it, I think with a smile. *She chased the dream.*

I know I should walk away. I know it would be an invasion of privacy to look at this script when she hasn't given me permission.

Knowing that can't overcome the strength of my curiosity, though. I take the stack and sit down in her armchair. Chase lies down at my feet, and I start reading.

A woman named Renee buys a large house sight unseen in a small town named Bethlehem. Her plan is to convert it into a Christmas-themed bed-and-breakfast. When she arrives, she's shocked to find that the dying town has rebuffed its Christmas namesake. She sets out to rally the people to embrace their Christmas connection in order to revitalize the town.

Renee has a run-in with Jack, a particularly grouchy member of the city council. As I read the descriptions of Jack's character—the rugged beard, tall stature, and grumpy moods—it's a view of myself in a Clara-shaped mirror.

The script so obviously reflects Clara's time in Noel, her time with me. There's no denying the connection. But as I read, I understand how Clara sees me. Really, truly *sees* me. The good and the bad.

She sees the hesitance to let people close. But she also sees the dogged love for the people of Noel. She sees the resistance to change. But she also sees the efforts, big and small, to be open to what's needed.

I stay up for hours, reading every line of her script. Chase snores softly at my feet as I turn the final pages. The story ends with Jack confessing his love for Renee, professing all the ways she's made him a better man. Acknowledging all the ways she's made the town better simply by her presence.

And then he kisses her under the mistletoe on her bed-and-breakfast porch.

Jack and Renee stare at each other with love in their eyes, the kind of love that fights through every obstacle, as the camera pans away to the town Christmas festival.

I stare at the final stage direction written at the end of the script, and my heart sinks. The reality of how much I hurt Clara slaps me across the face. This is the kind of ending she was dreaming of when she kissed me. But I froze up, acting as though I didn't *want* her kissing me.

Like I didn't want her.

I stand so abruptly, Chase jumps to his feet with a growl, searching for intruders.

"We have to make this right, Chase. You're gonna have to stay with Pops for a couple days because I have to go win Clara back."

CHAPTER FORTY-ONE

Clara

"How in the world are you done with all the newsletters already?" Madison asks me, incredulity in her voice and facial expression.

"I came in early." I shrug.

Her eyes narrow at me. "How early?"

I spin my ring and avoid eye contact.

"Clara Jane. Answer me."

"Fine, *Mom*, I came in at 4:00 this morning." I admit with an eye roll.

It's not like I was sleeping. I've barely slept since I returned to KC to lick my wounds. Every time I close my eyes, I see the shocked expression on Clark's face when I pulled away from kissing him. To add insult to the not-sleeping injury, my eyes are even more tired, considering my hasty retreat from Noel meant I left my glasses behind. I don't mention that extra detail to Madison.

I spilled everything to her the day after I returned. Mads came to my apartment with exorbitant amounts of sugar and watched action movies with me all day. Usually, Heartmark movies are my comfort watch in the midst of emotional turmoil. But they're the furthest thing from a comfort watch right now.

"That's it; leave this office right now," Madison commands.

I meet her eyes with a quizzical look. "It's the middle of a workday. I can't just leave the office, Mads."

"Clara, you've finished all the work you were supposed to do for this entire week. And you are a shell of yourself. He-who-doesn't-deserve-a-name has ruined enough of your favorite time of year already. Go do something Christmassy, right now. I'll cover for you here," she concludes.

I drop my head on my desk. "I don't feel Christmassy, Mads."

"Then go down to Crown Center. It's impossible to not feel Christmassy there," she states decisively. I turn my head on my arm to make eye contact, still sulking.

"Clara, please," Mads says, her tone of voice softening. "You need a change of scenery. Some Christmas scenery. Get out and be distracted by the holiday crowd for a few hours, okay?"

I sigh. "Fine."

CHAPTER FORTY-TWO

Clark

"Use the second from the left lane to turn left."

The GPS voice grates on my last nerve. My attempt to switch lanes at the last minute earns me a loud honk from the frustrated driver behind me.

Navigating this city traffic has me ready to give up driving forever. But I'm determined to make it to Clara's office if it's the last thing I do. I found the address for WritInc and drove straight here after dropping off Chase at Pops' place this morning.

No doubt, Pops has already filled the whole town in on where I ran off to today. But if their positive vibes can help my cause with Clara, then I don't even care who knows.

I park in the lot and step out of my truck, met with a blast of cold air. "Should have stopped to buy a coat," I mutter under my breath as I jog to the building.

Once inside, I take the elevator to the third floor. Inhaling deeply, I open the glass door labeled WritInc and step into the lobby. There's a woman behind a desk at the front. I'm not sure if she's an official receptionist or not, but she appears to be the first line of defense to the office.

"Excuse me?" I say, clearing my throat. She gives a cursory glance up from her computer screen. Once she looks at me fully, she sits up straighter with a smile.

"Can I help you?" she asks, smile widening.

I rub my beard, uncomfortable with her perusal. "Um, I'm here to see Clara Sullivan."

"I'm sorry, Clara's not in the office right now," she says, not sounding very sorry at all. "Is there anything that *I* could help you with?"

"Uh, no, unless you could tell me where I can find Clara."

"I'm sorry, I can't give out other employees' information," she replies. "But I could—"

"Clark?" I'm saved from the receptionist's next statement by the disbelieving voice of Madison speaking my name.

I look up to see her glaring at me, rage spewing from eyes. *Yeah, I deserve that.*

"Madison, can I talk to you?" I ask. She continues glaring. "Please? It's important."

She gives an eye roll that involves her entire head, but gestures for me to follow her to an empty conference room.

"Well? What could be sooo important from the jerk who broke my best friend's heart?" she spits. Guess I'm officially back on Madison's bad side.

I attempt to disarm her with honesty. "You mean the jerk who knows he messed up and desperately wants to apologize? Who is here to beg to put your best friend's heart back together? That's what's so important."

Madison's face softens. "You swear you're here to fix things and not make them worse? Because I don't know if you've caught on to this or not, but my Clara is a sensitive soul. And one more rejection from you might crush her spirit beyond recognition."

"I love her, Madison. I'm here to tell her that. I just have to find her," I answer truthfully. She nods her head in approval.

"In that case, I'll tell you exactly where to find her. Don't let me down, McScrooge."

"I—what?"

"Not important. What's important is that you hightail it over to Crown Center and look for Clara by the giant Christmas tree."

The drive from Overland Park to Crown Center in Kansas City, Missouri, is maddening. I'm tempted to sit on a bench for an hour by myself to regulate my blood pressure. But I'm more determined to find Clara and tell her how I feel before it's too late.

If it's not already too late.

The Christmas festival in Noel was uncomfortably crowded for me—but nothing could have prepared me for the sheer number of people packed into Crown Center. Young families taking their kids to visit Santa, an overflowing ice-skating rink, couples posing for photos in front of the Christmas trees. Even though there are still traces of daylight, the lights are turned on, filling the space with sparkle. It's easy to see why Clara expects Christmas cheer everywhere she goes if this is what she grew up around.

I walk slowly through the area, looking everywhere for her beautiful face. Not finding her right away, I brave the ice skating crowds to see if she's watching the kids out on the ice. No dice.

Panic sets in. Panic that she's not here any longer, that she left and I'm back to square one. I still have her father's number, but I'd much rather declare my love directly to Clara instead of having to explain to another person why I'm here.

Just when my hope is dimming, I spot the familiar shine of strawberry-blond curls. My breath catches in my chest as I watch her profile—sitting on a bench near the large Christmas tree, staring up at its lights.

There's a sadness cast over her features that I know I'm responsible for. A sadness that I'm determined to chase away for the rest of my life, if she'll let me.

I make my way toward Clara, my long stride quickly eating up the space between us. As I approach her bench, I call out her name.

She turns at the sound of my voice, eyes going wide when she sees me. "Clark?"

Clara stands abruptly, turning to face me but crossing her arms over her chest. "What are you doing here?"

"I have to talk to you, Clara."

"But how did you find me here?" she cuts in.

"I went to your office, but when you weren't there, Madison told me where to find you," I admit.

"Madison told you?" Clara sounds skeptical, confused. I nod. She must know that her bouncer of a best friend wouldn't have led me near her without good reason. I see her body relax the slightest bit, but her arms stay tightly wrapped around herself. "What do you have to say?"

"I want to tell you that I'm sorry for how I acted that night at the festival. The night you kissed me. It probably felt like I was rejecting you by not kissing you back—"

Her incredulous laugh cuts me off. "Gee, wonder why it would have felt that way?"

"But I wasn't *not* kissing you for the reason you thought I was," I cut back in. She's blinking quickly, trying but failing to fend off tears. I take a step forward and brush a stray curl off her forehead. "I didn't kiss you back, not because I didn't want to kiss you. I didn't kiss you back because I *did* want to kiss you."

Clara purses her lips and shakes her head. "That makes no sense, Clark."

I rub my beard and sigh. "I know. I'm trying to explain, but it's hard for me to explain . . . feelings." Her eyes soften enough to give me strength to continue trying.

"Clara, I thought that I was wrong for you. That if you were with me, you'd wind up miserable because of the type of man I am. I . . . I don't like needing other people. Quite frankly, I was determined *not* to need anyone, ever. But you get such joy out of helping other people, out of being needed, that I thought you'd slowly suffocate in a relationship with me. That my lack of depending on you would suck all the air out of your lungs."

"Clark, that would never—" She tries to interrupt, but I hold up a hand.

"Hold on, let me finish. That's the reason I told myself that I was pushing you away. But then I started to realize that it wasn't the true reason. It wasn't about protecting you from me. At least, not *only* about that."

I take a fortifying breath before admitting my next thought. "I realized that the way I *wanted* you felt a lot like *needing* you. Needing your spunky energy challenging my stubborn streak. Needing your smile making my heart catch. Needing your laugh brightening the air around me. Needing your kindness taming my grumpy side. Needing your concern for other people pulling me out of myself. Needing your eyes staring into mine every morning. Needing everything about you in my life, every day."

My words have grown shaky, and Clara's eyes have filled with tears. I reach forward and take her hand, the one that has been furiously spinning the ring on her pointer finger.

"Clara, I love you. I'm sorry that I wasn't ready to admit that when you tried. But now, I'm ready to admit that I need you, that I want Clark-and-Clara, all that we could be together. If that's still what you want."

She hiccups a sob. For a split second, the terror that I might have irrevocably screwed up my chance with her crashes into me.

Then Clara reaches her free hand up to my cheek, running her fingers down my bearded jaw.

"I love you, too, Clark. I still want us. I think I always will," she whispers.

I waste no time pulling her against me, leaning my head down to capture her lips. The sensation of her mouth against mine is as intoxicating as it was the first time she kissed me, but this time I give myself over to the rush. My hand reaches to cup behind her head, threading my fingers through her soft curls and angling her mouth against mine.

The moms who brought their kids out to visit Santa today are getting more of a scene than they bargained for, but I don't care. The string around my heart is humming in victory.

I never want to snap out of whatever spell Clara has me under. All I want is to stand here forever, kissing her lips with all the reverence and passion and tenderness and intensity that she deserves.

However, I do want to be respectful of how Clara feels about this PDA, so I break off our kiss to search her eyes.

"Nu-uh," she hums before pulling my neck back down to her. I gladly surrender, unable to stop a light groan from escaping my throat as I wind my arms around her waist, pulling her tighter against me. Locking her into my embrace like I'll never let her go—which is fully what I intend. Clara's arms loop around my neck, pressing even closer to me. The dam has burst, and every ounce of love for her that's built up inside me over the past year pours into this kiss.

The warmth of Clara's lips against mine—add that to the list of things that I *need*.

CHAPTER FORTY-THREE

Clara

Morning light streams through my curtains, but I'm reluctant to open my eyes. I want to stay in the perfect dream I was having; I don't want to wake up.

My eyes fly open with the realization that it *wasn't* a dream.

Clark-and-Clara. This is my new reality.

A grin spreads across my face, and I kick my feet under my covers. I stare up at the ceiling, replaying yesterday's events on a giant movie screen in my mind.

Clark driving to Kansas City. Braving the crowds at Crown Center to find me. Finally explaining the reasons behind his confusing behavior. Professing his love for me.

Kissing me. No more of the awkward Tin Man stiffness—he was *all in* those kisses at Crown Center. And every other kiss for the rest of the evening.

Clark Noel loves me.

I squeal.

After our, um, *extended* PDA at Crown Center, we decided to go to dinner and actually talk about our new relationship. It was torture to get into separate cars, but Clark followed me on the drive to The Country Club Plaza to eat dinner. We made a quick stop to purchase a coat for Clark before leisurely walking around to take in the Christmas lights.

Clark fulfilled another of my girlhood dreams by suggesting we take a ride in one of the horse-drawn carriages. He pulled me close to his

236

side and tucked the blanket tightly around our legs before draping his arm around my shoulders. As the white horse ambled us through the Plaza, Clark told me about his reckoning with Pops. Bless that old man's heart—I'm going to give him the biggest hug on record the next time I'm in Noel.

My heart was a puddle of warmth and gratitude and happiness until Clark filled me in on his trip to my cabin to water the plants and finding my movie script.

"Clark! You weren't supposed to read that!" I had exclaimed, cheeks coloring with embarrassment. He turned me toward him, taking my face in his hands.

"Don't be embarrassed about it, Clara. It was amazing. The way you brought the town and the characters to life was incredible. Renee and Jack feel like real people, as though I could walk down the street and bump into them. You are unbelievably talented," he'd assured me.

"Well, I suppose I did have some good inspiration," I said, smiling.

A mischievous grin spread across his face before he said, "I know a way you could thank me for being so inspirational."

Let's just say I'm glad the carriage driver's back was to us.

Clark followed me to my apartment to say goodnight and asked if I could take today off work. His eyebrows furrowed in confusion when I told him I already had the day off. "Tomorrow is my birthday."

Clark laughed, then he leaned closer to me, my back against my apartment door. He caged me in with a hand on either side. His voice was low and velvety when he spoke. "Of course, your birthday *would* be three days before Christmas, Clara, daughter of Joseph and Holly."

When he closed the gap between our lips, I thought my heart might implode from the weight of pure joy. My brain was overwhelmed processing all the addictive sensations—that soft tickle of Clark's beard against my face. The possessive grip of his hand on my waist. The solid mass of his biceps beneath my fingers. The leftover hint of the gingerbread cheesecake we'd shared lingering on his tongue.

Clark found a hotel a few minutes away from my apartment last night. After he left, I thought back on everything he had told me at Crown Center. His declaration of love was better than anything I could have dreamed up in a movie script. He explained everything I needed to understand about why his behavior with me had been so inconsistent.

And finally, I've figured out the Clark Noel Magic Eye illusion.

Underneath the confusing surface layer of closed-off grouchiness is the true image of Clark. And I think it's the spitting image of my cabin. Slightly dark on the outside, secluded, self-contained, hidden in the woods. But there's smoke rising out of the chimney from the warm, cozy fire inside. Clark may initially come across as unsentimental or gruff, and he certainly prefers solitude. But inside is a blazing, inviting fire, a sunroom full of bright light and life. A man who is steady, reliable, sacrificial, practical. A man who deeply loves his close circle of people, even if it might not look like cinnamon-roll-hero grand gestures.

A man who loves *me*. And good gracious, do I love him back.

My phone dings with a text from Sydney.

SYD

> Happy birthday, girl! Hope it's an amazing day?

I snort a laugh at the question mark at the end of her text. I'm not sure if Clark has filled Davis in on yesterday's events yet, so I call Syd. She answers after the first ring.

"Happy Birthday!"

"Thanks, Syd!" I smile as I tell her, "It's going to be an amazing day because I'm spending it with the man I love."

Syd's resulting scream likely alerted the entire town of Noel to good news.

"Ohmygosh! I've been dying to talk ever since Davis told me that Clark was on his way there but I felt like I should give you space and I didn't know how you would react and I've been DYING, Clara!" Syd gushes the run-on sentence so quickly I nearly miss half of what she says. Her voice sobers as she adds, "Seriously though, I was worried I might have lost you forever after Clark messed up."

"I would never have abandoned our friendship, Syd," I reassure her. "I may have had to get creative in avoiding Clark at all costs, but I never could have abandoned you or the town completely. But now, prepare yourself to get sick of me because I'm going to be there constantly visiting my man. Have I mentioned yet that Clark and I are in love?" I finish with a smile, earning another squeal from Sydney.

We talk for a few minutes until I realize that it's already 9:00 a.m. We hang up, and I shower quickly, scrunching in my curl cream and applying makeup in record time. I'm picking Clark up for a birthday brunch, and then we'll have most of the day together. Tonight, we'll join my parents for our annual dinner and *Nutcracker* ballet birthday tradition. When I called them last night to give an update on the Clark situation, they cheered with delight on speaker phone. Madison gladly gave up her claim to our fourth ballet ticket, happily insistent that I take Clark instead.

I arrive at Clark's hotel, and he's already waiting in the parking lot for me. He grins when he sees me pull in—the kind of smile that lights up his whole face. My eyes sting with tears of gratitude that I get to see this happy side of him. *I hope I see this for the rest of my life*, I think as Clark opens the passenger door.

"Happy birthday, gorgeous," he says before leaning over to kiss me. I think he intended it to be a quick "good morning" peck, but the magnetism between our lips quickly takes over and turns it into a deeper, lingering kiss. The love we'd stuffed down for so long finally has an outlet, and neither of us is trying to stifle it anymore.

Over brunch, Clark asks questions about my Aunt Gloria, somehow intuiting that today is a day that I miss her extra big. I share stories of her as my ballet instructor, as my babysitter, as the stereotypical spoiling auntie. I tell him about the day she gave me my birthstone ring as I twirl it around my finger, and he rubs his thumb across the back of my other hand.

Afterward, I take Clark to my favorite local plant shop with a coffee bar inside. As my birthday gift, he buys me the pricey Hindu Rope Hoya I've been denying myself for years. "You have to keep it at the cabin though," he says as the cashier carefully packages it for us. "I need to make sure you have motivation to make regular trips to Noel."

I reach up and run my fingers through the hair at the nape of his neck. "I have a much more compelling reason to visit Noel than a plant." He gives me a soft smile before I add, "I can't be away from Syd for too long."

Clark pinches my side before leaning in to press a kiss to my neck. The high schooler working the cash register obviously doesn't know how to respond, cheeks turning beet red. I smile at her and pull Clark's arm away before she melts into an awkward puddle.

After dropping the plant off at my apartment, we head to a department store to purchase something for Clark to wear to the ballet tonight. He can't exactly wear his token t-shirt and baseball cap. As big of a fan as I am of that particular ensemble.

He comes out of the dressing room wearing gray dress pants and a deep blue button-up shirt. Holding his hands out to his sides, he asks, "This okay? What do you think?"

I suck in a breath. "I think you're testing my self-control to not make out with you in the middle of the department store."

Clark's teasing smile reappears on his face as he grabs my hand to pull me to him. "What do I have to do to break the limits of that control?"

I give a wry smile back. "A song and dance might do the trick."

"Not happening." His expression softens into serious lines as he tucks a curl behind my ear. He leans in close, grazing his nose along my nose, my cheek, my jawline. My feigned resistance is already overpowered by the time he murmurs, "What if I told you I chose this shirt color to match your eyes? The eyes that have haunted my subconscious ever since the first night I stumbled into your bathroom. The deep, ocean-blue pools that I'd happily get lost in forever."

My pulse pounds in my neck, and my voice comes out as a whisper. "Well, when you put it that way." And then his lips are on mine again, dismissing all sense of time. One minute my hands are splayed flat against Clark's chest. The next, they're clutching fistfuls of his dress shirt as though that shirt was the only thing between me and a fall to my death.

Breaking apart, Clark glances down and chuckles. "I'd better go purchase this shirt before you do any damage to store property."

A blush floods my cheeks seconds before Clark leans in to kiss the heated skin. "Who are you, and what have you done with the grumpy Mayor Noel I know?" I tease back.

"What can I say? Clark-and-Clara brings out all the best in me."

After a lighthearted birthday dinner with Clark and my parents, we make our way to the Kauffman Center for the ballet. Clark even suggests taking a photo together in the lobby. I've been quietly in love with this juxtaposition of a man for a while now. But this extra-sweet, overtly thoughtful version of Clark has me ready to walk down the aisle tomorrow.

My mom takes several photos as we pose in front of one of the exquisite Christmas trees. Clark leans down and whispers in my ear, "Have I mentioned yet tonight that I love you in this dress?"

I giggle. "Only about twenty times."

He smiles down at me. "Emerald green is your color."

"Matches *your* eyes," I reply with a smile in return. He responds with a soft brush of his lips against mine, then threads our fingers together to head into the auditorium.

We take our seats, and I give Clark an overview of the story of *The Nutcracker* as the orchestra warms up. "What's your favorite part?" he asks.

"The snow," I whisper as the curtain rises. "It was Aunt Gloria's favorite role to dance."

Clark holds my hand on his thigh as we watch the ballet. I can't help sneaking glances over at him to take in his reactions. He's as transfixed as I feel every time I watch.

As the Snow King and Queen dance between the graceful Snowflakes, I'm physically overwhelmed by the gratitude and joy and happiness spilling over the edges of my heart. The fake snow slowly drifts down, swirling around the dancers. I peer over at Clark, and maybe it's just the blur of my own tears, but his eyes appear full of moisture.

I lean over and press a kiss to his cheek, relishing the sensation of his beard beneath my lips. He inclines his head to mine and whispers in my ear. "I get it now. I understand how Christmas is so magical."

My eyes sting with even *more* grateful tears. "I love you, Clark Nole."

He smiles at me. "Only for you, I'm Clark No-el."

CHAPTER FORTY-FOUR

Epilogue – Clark

One year later...

"Hurry up, hon! You can't miss the start of your own movie!"

"I'm coming!" Clara calls from across the room in the kitchen. She waltzes over, balancing two mugs of hot cocoa—mine plain, hers brimming with whipped cream.

I pretend not to notice the dollop of whipped cream Clara offers to Chase. Let's just say he's been spoiled with a *lot* of unsanctioned people food ever since Clara and I got married.

Our relationship might have seemed fast to some people. But we both knew the day we professed our love by the tree at Crown Center that we were in this forever. Not to mention, long-distance relationships are the literal worst.

Clara continued working for WritInc and living in Kansas City for the first three months we dated, but we saw each other almost every weekend. I took a handful of long weekend trips to KC to join her and her parents for their Thursday night dinners. But Clara almost always wanted to travel to Noel. That Hindu Rope Hoya I bought for her did the trick, apparently.

We've both made adjustments and compromises as we've learned to blend our very different personalities and preferences. Even without Syd's frequent reminders, I know that Clara has made me a better man. She's forced me to grow and stretch in ways that I never would have done on my own—like finally seeing a therapist to work through my complicated childhood and family loss. Admitting I needed Clara in my life opened the door to admitting I needed help from a professional, too.

When Clara's movie script was officially purchased for production by the Heartmark Channel, they asked her if she had ideas for additional films. Needless to say, Clara's mind is chock full of "Christmas love stories," as I affectionately refer to them. She resigned from her role at WritInc in order to move to her cabin in Noel and write movie scripts full time. Heartmark has already purchased the rights for two more, and I'm 100 percent confident that this is only the beginning.

Davis and Syd helped me plan a second annual float trip in June, complete with another "surprise injury" by Junior. Of course, it was a ruse for them to leave so that I could get down on one knee and ask to be Clark-and-Clara for the rest of our lives. Syd and Davis were ready with fireworks down the beach the moment that Clara screamed yes and jumped into my arms.

We got married in downtown Noel the day after Thanksgiving, surrounded by the Christmas magic that Clara dreamed up. It means delaying our honeymoon until after Christmas, but neither of us wanted to miss out on the second annual Christmas Fest—even bigger and better than last year.

The festival ended the day before the air date of Clara's Heartmark movie, "Christmas Saved Our Town." Syd is hosting a watch party at their house, and I'm sure every other television in Noel will be tuned to the channel tonight.

But Clara and I are curled up together on the couch at home, just the two of us. And Chase.

We decided that I would move into her cabin after we got married, rather than us living in my childhood home. My family legacy is still too complicated for me to want to begin my new family with Clara among the ghosts of those memories. For now, I'm renting the house out to Beau and Abby. The pet food production facility opened in October, and Beau was able to secure a position and wrap up his job in Joplin. They moved back to Noel just in time for Christmas Fest.

After several long conversations with Clara, Davis, and Syd, I resigned from my position as mayor. Emily took over the job, completely capable and willing to lead our town. Noland's has been doing well enough financially to hire more full-time employees. That means Emily has had more time—and far better ideas—to devote to the mayoral office than I ever did. She's also enjoyed lording her civic authority over their three teenagers to keep them in line.

Stepping down as mayor lifted a weight off my shoulders in more ways than one. It's freed me up to let go of some of the lifelong pressure I've felt from my last name. Allowed me to separate who I am from my ancestry. It's also given me more time to focus on my new wife, which is really the *only* thing I want to focus on these days. It turns out Pops was right—I've scored the biggest jackpot on earth in loving Clara. I have a hard time thinking about anything other than the incredible woman sitting next to me.

She takes a sip of her hot cocoa, then sets it on the table next to mine before burrowing under my arm against my side. "Even though I've seen bits and pieces of the footage, I'm so nervous to see the real thing for the first time," Clara says, face buried in her hands.

Grasping her wrists, I pull her hands away from her face. I press a kiss to each fingertip before angling my neck down to kiss her lips. "It's going to be perfect," I tell her.

She sighs and leans in to kiss me again, reaching one hand up to thread her fingers through my hair.

"Better be careful, or I'm going to carry you back to our room, and you'll miss your movie debut," I growl, only half teasing. Clara kisses the tip of my nose, then settles back in to watch the movie.

When Renee's character first encounters Jack on the screen, he's all rough edges and gruff bluster. "Hey, this guy is nothing like me," I whine, squeezing Clara's knee right where I know she's ticklish.

"Who said he was inspired by you?" she exclaims between gasping giggles. I narrow my eyes at her. "Okay, okay, he was 99 percent inspired by you. But you'll see past Jack's grumpy exterior to his heart of liquid gold soon enough."

Clara winks at me, and I'm tempted to make good on my threat to forgo the movie and carry her back to our bedroom. Instead, I tuck her tighter to my side, kissing her temple.

"The liquid gold might have stayed buried forever if not for the spunky, Christmas-loving beauty who came and rescued this grumpy Nole," I murmur. "Who knew I'd be saved by No-el?"

Clara untucks herself from my side and swings a leg over my lap, straddling me. She places a hand on either cheek and studies my face. My hands find her waist, and I study her back. After getting lost momentarily in her cornflower-blue eyes, I ask, "What is it?"

"You say you were saved by No-el, but you weren't the only one who needed a rescue. I don't know that I ever would have prioritized my own passion if I hadn't come here and met you. This movie"—she gestures over her shoulder—"literally wouldn't exist if I hadn't stumbled upon this town. Saved by Nole," she finishes with a thoughtful smile.

Clara leans down to press her soft lips to mine with all the tenderness mirrored in her eyes.

The tenderness quickly deepens into passion, and I kiss my way from her lips across her chin, down the slope of her neck.

"Clark?" Clara murmurs. "I'll watch the movie on rerun. I'd like you to carry me to our bedroom now."

I smile against her neck, then reach up to thread my fingers through her curls.

"As you wish."

Want to return to Noel and read Madison's story?

Scan here:

Acknowledgments

You know what I realized after writing my first book, *Love and Other Goals*? That I will never again skip the acknowledgments section of any book I read. The magic of seeing the village of people surrounding an author to make a book come to life—it's a thing of beauty to read about. So here's a look at my village (well, the small part of it that I can fit into a short-ish acknowledgments section).

Kyle, always. Not only are you the most supportive husband (better than any MMC I could ever dream up), this book wouldn't exist without you, yet again. Thanks for spit-balling this storyline with me on our impulsive drive to check out a cabin in the woods. Thanks for pushing me to actually write it down and turn it into a real book. Thanks for all the ways you have encouraged me and cheered me on (very loudly and publicly) in my new author adventure. I love how your Three energy matches my very intense Eight energy. I just love you.

Hannah, not only are you one of my most favorite souls on Bookstagram, you were the most perfect beta reader for this book. PER-FECTION. I'm so grateful for how you helped me develop these characters and the story from your Christmas-loving-reader's perspective. Thanks for all your encouragement not only about *Saved by Noel*, but about all the things. You know. Your voice memos and GIFs are the wind beneath my wings. Mark my words—we are meeting in real life someday soon.

To my other beta readers, Krystal, Paris, and Mandy, thank you for being amazing and for identifying spots in the story I needed to explain more (things always make perfect sense in my brain). Thanks for loving Clark+Clara and encouraging me with all your real-time reactions and comments. I don't think I can emphasize enough how much energy that gives to me to keep writing—we're talking triple shot espresso territory, at least.

Danae, thanks for being my final line of defense against typos going out in advanced reader copies. And for sending me a photo of you teary-eyed over Lana and Mateo, and for sending me sooooo many encouraging messages, and for just generally hyping me up as an author and a friend. I heart you.

Parker, this cover. You've outdone yourself. It's so beautiful and perfect and cozy and 1000% better than what I even imagined in my head. THANK YOU!!

Mom and Dad, thanks for raising us to **love** Christmas. I have so many fond childhood memories of our Christmas traditions, which made it all the more fun to write a Christmas book. Nothing gets me in my nostalgic, cozy feelings like listening to Mannheim Steamroller while putting up Christmas decorations.

To my sister, Mandy, thanks for always singing "Sisters" with the Christmas tree branches as our feather fan props. I love our mutual obsession with "Christmas love stories," whether in movies or books—AND how we're passing it along to our girls. Chase is, of course, in memory of your Chasers, the sweetest boy.

To my kiddos, Landon, Layla, Meili, and Mason, thanks for thinking it's cool that I'm writing books. Seeing your enthusiasm at my book launch party made my heart grow three sizes. Being your mom is even cooler than being an author, but I love that you all get so excited about me doing this thing. At least for now. Maybe when you're a little older, you'll get embarrassed, but for now, I'm eating it up. I love when you start writing down your own stories and say things like, "I don't know yet if I'll publish it, but maybe I will." It's possible.

Pops and Bev were written as a tribute to my four wonderful grandparents. My paternal grandpa was named Bill (William), and my maternal grandpa was an amazing carpenter who made the most beautiful furniture. If you ever see my gorgeous walnut bookshelves on Instagram, those were crafted by my grandpa. My maternal grandma was named Beverly, and my paternal grandma was a talented painter, especially of farm landscapes. I frequently got emotional writing Pops' scenes (though neither of my grandfathers were quite so cantankerous!). I miss you all.

There's no way I could possibly name every individual, but I need to give one big blanket THANK YOU to every person who supported me so enthusiastically when I published *Love and Other Goals*. For a lot of complicated reasons, I had a really hard time announcing to the world that I had written a contemporary romance book. To see the way you all came around me, cheered me on, pumped me up, shared about how much you loved Lana and Mateo's story—it has given me so much more courage and confidence to continue writing and publishing.

I'm going to get teary thinking about all the Bookstagrammers and real-life friends and bookstore owners and old college friends and fellow indie authors who have made this journey so special. I had the most amazing ARC team who took a chance on a debut author and became some of my biggest cheerleaders. I have a folder in my phone gallery titled "Author Encouragement" that is filled with screenshots of the kind messages you've sent gushing about why you loved the book. It's that energy that propelled me to write *Saved by Noel*. And I'll keep drawing from that well of encouragement for every other book to come.

Real-life references in the book:

The town of Noel, Arkansas, was inspired by the city of Noel, Missouri. I just kicked it across the border to NWA so I could create my own fictional town storyline and characters. Noel, Missouri, was founded by brothers Clark Wallace "C. W." and William Jasper "W. J." Noel—so I made my MMC's name Clark "C. J." Noel.

Take a *Saved by Noel* inspired tour of the Kansas City Metro—you'll need to stop at McClain's Bakery (multiple locations) for bakery treats or enjoy their delicious lunch selections.

Don't miss Joe's Kansas City BBQ (multiple locations). Be sure to take Clara's advice and try the Z-man sandwich with a side of fries (ask for extra crispy). You could also just try one of everything.

If you want the greatest cookies ever baked, swing over to KCOOK-IES in Olathe (kccookie.com). The flavors rotate, but my personal favorites are the tiramisu and the raspberry sea salt chocolate. You literally can't go wrong, though.

Cap your tour off with a stop at one of Family Tree Nursery's locations to get a cup of coffee and a plant to take home.

If you want to keep your new plant alive, follow @happyhappy-houseplant on Instagram and buy her plant fertilizer. She's the "plant lady" I alluded to in the book, and discovering her right after purchasing my first plant is the one and only reason I have plants that thrive.

About the Author

Tracy Baack connects with readers through relatable romance. She enjoys writing character-driven contemporary romance novels with so much character depth and development, you just might think they're real people. Her books are always closed-door but full of heart-melting swoon, and they end happily ever after (after a little dose of angst).

Tracy lives with her husband and four children in the suburbs of Kansas City, Kansas, where she loves supporting indie bookstores. Her primary love language is sending the perfect GIF for any moment.

Tracy is the author of *Love and Other Goals, Love and Other Chances, Saved by Noel, Home Safe,* and *Joy to Noel* (with more on the way because she just might be a writing addict).

Connect with Tracy on Instagram at @authortracybaack or through her website www.tracybaack.com.